A
Harlequin
Romance

DESTINY
IS A FLOWER

by

STELLA FRANCES NEL

HARLEQUIN BOOKS   TORONTO
WINNIPEG

Original hard cover edition published in 1970
by Mills & Boon Limited.

© Stella Frances Nel 1970

SBN 373-01743-X

Harlequin edition published December 1973

Printed in Canada

1743

CHAPTER ONE

THERESA STANTON watched the train disappear into a curve of tall, thorny scrub and was quite sure the tail end of the last coach flipped a cocky snook at her as it too was swallowed by the prickly jaws of waiting greenery. She forced down rising hysteria – the heat was causing strange hallucinations – and brought her gaze back to the dusty wayside station. She seemed to be in solitary possession at the moment. With sudden apprehension she drew a letter out of her bag and scanned the contents again.

A sigh of relief escaped curving lips. She was in the right place, at the correct time and on the appointed day according to this letter in her hand. So where were Dan and Mary? Theresa hoped sincerely that the delay in meeting her was not caused by a breakdown or trouble with their car. She studied the letter for the umpteenth time.

'My dearest Terry,' wrote Mary Rourke, 'Dan and I are very pleased that you have accepted our invitation. It's high time anyway, we haven't seen you for ages and your constant promises never seem to materialize. So at last, with your resignation (why?) we'll have the pleasure of your company. What does the haughty Doctor Derek think of your leaving his precious nursing-home? Do I hear the distant sound of wedding bells? Don't mind me, honeychile, I'm dying with the disease that killed the cat, but I guess I can hold out if I take a deep breath and wait for you. You'll love our poppet (Glynis Theresa Rourke), she's rather superior for the wise old age of four months. When I tell her Auntie Terry is coming at last she gazes into the distance superciliously and gives a wet, knowing grunt! Well, all can wait until I see you in person. Dan is still a pain in the neck to me and I'm looking forward to a demolishment of his flirtatious manner with one look from your cold violet eyes. 'Nuff said! We'll meet you, providence willing our mechanical contraption doesn't have its periodical inner tantrum, at Guntha siding on Friday morning 10.30 a.m. That's the appointed time the train should arrive but never does. Don't do your block, honey, we'll be there even if I have to call the faithful wheel-barrow into mobility. Dan pushing, of course. . . .' Further details followed, and Theresa smiled in genuine amusement at her friend's quaint ramblings.

Her expressive face sobered as she thought of ex-planations she would have to disclose on the subject of her broken engagement. Slim fingers ran through honey-blonde hair in a distracted movement and blue eyes darkened as bitter thoughts clouded her tired brain. A very grizzled old man suddenly appeared from the direction of a tiny shack on the opposite side of the track and ambled towards her. After all, she was not alone in this desolate speck of nowhere! Theresa walked eagerly to meet him. Old Truscott studied her intently for some moments, then took the chewed-up match from his mouth with gnarled fingers.

'Could be you're the young lady for Windimount. A bit young for the job, I'd say. Miss Melinda be a handful for the likes of ye. What's come over that Master Scott?'

Before she could answer his enigmatic query he turned away to watch as a low-slung grey car came to a smooth stop at the siding.

A perplexed girl and an inquisitive, expectant old man watched as the deeply tanned hands of the dark man at the wheel opened the door and he climbed out with a quick, lithe movement. Smoky grey eyes met Theresa's gaze and he stopped with a startled exclamation. Swift, circling scrutiny took in her cinnamon-brown summer suit with the tailored yellow blouse showing at the pure column of her throat. His gaze dropped to high slim-heeled sandals and a matching bag. Hot sunlight sparkled on shoulder-length hair accentuating, in startling contrast, eyes that were the deep blue of hyacinths.

In turn, Theresa stared into the arrogant, sun-tanned face of the man facing her. For some reason he seemed to be angry. His eyes had darkened and she had the wayward thought that never had she seen such dark, absurdly long eyelashes on a man. High cheekbones planed down to a square jaw, but this chin was redeemed by a vulnerable-looking cleft or dimple. He had a well-defined mouth which could well be humorous but was drawn into a grim line at this moment. Dark hair was relentlessly brushed back. He was tall and slim-hipped, resilient grace being apparent as he slipped his thumbs into the waistband of tan whipcord slacks and surveyed her, almost contemptuously.

'What the devil – that woman must be out of her mind! I distinctly wrote her to send someone older and qualified!' His voice was deep and matched the quality of his arrogance.

'I don't qualify? How utterly devastating! In what, may I ask?' Theresa had found her voice and the words were uttered before she could bite them back. A tiny pulse started in her throat as her sarcasm matched his.

'Good grief, ignorant of the necessary qualifications as well! This is the end!' He turned to the old man. 'All right, Mike, party's over. You can draw up your chin.'

Taking a firm grip on Theresa's bags, the tall stranger slung them through the back door of the car on to the seat. 'You must be tired after the long trip, Miss ... er ... so come along. We'll discuss what's to be done at home when you're rested. The front seat, please – I'll think of your name in a moment.' He held the door politely.

'Theresa Stanton. How do you do Mr. ... er ...?' She remained where she was and her own firm chin lifted a fraction higher.

'That's not the name of the applicant—' He swung around and smoky eyes studied her again. 'Stanton? That's the girl Dan was expecting – the bluestocking. I beg your pardon. Thank goodness you're not the one for Melinda. What could have happened to the silly woman?' He gazed around as if expecting someone to materialize out of thorny scrub and then recollected himself. 'Forgive me, Miss Stanton. Scott Milward's the name. Dan seems to be somewhat delayed. May I take you to your destination? It's not far out of my way.' Scott Milward waited, an enigmatic look closing his face as he watched the girl.

Theresa was fuming with indignation, but she took pride in her outward coolness. She heard another car approaching and knew instinctively it would be Dan or Mary.

'Thank you, Mr. Milward, it won't be necessary for you to go out of your way at all. My friends have come. May I have my bags? And I second that very expressive remark of yours.'

'Expressive remark?' Puzzlement clouded his face.

'Thank goodness I'm not the one for Melinda, whatever that may imply. Hullo, Dan darling, the train was on time for once.' Let the autocrat put that in his pipe and smoke it!

Theresa almost hurled herself into Dan Rourke's arms as he joined them. With a great shout of laughter the stocky new arrival gathered the girl into his arms, swept her up and planted a whacking kiss on her lips.

'It's me own darling, come to lighten up me dark days. Begorra, girl, 'tis good to see you. And lovelier than I remembered!'

'My word!' Mike Truscott's grizzled chin hung down as far as it could go.

'Yes, Mike, ain't she gorgeous? No skidding to Mary now, you old reprobate. Hi there, Scott! Didn't your baggage turn up? Mine did, and she sure ain't dowdy, hmm? Mary couldn't come, dear, Poppet has a slight hangover from earache – nothing to worry about. Have you met Scott, honey? Our local candidate for the mommas' and lassies' caps.'

'We have met, Dan.' The ice in Theresa's voice cooled Dan's exuberant spirits somewhat and his bright eyes swivelled from her to Scott's uncompromising face as he climbed into his car.

'Yes, we have met. There was a slight case of misunderstanding, mistaken identity for which I apologize—' a mere hesitation as the man eased himself into the seat '—if an apology is called for—' a wave of a hand and he was gone.

'Well, of all the—' Theresa turned and spoke in urgent fury to a bewildered Dan. 'Who and what is this baggage that was supposed to be on this train, Dan?'

'Scott was expecting a governess for his daughter, Melinda—' Dan began.

'If an apology is called for? Not if I look like an ordinary, dowdy governess – do I look like one, Dan?'

'Of course not, honey, you look every inch a queen.' Dan eyed Mary's friend, drawn to her full height, a haughty tilt to the delectable chin. Trouble in store for someone!

'So I rate an apology, then, not so? And he deliberately said "*If* an apology is called for." I'll call for one if it's the last thing I do, *and* expire in the attempt!'

8

'Ha, Mister Dan, she sure are a spirited filly, begging your pardon, miss. You'll need it to stand up to that Mr. Scott, that's for sure.' Mike showed his glee by demolishing another match between surprisingly strong white teeth.

'Did you not enlighten him as to who you were?'

'I had no chance, Dan. He simply stood there and tried to mow me down with sarcastic remarks on my youth and capabilities. When I eventually introduced myself he called me a – bluestocking!'

Theresa suddenly fixed a suspicious eye on Dan. That individual hastily turned to her bags and deposited them with great care on the back seat of the vintage station-wagon. 'Shall we go now, sweetie? Mary's quite likely to start walking to meet us. She's that excited about your visit.'

Theresa got in beside him, her fury subsiding. Blow Scott Milward and his would-be 'baggage'. She was going to see her very dearest friend again and see the baby she had heard so much about.

Mary had met and married her Rhodesian farmer after a whirlwind courtship, leaving almost immediately to settle in this forsaken-looking place where Dan evidently cultivated tobacco. She waved her hand to Mike and the old man gave back a courteous salute.

'Sorry I was late, Terry. This old wagon played up again and, for truth, it's time she was pensioned off. Just this coming month I'll endeavour a trip to Salisbury and come back in a spick 'n' span what-have-you with luverly shining trimmings, so help me! How was the journey up? I guess I needn't ask – long and tiring. How much illegal goods confiscated at the border – surely not that case of whisky you so stealthily slipped under your mini-skirt?'

Theresa laughed in delight at Dan's anxious expression. 'Oh, Dan dear, I had the bottles strapped around my waist under said mini, but the Customs chappie said I looked too suspiciously like Annie Oakley. So I had to haul them out, and one by one we solemnly drank the contents. Not a tooth-ful left for Danny Rourke.' She looked suitably ashamed and regretful.

'They come and go, mostly go.' Dan sighed, looked darkly at her. 'I might just spare a toothful of my own precious stuff for you, but not if it's a hollow tooth. Not that much!'

'Thank you, kind sir.' Her eager eyes watched the road. 'How far still?'

'It's only an hour's drive from the siding. This is where my land starts.'

'And all those weeds – aren't they tall?' Theresa spoke mischievously.

'Weeds indeed! I'll have you know those are not weeds, it's tobacco—' he caught her sidelong glance. 'Away with you, begorrah, you ignorant city miss!'

Mary Rourke was waiting on the steps of the wide verandah as they drew up with a flourish. She flew down to envelop Theresa with loving arms. 'My Theresa, come at last, and more beautiful than ever! Let me look at you, just stepped out of a fashion page and not a dusty train, I do declare!' She stepped back. 'A bit on the thin side?'

Sudden tears threatened and Theresa's eyes sparkled as she greeted her friend. 'Mary darling, it's good to see you again. Now don't give with the mother-act, I can see it surging to the fore. I'm not thin and my health is good, I still have my own teeth, no hollows unfortunately.' A quick, naughty glance at Dan.

Dan grinned, 'All right, girls, stop drooling. Step smartly, I hear tea things. How's Poppet, Mary?' He led the way into the large, cool living-room.

'She's sleeping. I think her troubles are over now. We'll have tea and then Terry can meet the queen of the house.' Mary made bustling sounds at the tea-trolley which a dark, smiling maid had wheeled into the room.

Theresa sank into an easy chair and kicked off her sandals with a sigh of contentment.

Mary smiled at this familiar gesture which she remembered from the days when they had shared a flat in Pretoria. Theresa might have contradicted her remark that she was thin, but Mary could see the difference. Also something – sad? – that lurked in the blue eyes usually so gay with joyous love of life. What had saddened them so?

The sitting room was furnished to induce contentment. A soft green wall-to-wall carpet, beige curtains across wide windows and easy chairs ranging in colours of brown to a light tan. One deep rocking chair with a high back looked startlingly lovely, covered in a material of deep bronze with a slight tracery of green. The walls and ceilings were white and Dan's bar fitted into the lower curve of the L-shaped room where the natural redwood used for the counter and fittings gleamed richly.

Dan had his tea and left them with a muttered remark that 'man's work was never done'. He turned at the doorway. 'Scott's gal didn't turn up, Mary. If you stop delving into your lurid past Terry will tell you all about it. She has first-hand knowledge, having met the lord of Windimount at the siding—' His voice trailed off as he hastily made his exit.

'So you met Scott. Isn't he just the mostest?' Mary asked eagerly.

'The mostest? The leastest as far as I'm concerned,' Theresa retorted. 'He has the manners of a – a savage! At least you know what to expect from the species, who gives warning when you're expected at his next meal.' She went on to relate the incident which led to the introduction of Scott Milward.

Mary laughed unexpectedly. 'Oh, that sounds just like our Scott. He's nothing if not straightforward, and you must forgive him. He must have received a shock when he saw you, not the staid lady he expected to see! The woman in charge of Melinda is leaving soon, to be married, and he was counting on this other one to get into the routine before that time.'

'Where is his wife, and how old is Melinda?' Theresa was suddenly curious about the Rourkes' tall, outspoken neighbour.

'Melinda is four and a sweet, precocious little handful. Scott adores her. Elaine, his wife—' Mary hesitated, '—she left him almost two years ago. I believe she's in Pretoria. Scott is very bitter.'

'Why did she leave him?' Theresa asked bluntly, shocked that a woman could simply walk out leaving a small child. Could there possibly be such extenuating circumstances as to warrant such an act of desertion?

Mary remained silent for moments. 'Well, Terry, it's hard to explain. Elaine is a city girl, she's American and very glamorous. Scott is very tight-mouthed about the

11

whole affair. He met and married her in New York, and she wasn't very happy here in the wilds, as she called it—' A sudden wail reached them and Mary started up. 'I'll tell you more about it later. Come and meet Madam, that's her imperious call you've just heard.'

'She's lovely, absolutely adorable!' Theresa cuddled Mary's daughter on her lap.

'Glynis Theresa Rourke likes you too, love.'

The eyes of the two friends met above a cooing roly-poly baby in the younger girl's arms. Mary noticed a wistful darkening of blue eyes.

'Something is troubling you, Terry. Would you care to tell me about it?' she asked quietly.

'I don't know how – Mary, I can't bear it – I – ' Theresa's usually clear voice came to a stammering stop. There was a frightful choking in her throat as she looked into Mary's kind, inquiring eyes.

Mary Rourke lifted her baby from the girl's arms. 'All right, honey, give Poppet to me. You can have a shower and climb into something more comfortable. Jeans are quite in order, that's my national dress these days. Lunch will be ready soon and then we can gossip some more. You need only confide as much as you think fit and there's all the time in the world. Come, I'll show you to your room.'

Briskness hid her sudden uprush of love for this quiet, unsure girl. Something awfully upsetting must have happened, for normally Terry was a vibrant girl full of joyous laughter and vitality. And she had not mentioned her fiancé, not once. In her third year of nursing and a glowing future before her, affianced to one of the smartest doctors in the Transvaal, Dr. Derek Mann, Terry was devoted to her profession, so why had she suddenly resigned? Mary had a dark suspicion that it had to do with Derek. What had that superior (*she* was not too taken with him) medico done to her Theresa?

Theresa gratefully accepted the offer of a shower and changed into white jeans and soft yellow shirt. She brushed her hair, slipped a white band on to keep the honey mass off her face.

A delicious lunch comprising cold ham and salads made her realize how hungry she had been. Disillusionment in her love-life by no means deterred a young, healthy appetite!

Dan left and Mary practically ordered her to rest a while during the hottest time of day. Later the two friends sat in grass-woven easy-chairs on the cool side of the verandah. Baby Glynis was dumped on a blanket and they watched her antics in amused silence. Intent on the embroidery work in her hands, Mary started to talk about mutual friends they had known when they had shared a flat together in Pretoria.

This came to an end eventually and a long silence ensued. Theresa looked up from the book on her lap and watched her friend's busy hands while 'poppet' gurgled at her feet.

She spoke then. 'Mary, I must tell you what happened. You're my friend and, as such and in respect of, an explanation is due to you.' A restless hand went to her hair.

Mary put down her work. 'Fire away, lassie.'

'I can't think how it all started, believe me. I'd loved nursing, as you know, and Derek and I were the proverbial happily engaged couple, at least I thought we were. Oh, Mary, why couldn't he trust me? I never thought that word – trust – would ever be needed!' Theresa was quiet, lost in bitter memories. She drew a ragged breath. 'I guess it did look rather compromising to other people. Do you remember the estate agent who found our flat for us?'

'Mitch Saunders, yes. He was rather sweet on you and pestered us for quite a while before you managed to drum home your engaged and unavailable status. You can be an iceberg at times, honey, and I'll never forget that Don Juan's face when you showed him the door! Go on.'

'Saunders also had a sister, Sylvia. Widowed and stinking rich.' Theresa clenched her slender fists.

'So?' Mary ventured to break the silence.

'So she fancied my fiancé. In a big way. You see, he had everything she wanted – a good position in society, rich in his own rights, a lovely home in the right snob centre – Mary, I'm almost certain she engineered the whole – this difficult position I'm in at present. And I would not fight back because – there was no trust in Derek's make-up. We met her quite often, at parties, etc. She was always underfoot and made a big play for Derek's attention. The flattery that man can swallow amazes me, and my handsome doctor swallowed elephantine gulps and loved it. Don't get me wrong, he was just as attentive and loving to me as ever, but the way was being paved for him, poor man. I can even pity him now.'

Theresa looked out at the sunlight playing on the leaves of a tipuana tree. 'What I can't forget or forgive is his lack of trust and pompous disinclination to believe my true version of what followed. "His own eyes could not deceive him, not only once but twice" was his verdict, so that was that.'

'What was what?'

'I can only go on if I know you're going to believe me.'

Mary studied her intently without a word. The girl met her eyes and sighed with sure conviction.

'Thank you, Mary, forgive my doubting mind. I should have known, but my ideals have been somewhat shaken. You can't imagine what two silly episodes can do to one's morale – not the episodes in themselves but the misconstrued conception as they appeared to others, to Derek mostly. I'm dithering and can't seem to get to the point—'

'Dither along, darling, if it helps. I'm not going to vanish.' Mary's quiet, compassionate voice soothed the girl's taut nerves.

'Well, Mitch Saunders phoned one day and seemed so upset he could hardly speak coherently. It was about his sister and he desperately wanted my advice seeing I had knowledge of medical procedures. I told him I was only a third-year nurse, why didn't he call the right authorities, meaning a doctor, but he interrupted insisting that he would like to talk to me first, and I could then advise him what to do. I asked him what was wrong with his sister as she looked in splendid health to me. He was quiet for so long that I thought he had rung off, and then his voice came over rather ashamedly admitting that he had pried amongst Sylvia's private papers and had made a startling discovery about her health which upset him very much. It was quite evident that she wasn't doing anything about said health. He was fond of her etc., etc. I've since found out that she was very generous with her money, so he would be fond of her!' The sarcasm slipped out and Theresa shook her head as if to clear it of cobwebs. In a toneless voice she continued, 'I ventured that he should insist on medical attention and he replied that

14

Sylvia wasn't the kind anyone could force, least of all her brother! Please would I meet him somewhere to discuss the matter and if I thought it proper maybe I could confide in Dr. Mann and he, in turn, could speak to Sylvia? He promised to disclose the full story appertaining to her health, having confidence in my integrity (what a word!).

'I told him to come to the flat, but he refused, saying he wouldn't like to jeopardize Dr. Mann's fiancée in any way. Well, to be brief, I agreed to meet him at a certain restaurant in Church Street. The moment I replaced the receiver the phone rang again. Derek informed me that he was free for the evening, would I like to go places? I was in a quandary and after some hesitation (which incidentally was pointed out later) told him I'd rather have an early night. Please believe me, I had no intention of deceiving him. Having given my promise to Mitch the matter was confidential at this stage, or so I thought. Mitch's story was plausible and I was a gullible ass.'

'His story was very good so far. What then, Terry?' Mary leaned forward, following Theresa's narrative with thoughtful interest.

'I found Mitch sitting in his car at the kerb in front of the stipulated restaurant. He was very jittery and said the place was full and recognized acquaintances might gossip. The fleeting thought did pass through my mind that he was suddenly very careful of my reputation, but he looked so worried that I agreed to drive with him to another place. No one was more surprised than I when he turned into the circular drive of the Union Buildings. Before I could protest he reached the top and parked the car facing the lights of the city.

'I waited, thinking he was trying to formulate a way of telling me bad news. He asked rather hesitantly after my health, not having seen me for some time. I assured him that I was quite well and would he come to the point; why this devious, unethical way of discussing things, realizing afterwards that he was watching the curve of the road rather closely. Another car was coming up slowly and Mitch moved closer to me as if to avoid the glare of its headlamps.'

Theresa unconsciously rubbed her ringless fingers as she

15

gazed at her friend.

'The car came to a standstill and Derek stepped out! Dramatics? Oh no. He opened the door on my side, asked politely if he could drive me back now that I had received the required fresh air. Mary, it was – it was funny – so funny that I nearly burst out laughing!'

'Pompous ass!' The invocation was involuntary.

'Oh no, darling, he was every inch the gentleman. No scenes, that could wait. I turned to Mitch expecting him to explain, but he moved behind the wheel, muttering that the matter could wait, he would get in touch. The wretch! Dear Derek couldn't help a slight descent from dignity, for he retorted, not if he could help it – goodnight Saunders.'

Theresa relived the time, later, when they were back in the flat.

Derek Mann was tall and fair-haired. His light blue eyes stared down at her accusingly, making her feel small, definitely giving her a feeling of guilt. She stood facing him proudly, her hand resting lightly on the chair beside her.

'Well?' Derek teetered casually on his feet, but his hands were tightly clenched. 'Did I interrupt your "early night"!?'

'I still intend to have that early night, Derek. This was a confidential matter that came up—'

'Oh, very confidential, I noticed. He was sitting very – er – confidingly close.' Sarcasm dripped.

Theresa kept her tone even. 'Mitch rang and wanted to see me on a private matter which he promised I could discuss with you later.' Something was trying to get through to her and she had a moment of puzzlement.

'So private that you had to leave the privacy of your flat and drive to the very public place, where couples are notorious for their confidential secrets—'

'Oh, don't be silly, Derek, it wasn't like that at all. It was a medical matter, if you must know.' Theresa was suddenly impatient with his lack of understanding.

He looked at her contemplatively. 'If I must know? A medical matter? What's the implication, is Mitch in trouble with some woman and is he seeking your assistance?'

'Not as far as I know. He has a problem concerning a woman, but not the way you mean.' Theresa was suddenly furious with him for daring to think she would help anyone in the way he was insinuating. 'How dare you suggest that I would meddle—' and then it hit her. 'How did you know where to find me?'

'I received a phone call. Anonymous.' He watched her and his cold manner warmed as indignation made her more vitally alive and beautiful.

'Anonymous!' Blue eyes flew to his in amazement. 'This is a put-up job, Derek. There's nothing wrong with Sylvia, and Mitch is in this up to his traitorous eyes!' she stated flatly.

'Sylvia? Should there be something wrong with her? You'd better explain, my dear.' Derek was clearly puzzled at this enigmatic statement.

'Mitch phoned and wanted a private talk about some illness of Sylvia. He sounded extremely agitated, that's why I was with him.'

'And why should someone phone me and say that it wasn't the first time they had seen you in that particular spot?'

'Good heavens, Derek, you can't believe that of me? You trust me, surely?' Theresa sank down into the chair in complete bewilderment.

Derek said slowly, 'Sylvia did come to see me today at my consulting-room. I've started treatment of a slight – indisposition. Nothing serious enough as your version of Mitch's agitation.'

'My version? That sounds as though you don't believe me? Oh, forget it. Sylvia coming to see you is proof of my explanation anyway. But the phone call, that's deliberately malicious. Have you no idea who it can be, was it a woman or a man?'

'I can't say. A muffled voice which could have been of either sex.'

'Why didn't you tell them to go to hell and slam the phone down? Or did your curiosity overcome your trusting nature?' The scorn in her voice in contrast to the bland innocence of her face startled the man.

'Well, after all, Terry, I have my good name to watch, and if any of our friends had seen you there they would have jumped at the chance of misconstruing the whole episode.

That's reasonable, isn't it? I had to satisfy myself and I can tell you it was quite a shock when I found you there. Anyway, you seem to have explained the whole occurrence, so I'll forget it. Just don't get yourself involved again, sweet, send would-be patients to me. I'm the doctor.'

After he had left, Theresa looked at the door contemplatively. Had Mitch deliberately tried to compromise her? Who else had known they would be there, why did he drive to that particular spot? She had an instinctive feeling that his sister was the mainspring of the plot to discredit her in Derek's eyes. The phone call? To top it all ... Derek's insinuation that she, a nurse, would possibly dabble in illegal abortion!

Oh, to the devil with it! Theresa stripped, showered and scrubbed as though trying to cleanse herself of an unholy taint. ...

'That was the first time, Mary. Two weeks later came the anti-climax. I always thought of love as a "many-splendoured thing" and I sure crashed on that mythical rock. Love would see to the core of things, see through pretence – Oh no, love is a delusion!'

'Hey, pet, hold your horses! Your view is a bit cloudy at present, and I don't blame you. Carry on while I dry Poppet's tail. So Madam Sylvia didn't stop there?'

'I'll make it short and should I say sweet – it leaves a bitter taste in my mouth. I was doing my bit of district duty – it does land me in some queer places – and a call came from a flat in the better part of town. I didn't question it, so you can imagine my fury when Sylvia opened the door. I prepared to blast her when she suddenly staggered and clutched at me, spilling a small glass of tomato juice down the front of my uniform; it was in her hand when she had opened the door. She looked near to collapse, so I helped her to the bedroom and did the usual things a nurse does for a fainting person. She recovered mighty quick. Thanking me, she explained that the flat belonged to a friend whom she expected any minute. I asked why she hadn't sent for Derek and she said she had tried but he wasn't available. Very upset about the mess on my uniform, she insisted that I remove it and sponge it as best I could. I slipped into the large paisley gown hanging behind the door and took my uniform to the bathroom. Busy cleaning it, I heard the front door open and close and wondered if her friend was a male. Going back to the bedroom, I discovered Sylvia was gone!

'A knock on the front door and I was still standing in stunned surprise when it opened and Derek confronted me. To cut it, the flat belonged to Mitch, I had on his dressing-gown, another anonymous call to the good doctor and there you have it! His accusations were flung at me before I could pull myself together. They were so brutal and demeaning that, without bothering to explain, I handed back his ring. My pride was up in arms, Mary. If a man didn't have enough trust to wait for explanations, I wanted no part of him. I resigned the next day.'

'And Sylvia?'

'I never saw her again.'

'So you ran away?'

'You can call it that, which probably made the situation look worse than ever, but I didn't care a damn. Derek tried to get in touch again, but I refused to see him or speak to him except to inform him that Sylvia could supply the details. Matron was upset and difficult, but ended up giving me favourable credentials.' Theresa hesitated, her face pale and withdrawn. 'I've thought of going to Salisbury or some other hospital, I could carry on nursing. Money from Dad's estate is still in the bank, but it's not going to last for ever—' She lowered sudden moist eyes and bit her lip.

Mary saw, and knew that Theresa was thinking of her parents and that tragic air disaster that had left her an orphan at the age of seventeen, more than three years ago, but the heartbreak was still there. She had turned to nursing, a profession she had yearned after since childhood.

'Well, I do think you acted tempestuously, honey. Not but that I would have probably done the same thing. However, thanks for telling me. I can read between the lines and realize that you haven't revealed how much you must have suffered because of that obnoxious couple, there should be a law against types like that. As for the high-handed Derek, I confess now that I never liked him anyway, you're well rid of him – knowing your pride— You're very welcome to stay here as long as I can manage to keep you, and that's as long as I have breath in my body!'

Theresa swallowed back the lump in her throat and spoke quietly. 'I'm blessed to have friends like you and Dan. Thank you. Please let me help in any way possible. I'm not afraid of work.'

Mary smiled. 'Go on with you! Everything is run on oiled wheels, there's not even enough for me to do except care for Dan and that young miss. I know of your propensity for work, you'll find something to do if it kills you! You're here to have a good rest, so relax and forget the past. We have some top saddle-horses, you can ride and explore to your heart's content. Our village club provides tennis, dancing and golf – believe me, there are scads of eligible males who would jump to partner you and take your mind off other problems.' The smile turned into an irrepressible chuckle. 'I'm sorry, Terry, but I've suddenly had a clear picture of you standing in a man's flat and a disapproving doctor looking at you with deep suspicion. Picturing Theresa Stanton drawing up her haughty five-foot-what-have-you, in a man's dressing-gown, and imperiously handing him the ring!'

Theresa smiled too and a heaviness lifted from her heart. Mary was right, it did sound real corny, the way to view it was lightheartedly. Somehow, Derek's suspicions and distrust would be seen in its right perspective and she would be wary of so-called love in future. The shock of disillusionment had been painful and in the days that followed left a gap similar to having an aching tooth extracted. The idea of eligible men in the neighbourhood left her stone cold. She did not voice this feeling to Mary, but decided to be more circumspect in her dealings with the opposite sex in future.

Humour came to her rescue and lit her eyes as she wondered how Dr. Derek Mann had explained his sudden loss of a fiancée to his society friends. Her name must be well coated with mud by this time! Well, Sylvia had the field now. Was it possible to fake a faint as well as she had? Theresa came to the conclusion that she was not such a good nurse after all, not to see through or diagnose fake from reality.

CHAPTER TWO

STANDING on the verandah, breathing deeply in the fresh
morning air, Theresa looked at the distant hills and reflected
that her first impression of the country was definitely wrong.
It was not desolate or forsaken at all. Across the tobacco-
lands umbrella trees dotted the landscape and the veld was
lushly green – ideal for cattle farming, Dan had informed
her. Beyond the deep green line of trees that grew along the
river-bank and which delineated his land from Milward's
vast cattle ranch she could see softly rolling hills, the early
morning haze giving them a wavering, unreal appearance.
Later, the harsh, hot sun would reveal outcrops of huge
rocks with thickly-fleshed aloes and other strange plants
growing in crevices and gullies.

Land of the Flame Lily! A curious thrill of excitement
coursed through the girl's body as she stood looking into the
distance. It seemed to beckon to her with impelling, expectant arms as if willing her to come, 'come and discover what
mysteries we hold for you, girl, come and explore nature in
its beauty'.

'It's a lovely view, don't you agree, Terry?' Mary joined
her and sat on the encircling wall. 'Although that same view
can turn out excruciatingly hot and unnerving if you happen
to be out there later in the day. Don't ever go out riding or
walking without a hat, it's fatal.'

Theresa turned an eager face. 'Oh, Mary, could I take a
horse after breakfast? My riding has gone rusty, but I'll be
very careful and promise to glue my hat on. I'm so intrigued
to see what's down there amongst that line of green trees. I
can almost hear them calling me.'

Mary looked into her friend's face, noting that blue eyes
held a sparkle which had not been there the previous day.
That lost look was not in evidence and she hoped sincerely
that it would be banished entirely during Terry's stay at
Oaklands.

' "The Call of the Wild". It's getting you already, pet.
Either you remain immune or its velvet claws hold you in a

passionate embrace from which there's no escape. One or the other, there's no in-between.'

Mary spoke dryly, but the look in her own eyes belied the even tones. This land had already claimed her in joyous bondage.

'That sounds wonderfully romantic and you've got it bad, that's for sure, friend.' The misty outlines drew Theresa's eyes again and she added contemplatively, 'Yes, I guess it could enthral one very easily if one were so inclined.'

'Even against one's inclination, my dear girl. If you answer that call just once then you're sunk, for good and all.'

'Scott Milward's wife, were her ears deaf?' Theresa's question, coming up suddenly from the depths of unconscious thinking, surprised even herself.

Mary considered. 'Elaine was simply not cut out for this kind of life. Scott indulged her recklessly. She's spoilt and very lovely, but—' she hesitated.

'Did he – does he love her very much?'

'He worshipped her,' Mary stated flatly.

A dull ache of pain at her own lost love was suddenly affiliated to that of Milward's awry love and marriage and Theresa shook the bitter mood, as if it were a heavy black cloak, off her shoulders. She spoke with enforced brightness. 'Well, I hope the claws are sheathed this morning, I only want to explore a teeny and won't heed any clarion calls. Do you think Dan will let me have a horse?'

'Of course. But you must promise to be careful and not go too far. The boys are busy in the lands and I haven't anyone here to go with you. I can't get away on account of Poppet, if you promise—'

'Cross my heart and hope—' Theresa chuckled at Mary's earnest expression and gave her a quick hug. 'Let's grub, I'm famished. I'll have to watch my figger at this rate!'

'Ha! From what I remember you could eat lashings of everything without any noticeable difference to your vital statistics. I was the one who dared not look at a cream-puff but I felt the expansion!'

Dan came round the corner of the verandah. 'Do I get breakfast, or are you two going to stand in mutual admiration all morning? I'm a working man, alas, otherwise it would pleasure me greatly to spend my days gazing at the view.'

His twinkling eyes travelled slowly over the slender figure of the girl at his wife's side. Theresa stepped back in mock alarm.

Mary put a fist under Dan's chin. 'Stop leering, Casanova, come and eat, and take that hungry look off your silly face.'

'Jealous spoilsport!' Dan grinned wickedly and slung long arms around the girls' shoulders as he led them in.

Theresa dismounted and tethered the horse to a stout branch, then made her way to the water's edge. The river was rippling cheerfully over shallow rocks to settle into deep pools fringed with tall grasses and reeds. Wild bauhinia and spathodeas were struggling to reach for sunshine amidst tall gums. Masses of swordfern grew in damp crevices on the banks and a fascinated girl followed the course, stepping over fallen branches and undergrowth.

A slight rustle in the reeds startled her and her heart started to beat heavily. Heavens, she had forgotten that Dan had mentioned many types of snakes to be found hereabouts! Theresa stood perfectly still, her eyes glued to the spot from whence the noise had come. Not even a stout stick in her hands for protection; there were plenty lying around, but she dared not move for fear of attracting attention.

The silence lengthened, and just as she decided to move the sound came again and she was staring straight into the large velvety eyes of a small furry animal. Hypnotized blue held equally mesmerized brown for seconds on end and then Theresa expelled her breath with a gasp. A startled squeak at the unexpected guest and the furry ball backed out of sight!

Theresa moved out of the brush and found a large boulder jutting into the water, its smooth top already warming in the sun. She sat down on it, her legs suddenly weak, and fumbled for a cigarette. If a small animal could frighten her like that, what would happen if she met up with crocodile or hyena or ... were there lions in this vicinity? Her hand shook as she inhaled deeply and stared across the river apprehensively.

'Coward!' she castigated herself sternly. 'The wilds call with the rustle of a small creature and you nearly die of fright. Shame on you, Theresa Stanton!' Her eyes roved on and rested on an outcrop of rocks limned with a brush of golden sunlight. A brilliant flash of scarlet flowers bloomed in a pocket of ground amongst the rocks and their regal beauty drew her delighted gaze. In no time she had found a crossing of flat rocks. All thoughts of fearful animals were forgotten as Theresa climbed the outcrop and peered into the earthed crevice at this blaze of colour and beauty.

Could it be the St. John Lily? she wondered. It would be sacrilege to pick them, they looked so right in that setting. She would leave them just so, her own private treasure trove, to come and gloat over and over again. With a sigh of pleasure the girl backed down and walked around the rocks seeking more beauty.

A deep, blowing grunt close to her unsuspecting back spun her round and again she was staring into large velvety eyes! The large gleaming eyes of the biggest domestic beast she had ever seen. One involuntary leap and Miss Stanton was up on the rocks again!

Looking down, with her heart in her mouth, she observed that it was not a cow but a very red, fearfully humped, ferocious-looking bull. The red, fearful, ferocious bull grunted again and she drew her feet up in agitation; could that hulk of animal climb rocks? His eyes were also red in close-up, probably a stud bull with the usual bad temper accorded to the breed. . . . Thus, again Theresa sat perfectly still, her mind desperately seeking a way out of her predicament, while the animal stood below her with swishing tail (getting ready for the charge?).

With relief she espied a horse and rider topping the rise several hundred yards away. She was afraid to move in case the animal became excited, but the rider, unaware of impending tragedy, had turned away. In desperation a piercing whistle left her lips and the horse reared in fright.

Calming his horse, the man faced around to take in the situation at a glance. A golden nymph huddled on a large boulder while her red-eyed captor emitted deep noises from a well-developed neck and throat. To Theresa's ears came the heart-relieving call as Scott Milward rode nearer.

'Sit very still, I'm going to rush him, frighten him away. Be ready to jump on my horse when I stop. Here I come!'

A shrill, cowboy-like yelp rent the air and hooves thundered as he dashed forward and the startled beast below her turned tail and fled. With a flourish the rider drew up, in an instant he had scooped the nymph into the saddle and they were away!

Flying across the veld at this speed brought more terror to the girl. She had been rescued from one hazard only to be flung into another, a broken neck to say the least. 'Stop, oh, stop, please!' Theresa screamed into the passing wind. Scott slowed down and she stammered in a choked voice, 'You're going in the wrong direction. M-my horse is–is over that way.'

He veered around and slackened speed as they neared the the river, finally stopping at the crossing where Theresa had left her horse. Scott loosened his firm grip on her waist, dismounted with a lithe movement and lifted the trembling girl down. Theresa's legs were fluid and Scott held her with strong arms while she steadied herself.

Breathlessly she looked up at him while endeavouring to stand firmly on her own stupid feet. Grey eyes gazing down into hers suddenly made her feel more limp than ever, as if she was being hypnotized. For the third time in one morning and, inexplicably, she was most afraid of the eyes now holding hers, if she wasn't careful she would surely drown in the depths of those smoky-grey pools!

Slowly Scott dropped his arms and stepped back, and Theresa experienced almost a physical wrench when his eyes left hers for a casual look at the river. 'You'll be all right now, Miss Stanton. I guess your fiery beast is over the horizon by now.'

She stammered, 'I don't know how to thank you, Mr. Milward. I was terrified – it was very good – I mean courageous of you to rescue me in that reckless fashion—'

''Twas a pleasure, ma'am, think nothing of it.' He touched his hat.

Did Theresa detect slight sarcasm in his manner and the way a sudden dimple played at the corner of his mouth? The humble touch of hand to hat somehow did not accord with the autocratic bearing of the rest of that sun-browned body and compelling face.

'Well, I'm indeed grateful,' she reiterated. 'I wonder who that beast belongs to, and is he as fierce as he looks? Whether he is or not I'd hate to meet up with him again. He did get a fright when you descended on him with that heathen yell!'

'I agree, a yell of such proportions would frighten the devil out of his lair. Forgive the spectacular rescue, my dear. Boys will be boys even at my age. You'll find your way home from here?'

The hooded eyes and change of manner bewildered the girl and the cold dismissal in his question was so evident that she felt a chill clamp coldly around her heart.

Theresa collected herself and her voice was equally cool and casual. 'Thank you, yes. Again, many thanks for your help and the trouble I caused you.'

She turned on her heel and very carefully stepped on to the stones crossing the river. Only when the opposite side was reached did she hear the sound of his departure and she watched as horse and rider vanished from sight. What a strange man, and how moody could one get? Why in heaven's name did he apologize for rescuing her, and that crack about boys being boys? Scott Milward was certainly a contradiction of sardonic inflections and quick, warm actions. Theresa still felt breathless when she remembered his incredibly swift movements as he swept her off the rock on to the horse, the sureness of his arms in that mad gallop.

Absorbed in her thoughts, she scarcely noticed the time or distance, surfacing only when her horse ambled through the home-gates. Dan was climbing out of the jeep and they met on the front steps.

'Have you been out all this time, doll? That was real naughty of you.'

'Oh, Dan, the time has flown, is it really midday? I hope Mary isn't angry with me.' Theresa removed her hat and felt anxious as Mary, appearing in the passage, stopped to survey her, arms akimbo.

'I'll cancel that call I put through to the local police-hounds,' she remarked evenly. At the girl's shocked face she continued chidingly, 'Anyway, I was going to put a call out for you, but I didn't, so now I don't have to cancel it, do I?

Lucky for you, my girl, because if I had I would—'

'You're getting slightly tangled in the tongue, Mary *mia*. Give the girl a chance to explain her tardy appearance.' Don slapped his wife's rear affectionately.

She glared at him indignantly. 'Don't get fresh with me, Daniel Rourke, I'll have you know I'm a respectable married woman. Come on in, Theresa Stanton. ... Now sit down and explain.'

Grinning at her friend's stern countenance, Theresa sank into a deep armchair. 'You'll never guess what I went through this day. I met up with three wild creatures! The first one ran in fright (so did I), the second cornered me on a rock and the third – the third, on a horse, rescued me from the second one, so there!'

The Rourkes stared at her and looks of amazement on their faces were so similar that she burst into delighted laughter. Mary gave Dan a meaning look. He started loosening his belt in a threatening manner, his dark gaze on the laughing girl.

Theresa stopped abruptly. 'All right, Dan, don't spank me! I'll be more explicit for your dense benefit, although my condensed effort was rather fabulous, don't you think?' Dan threatened again and she continued hurriedly. When she came to the end of her story Mary's face was a study in blankness and Dan was equally poker-faced. She looked from one to the other in puzzlement. 'Neither of you seem to be enthralled at my tale of gallant rescue—'

'I think it's absolutely astonishing—' Mary came alive, but her husband forestalled her, drowning further words in a loud voice.

'Yes, yes, colleen, it was a good thing Scott was in the offing, wasn't it, otherwise you never know what might have happened.' He strode hurriedly to the door and turned. 'You did say it was a ferocious beast that confronted you?'

'Yes, that's what I said.' Uncertainty clouded Theresa's voice, for a humiliating suspicion was taking form.

Dan remained deadpan. 'Mm, that's what I thought you said. Excuse, please, I must wash my hands.' He disappeared.

'Mary—?'

'Darling, it must have been thrilling, especially that ter-

27

rifying ride—' in a darkening tone. 'I'll speak to that Milward! Oh, heavens, I smell something burning!' That young matron smartly exited, blowing vigorously into her handkerchief.

Theresa lay back and darkly nursed indignation. 'So!' she snorted aloud, 'it was a big frame-up. And my two very good friends have realized that. How tactful of them to disappear so conveniently. Not a ferocious beast at all, only wanting to be friends, *and* belonging to that odious man, I presume. Boys will be boys, eh? That's why he did have a scrap of decency to ask forgiveness for the spectacular rescue. How big of him, Mr. S. confounded Milward!' She stopped, her fury choking her. But her thoughts were savage and precipitated hot colour to her cheeks as she dwelt on the person responsible for her humiliated senses.

When Dan came back Theresa was cool and composed. 'Is lunch ready, Dan dear?' Her smile was transparently ingenuous. 'What's wrong, dear man? Is my face dirty, you're looking so hard at me. I shall wash immediately, sir!' Theresa blew a fluttering kiss and ambled out, swaying slim hips in an exaggerated motion.

At lunch she rubbed it in good and hard. 'Mary dear, I am so sorry I caused you worry by staying away so long. Surely now that you've heard of my terrific experience wouldn't you say it was worth it?' Clasping her hands together, looking dreamy, she continued, 'And that fabulous, brave man, his heart must have stopped when he saw my danger—'

Her friend looked worried. 'Really, Terry, I think I should – I think, I mean – you should really know that—'

'Please, Mary, you should try not to repeat yourself so often, try not to stutter, it will be a bad influence on Glynis Theresa.'

'Would it?' Mary caught herself. 'Oh, Terry, I don't always stutter! It's that I – I should tell—'

'There you go again. Dan, you should look into this.' Concern was in Theresa's voice and then she brightened. 'But of course, how silly of me. You're worried, hence the stutter. Not to worry, honey, I know what you're trying to say and, forgive me, I know my manners. I'll thank the obnox— the gallant Mr. Milward very sweetly when next I see him. Oh, be very sure of that!'

Theresa smiled radiantly at her hosts and changed the subject, speaking rapidly of other things. How was Poppet's earache? So glad she was better, could she take her for a walk later? How were the boys doing on the land and at what stage was the fertility of the dear little tobaccos? Theresa jabbered on until it was time for Dan to leave.

Her dismay showed for an instant, when he stopped at the door to remind his wife that Scott was coming to dinner. When Mary turned back she was brushing breadcrumbs into a neat heap on her side-plate.

'I feel sorry for Mr. Milward. Know what, Mary?'

'Yes, dear?' Mary's voice quavered.

'I have a good mind to offer my services to him – for Melinda. After all, he saved my life, and with nursing experience I should qualify, not so? She's too young for schooling, so a nurse would be more suitable, I should think.'

'No! I don't think you should—'

'Thinking again, you were certainly more sure of yourself in the old days. Darling, I'm only teasing, don't look so upset. You mean I'm too young, as Scott remarked at the time of mistaken identity?'

'No, not really, but – well—' Mary tried again.

Theresa decided she had gone far enough, stood and stretched her arms. 'I'll put it to Mr. M. when I see the old dear tonight. Time for the universal siesta. Boy, do I need it! See you later, dear friend, dear friend.' She sang loudly as she walked down the passage to her room, twisting the placement of words in an old song, 'A friend is just a stranger you'll never know!'

29

CHAPTER THREE

THERESA gave a last glance at her reflection in the mirror. Hair piled in a neat swirl on top of her head, slim body enchantingly sheathed in creamy, embossed linen featuring a high front neckline that dipped daringly low down her back. Light make-up accentuated thickly-fringed blue eyes. Amethyst ear-rings and gold sandals completed her dress.

Full battle dress – to meet Mr. Joker Milward!

Mary raised an admiring eyebrow and Dan raised his glass when Theresa joined them at the bar. Sundowners were enjoyed while they waited for the dinner guest. It came as a slight shock to the girl when she suddenly realized that Derek had not touched her thoughts for a full day. That did not mean she had forgotten and at the moment she was only concerned with would-be jokers. Scott Milward evidently regarded her as a silly girl who needed thrills to disperse boredom. A thought struck her and she looked long and hard at Dan and Mary.

'By the way, how come I was called a bluestocking by your neighbour, at the station?'

Dan opened his mouth guiltily, but his wife forestalled him.

'My fault entirely, Terry. When we mentioned your visit I rather harped on your classical background. Knowing, having known the Professor, your dad, so well, I often spoke of his brilliance and personality when Scott was present. I guess that gave him the impression you were a bluestocking. It's not an insult, dear, for you to have a cultural background. Your daddy was the finest man I ever knew, and his love of the classics has rubbed off on you as well; I recall quite clearly that you always preferred the opera and would rather browse in his quite fantastic library than lead a gayer life of dancing, parties, etc.'

'Oh, I see.' Theresa accepted the explanation, so did not pursue the subject. Mary must have told Scott that she was also a nurse, but he probably ignored it and thought she was merely after the glamour of the profession, not as a serious occupation.

The sound of a car outside put an end to thoughts and she stiffened slightly as Scott walked into the room. She studied the man as he greeted Mary and Dan in a courteously familiar way. He really was incredibly handsome and looked cool and suave in a light tropical suit. Darkly-lashed grey eyes turned now to her and a smoky flame flickered in their depths as his swift appraisal started on gleaming hair, circled her face and came to rest on the full curve of soft lips.

'Good evening, Miss Stanton. How are you?' Scott held out his hand to enclose hers in a warm clasp.

'Very well, thank you, Mr. Milward. I hope the same of you.' A queer tingle ran up her arm and she was very conscious of his long brown fingers.

'I'm fit, thanks.' He dropped her hand suddenly.

'The usual, Scott? I'm sure Terry and you need not be so formal. Theresa, meet Scott.' Dan handed him a glass.

Scott Milward's sudden smile transformed his imperious face into lines of boyishness. 'Hello, Theresa.' Her name on his lips had a caressing quality.

'Hello, Scott.' An inner tremor softened her voice and Theresa gave herself an invisible, angry shake. 'Don't get soft now, simpleton. This is the man who took you for a ride in more ways than one, and don't you forget it just because he has a dimple in that brown cheek and his mouth looks generous, vulnerable. A double-crossing face!' Thus Theresa admonished herself while she smiled sweetly and accepted the glass handed to her. To Dan she said mildly, 'I shouldn't really have so much to drink, Dan dear, you know how silly it makes me.'

That worthy raised surprised brows at this blatant lie, but she had turned back to Scott. 'Mary told me about your daughter. How is she?'

'Melinda is fine, thank you. A little put out because she couldn't come with me.' A light gleamed in his eyes at mention of his daughter.

'Have you solved the mystery of the missing – governess?' Sweet venom showed for an instant.

Scott studied Theresa intently for a moment and then

31

answered, noncommittally, 'Yes. A phone call, late this afternoon. Of all things, the unfortunate woman developed mumps and there's no available substitute at present. I mean no one who is suitably qualified.'

'A qualified nurse? Staid and not too young?'

Mary interposed hastily, 'I'm sure they'll find someone for you before Vera leaves.' She flashed a warning glance at her friend.

That damsel smiled enigmatically. 'Dear Mary is so worried about you and Melinda, Scott. I have a proposition to discuss, later, if you care to listen—'

The maid announced dinner and Mary quickly led the way, giving Theresa's arm a pinch in passing. The girl gave her a surprised, innocent look of reproach. However, she did not reopen the subject until dinner was over and they sat sipping coffee out of diminutive cups.

The conversation covered recent films and shows, and Theresa took her cue from there. 'I like good shows, but you'd never guess what my favourite films are.' She looked dreamy, then opened her eyes wide as Scott raised an inquiring eyebrow. 'Westerns! Oh, those cowboys!'

Three pairs of incredulous eyes met her wide blue gaze.

'Do you know, Scott, I have a sneaking feeling that my friends think I'm slightly highbrow, but they're so wrong. And that's why I want to thank you again for our thrilling ride this morning – it put me right into my favourite picture. Handsome hero rescues desperate maiden! Of course—' she added deprecatingly, 'you didn't realize that the poor little beast was only being friendly and there wasn't any danger really. I'm glad, though, because it was exciting, and you do ride superbly well. Please forgive me for not putting you wise to the real facts, but I couldn't resist the Western melodrama of it all. My piercing whistle was most realistic, wasn't it? And you responded so gallantly. Am I forgiven?' bland innocence entreated.

Scott Milward looked at her steadily. 'Touché' he murmured softly. (Her eyes were definitely the colour of rain-washed hyacinths). 'You're forgiven, Theresa. I'm pleased to have given you the thrill of living up to your favourite – Westerns.'

'Thank you kindly, sir.' Theresa turned her attention to

the silent, dumb-struck Rourkes. 'I did put it over you as well, and I'm sorry, but it was such fun watching your faces. Deadpan Dan and Muttering Mary listening to the escapades of Titillating Theresa! Well, now that we're all friends again, my proposition—'

'Theresa!' Mary found her voice.

'Yes, dear? Oh, I know you're going to warn me that Mr. Milward – Scott – will turn down my proposal, but I'm going to put it to him, regardless.' Theresa looked serene, but her insides began to wobble as she met Scott's disconcerting gaze. She was quite certain he would not accept her offer, yet something was driving her; she wanted to see that look of acidulous contempt appear and then inform him that she was only joking, blithely and amusedly.

'I'm a third-year nurse, which includes extensive training in the children's wards. If I can be of assistance in caring for your Melinda, at least until such a time as you find another – governess or nurse, I herewith file application for said vacancy.'

A long silence ensued. She asked timidly, 'Or am I too young and flighty, perhaps?'

Acidulous contempt was not forthcoming. Scott considered her with unreadable eyes, his expression inscrutable. 'May we adjourn to the lounge, Mary, while I consider Theresa's generous offer?'

'Certainly. I'll – er – I'll follow as soon as I've pacified Poppet, I can hear her grumbling.'

Dan also found a farm matter to settle, so Theresa and Scott walked in silence to the sitting-room. She seated herself and he wandered over to the window and stood with his back to her. An uncompromising back, straight, autocratic. . . . A peculiar feeling feathered over her scalp as she waited for him to speak. All of a sudden Theresa did not want contempt or any other form of sarcasm from this man and was bitterly sorry that she had deliberately invited it.

He turned, at last, to face her. 'Would your doctor-fiancé approve of a position for you as nursemaid to a divorced man's daughter?'

The question came so casually that it took a moment for Theresa to assimilate its content, and then she was shaken at the pain that gripped her heart. She looked down at her hands, fighting for control. Did that pain stem from her own broken heart or was it pain for his casual admittance of the final wrench from the woman he adored? She still did not know, when a proud head was raised and she stated simply, 'Derek and I are no longer engaged. I've also resigned my position at the hospital.'

'I see.' He rubbed his chin reflectively. 'Well, I'll take you up on that offer, Theresa. You may want a day or two to visit with Mary. Let's see, it's Sunday tomorrow – I'll call for you on Wednesday. Suit you?' The question was shot at her in a brusque, husky voice.

Theresa stood up suddenly, walked away from him and leaned her elbows on the bar. The shock of his acceptance of her impulsive offer was like a blow between the shoulder blades, coming on the heels of the swift pain that had shaken her. She felt his presence beside her and his elbow brushed against her arm as he idly fingered an ornamental opener.

Scott spoke then sardonically. 'It evidently doesn't suit you. Well, I don't blame you, you're entitled to have your holiday and good times. I'm afraid my predicament is rather urgent as Miss Smith is leaving quite soon. Getting married, hence the hurry, poor girl.'

The bitter sarcasm brought a quick retort. 'There are happy marriages too, Scott. I've lost a fiancé and you've lost a wife, so we don't see life through rose-coloured glasses at present. Dan and Mary, for instance, who could be happier than they—?'

'You're still young, my dear Theresa. Quite possibly there will be a reconciliation with your doctor, or you may find so-called love elsewhere. So don't couple my troubles with yours.'

'But you're not an old man, Scott. Pain recedes after a while, soon one finds new horizons and other compensations follow. You have your daughter to love. To me love is an illusion—'

Scott cut across her words with grim finality. 'Spare me the relevant details. We seem to have deviated some-what.'

Dan had an affectionate arm across his wife's shoulders as they came and joined the couple at the bar. 'Serious discussion, what?' he asked jocularly.

'Ah, very serious. Theresa's love life has gone awry, so has mine. We've been commiserating. Also, because of that I'm about to lose a would-be applicant, if my guess is right.' The mocking eyebrow was high and grim amusement glinted in imperious eyes.

Theresa was seething with fury at his curt dismissal of her attempt to comfort him. Their eyes met for a timeless moment while wills clashed, one arrogantly confident, and the other indomitable, spirited. Theresa turned away from the magnetic personality of the man and slipped her arm through Mary's. 'Scott, or should I say Mr. Milward as he's my future employer, has accepted my application and I'm to start on Wednesday. Not having met Melinda I can't conceive what my duties will be, but if she's as kind and gracious as her old dad, I have no need to worry. Don't look so surprised, Mary, I'm sure to have a day off occasionally to visit you and enjoy other exciting times that my extreme youth yearns for. Whew, that calls for a drink! What say, fellow countrymen?'

Scott spoke imperturbably. 'It certainly does, especially for you, after that noble speech. You may call me Scott, I won't consider it an impertinence. Dan, don't be mean with your hooch, fill 'em up and drink to this charming girl's and my grateful alliance.' He added, almost as an afterthought, keeping his voice deliberately casual, 'I've told Theresa, and I want you to know as well, my – separation – is finalized.'

Mary spoke quietly. 'Scott, I don't quite know what to say. Candidly I think it's better this way.' Her eyes were shining with compassion as she placed a comforting hand on his arm.

Dan looked at his friend wordlessly, a world of feeling in his warm eyes.

'Cheers, folks. Here's to your freedom, Scott Milward, and to my slavery!' Theresa challenged him to break the pall of bitterness that threatened.

'Thank you, Theresa. Sunshine gal, you're good for the morale,' Scott smiled, and lifted his glass in arrogant salute.

The party suddenly became happier as Dan took over and channelled everybody into a brighter mood. His spirited

Irish humour and Mary's dry repartee kept them vastly amused. Scott was not lagging and Theresa was amazed at his easy, descriptive knowledge of people and countries he had visited. She noticed that he did not talk of America, even though he had met and married Elaine in that country. His ex-wife now, the woman he adored, so Mary had told her. Was that adoration a thing of the past or was it still in his heart?

When Scott announced that it was time to depart he turned to Dan. 'Bring the girls over for tea tomorrow afternoon. Melinda worries because she hasn't seen Mary and Glynis for some time and it will give her and Theresa a chance to become acquainted.'

'Sure will do that, chum,' Dan acquiesced, and Mary seconded the invitation.

'Good. Thanks for the dinner.' A salutory wave and Scott strode out.

'Well now, my girl, explain your wily ways. I could have cheerfully conked you one at the dinner table. What have you let yourself in for?' Mary demanded.

Theresa giggled deliciously. 'Oh, dear, my tale of rescue—'

'I gathered that you'd cottoned on and you turned the tables very neatly, you had us all tongue-tied. So much for that, now what about this job business?'

Theresa sobered. 'Yes, Mary, it started as a joke and boomeranged with a vengeance. I never dreamt Scott would accept my offer. My pride wouldn't let me climb down after he remarked that, being fond of my pleasures, I probably wouldn't like the idea of starting immediately. That's my case in a nutshell.'

Mary considered thoughtfully. Dan came over and squatted on his heels. 'As master of the house, may I say what I think? I think it's a very good thing. Theresa will be near us instead of miles away as she would be if she goes nursing again. Scott is a good man and will look after her interests. She'll soon show him she's not too young to take the responsibility of caring for his daughter. He really needs a nurse and companion, not a governess. That word is extinct anyway, and being companion-nurse is not demeaning in any way. It's a responsible and worthy vocation, and

Scott will be generous with salary. Have you discussed the financial side with him, Terry?'

'I never gave it a thought!' she exclaimed.

'If you're set on taking on the job, I wouldn't worry. Scott isn't mean, especially where his daughter is concerned.'

'I'm taking it because I've given my word, also to show him I can do it! After all, I have you two at my back, if he should become – obstreperous.' A defiant tilt of chin testified that heaven help the one who dared become difficult with her.

Dan laughed. 'Obstreperous ... Scott? Never that, dear girl. Elaine cured him of any yen or leanings that way. I wonder how he really feels about his decree nisi. He's always been a dark horse—' Dan stopped smiling as he reflected on the inner feelings of Scott Milward.

The family passed a leisurely Sunday morning. Theresa washed her hair and dried it in the warm sun on the lawn while baby Glynis sprawled on a blanket at her feet. The little imp was trying her utmost to reach the green grass so aggravatingly out of reach.

Mary called her in to lunch and she had difficulty in wading through the heavy meal of roast beef, Yorkshire pudding and vegetables with a baked honey sweet to follow. The heat was unnerving.

Back in her room Theresa took off her dress and sandals and flopped on the bed. A questing breeze blew through the open window, cooling her hot brow slightly. She dozed off for a while and was amazed to find the time near to three o'clock when she awoke. A slow surge of excitement welled up at the thought of afternoon tea with Scott Milward. Of course, it was only curiosity to see his daughter and their home. He had been cynical about his lost married status last night, but Theresa was sure it was merely an outer cover for feelings that ran deep. She sensed unplumbed depths in him, a passionate savagery that was curbed with supreme mastery under a show of nonchalance.

After an invigorating shower she slipped a light, square-necked cotton dress over her shoulders and brushed her hair into a smooth cap that flipped out at the ends. Dainty white sandals completed her attire. She looked cool and fresh as she waited with Mary and Glynis for Dan to bring the car.

A symphony of green and white met Theresa's gaze as they drove up the long avenue leading to Scott's home. The stark white of the house stood dappled in golden sunlight amidst the green of tall trees. A swathe of smooth green lawn sloped from the front entrance down to a circular driveway. A woman was seated in one of the chairs under a cool shade-giving tree and her little companion jumped eagerly off her chair as the car stopped in the drive.

Theresa had her first look at Melinda Milward. The child threw herself into Dan's waiting arms with a cry of glee and then wriggled down to hold up her lips for Mary's kiss. The most important thing came now as she was very carefully allowed to carry Glynis (Mary's hands held in protective readiness) across the lawn.

Theresa followed slowly, her eyes on the little girl, a startling miniature of her father – the dark hair, cut short in gamin style, grey eyes also thickly fringed with dark lashes and the same proud, easy grace that he had. Bare-footed, she wore only a scanty white top with red shorts.

Dan had the blanket on the grass and Melinda bent down slowly and, with infinite care, deposited her treasure on it. She turned to regard Theresa with those amazing eyes, in silent scrutiny.

Theresa gave an audible breath as she lifted her own eyes to find an identical pair studying her with the same intensity. Scott had appeared suddenly and was standing a few yards away. He wore tight-hipped brown slacks with a creamy, open-neck shirt which deepened the tan of his neck and arms. With quick, easy strides he closed the gap and put his hand on his daughter's head. Turning to the woman who was standing now, he spoke. 'Miss Smith, meet Miss Stanton.' They acknowledged the introduction and Scott looked down at his daughter. 'Miss Melinda, meet Miss Theresa Stanton.'

Theresa smiled and held out her hand to her future charge. Melinda put a small, sun-browned hand into hers and announced gravely, 'Your hair is like sunbeams and your eyes is like – what, Daddy? – I know, like the sky.

Tresa am very pretty, isn't she, Daddy?'

Theresa thought her voice had the same caressing quality as had her father's when her name, Theresa, was spoken.

'I like you too, Melinda,' she answered quietly.

The strange spell was broken as Scott turned to speak to his other guests and Melinda sat down next to the baby.

'I'll organize the tea.' Vera Smith moved away, but Scott called her back.

'Everything is organized, Vera. Don't run away, get acquainted with Theresa (that inflection again!). I'm hoping she hasn't changed her mind and will be relieving you very shortly.'

He held a chair for Theresa and lifted a quizzical eyebrow. 'My daughter waxes rather lyrical at times. She has her father's love of nature . . . and beauty. You and she should get on well, I hope.' The last came out with sardonic inflection and she shot him a hostile glance before answering with smiling venom.

'I don't doubt that we shall get on very well. What I am beginning to doubt is whether I should like the constant proximity of her father!'

Scott sat down on the chair next to hers and leaned forward. 'Does my charming presence disturb you so much, or is that merely an excuse to vacillate?' he asked softly.

The aura of his presence was magnetic and Theresa drew back slightly to fight a sudden pounding in her ears.

'I am not the vacillating kind and will keep my word, nor do I make a habit of thinking up excuses.' With an effort she turned to Vera. 'I believe you're to be married, Miss Smith? Please accept congratulations and wishes for a happy future.'

Vera Smith had brown hair with bright bird-like eyes of the same colour, and Theresa guessed her age somewhat near the thirties. Her very ordinary features now lighted up into a lovely smile.

'Thank you, Miss Stanton. I'm quite sure Dick and I are going to be very happy. He owns a small garage in Salisbury and he's worked hard to buy a home for us. We've waited a long time and now at last we can afford it. I'm so glad you're coming to help Mr. Milward, although you are a bit young –

39

I mean—' she stammered, and glanced at the small girl who was chattering animatedly to Mary, 'Melinda is a darling but quite a handful – a bit spoilt and—' her face went scarlet as she caught Scott's amused glance.

Theresa came to the rescue. 'I'm twenty-one, have a nurse's qualifications and am quite able to face responsibility, Miss Smith, whatever they may be.' Defiant blue eyes challenged the man sitting next to her. He looked so amused and vital that she could, quite easily, kick him hard! (If she were not a poised twenty-one-year-old.) 'So I'm not as young as you think. I hope Mr. Milward doesn't share your views.'

'Not at all, dear *old* thing, I'm sure you'll cope with Melinda's tantrums.' The wicked gleam left his eyes. 'We'll discuss the proposition later, in my study.' Abruptly he dismissed the subject and drew Mary and Dan into conversation.

'I'd like you to see the horse I bought from Colonel Strang's stables, Dan.'

'I believe that stallion's quite something to look at. Bit on the wild side, so the colonel's yardman told me, and will take some taming.'

'He's a gorgeous hunk of horse. He'll ride tough and he's got a hard mouth. I'll tame him.' Scott stated this fact with a simplicity that was the negation of boastfulness. Theresa thought he looked like a man who would tame anything by simple, arrogant domination if nothing else. His decision would be his law.

'If anybody can you will be that one,' Mary exclaimed. 'You have yet to see Scott Milward on a horse, Terry. It makes my blood run cold if I happen to be in the vicinity when he's busy taming a wild horse!'

'I've seen him on one,' Theresa dryly recollected.

'So you have, but not on a half wild one. By all the laws of nature his neck should have been broken by now.'

Scott grinned. 'Necks don't break so easily, my bloodthirsty one. Not as easily as—' He stopped abruptly.

'As hearts, you were going to say?' Theresa laughed, to cover her confusion. 'But then necks are literally broken while hearts break figuratively speaking and can be mended, with time.'

'Yeah, when your neck is broken you're good and dead, you've had it, as they say in the classics. Thanks be, horses don't break their hearts, Theresa. That's a privilege of the human race, the superior, heartbreaking human race. Ah, here comes the tea. Vera, you may do the honours.'

'Come'n see my baby, Tresa. She's sleeping now, so we must be ver' quiet.' A small, commanding hand tugged at the girl's arm.

'Theresa will have her tea first, Mel.' Scott was firm.

'But, Daddy, I want Tresa to see her now 'cos she closes her eyes just like Glynis does.' Petal lips pouted in appeal.

Scott hesitated and glanced from her to Theresa.

'When daddies speak to their little girls they must always listen.' Theresa added earnestly, 'And you must teach your baby to listen when you talk to her, Melinda. Then she'll be a good girl too, just like you.'

Melinda stopped pouting to consider this statement. 'She's very naughty, I spec's 'cos she's small, but I'll learn her.' A confident elbow dug into Theresa's knee.

'Teach her,' Vera corrected automatically.

Melinda looked her scorn, turned back to her new friend. 'Is your tea very hot? I'll give you a cookie. This's my fav'rit, you can have it.' Magnanimously, the plate was offered.

'That's very kind of you, I also like the gooey ones, thanks.' An inward shudder as she took the proffered creamy concoction.

Melinda promptly relieved her of the empty cup when she finished her tea. 'Now may she come, Daddy?'

'If Miss Theresa wishes,' Scott smiled at his daughter.

Theresa was led on to the wide verandah into a roomy lounge. Her quick eyes took in the bulky furnishings. Large windows were heavily curtained in maroon velvet which made the room dark and close, not counteracting the hot, humid climate at all. Furnishings should be light and airy, to give an illusion of coolness, was her thought. The passage to the bedrooms was carpeted in dark green. Melinda's room was big and airy, the juvenile bed and cupboards painted a dull, drab brown.

Theresa duly looked and admired the quite exquisite

41

baby doll lying in its own little cot. Roughly clothed, the frayed squares of covering were tenderly straightened. (Miss Smith was certainly not imaginative or needle-minded.) Theresa made a mental note to do some sewing for Melinda and wondered if the household sported a sewing-machine. She asked the child to show her the bathroom and was amused when asked, 'Did Tresa want to use the jazz?'

'Yes, dear, but I call it toilet.'

'Vera does too, but Daddy and me say jazz.'

So whatever Daddy says or does must be right! Theresa pondered while she washed her hands. She could foresee a few clashing of wills if Daddy was the fond, spoiling kind. Oh well, she would cross the bridges as they came.

Her heart wept for the motherless child and unwittingly to the wifeless man as well. If he loved Elaine so much it must hurt unbearably at times. And Melinda barely four years old! What had been the cause of her desertion, surely something deeper than dislike of environment? The house looked strongly built, the rooms she had seen were large, but no effort had been made to make use of wide windows or lighter, brighter furnishings. There was not the touch of wifely pride in a home. Elaine might not have had an eye for decor or was it simply that she did not care?

Theresa simply itched to pull down those dark curtains and turf out the stuffy furniture of the lounge! Light, sun-filter curtains and furnishings in green and autumn shades . . . she stopped her wandering thoughts as Mary called from the door.

'Have you gone down the drain, honey? We're waiting for you, come and see the fabulous horse.'

'Coming, Mary!' She opened the door and they walked back to the lounge. Mary stopped and wrinkled her forehead. 'I do wish Scott would do something about this room—'

Theresa laughed. 'It's quite hideous. I've just been going quite mad in the bathroom, thinking of what I would do to it if I had the chance.'

'Oh, you have?' Mary studied her thoughtfully. 'Well, perhaps you can do something. It doesn't seem to bother Scott unduly, but maybe if you play it right things can be—'

Theresa interrupted swiftly, 'It's Scott's house and I'll be an employee, don't forget.' She ran her fingers through her hair and continued, 'One thing I am going to do and that's fix Melinda's room, paint or replace that drab furniture, if I have to do it myself. Do you know if this establishment possesses a sewing-machine?'

'Not that I know of, but you could borrow mine.'

'What needs to be borrowed?' Scott inquired from the doorway.

'Terry wants a sewing-machine and I said she could borrow mine,' Mary explained.

'What for?'

'For the normal use, to sew and mend.' Theresa showed amused sarcasm for the density of males while she hoped uneasily that he had not heard her remarks on the hideousness of his lounge.

His eyes held hers, tiger-yellow lights flickered in their smoky depths when he spoke. 'I am enlightened. Are you two coming to the paddock? Dan wants to look at the horses.' He turned on his heel and the two girls hastily followed his long-legged stride.

Theresa leaned her arms on the rail next to the others while Scott vaulted it with lithe grace. Three of the horses cantered up confidently, the fourth one watched them warily from a distance. He was a magnificent animal with a glistening sherry-brown coat and silky blond mane. The two men watched admiringly and waxed enthusiastic on his finer points. The dappled horse at the rail came up to Theresa and nuzzled her arm sharply. At her sudden exclamation Scott turned and extracted a sugar lump from his pocket.

'Frost has taken a liking to you. Give him this, he has a sweet tooth. You may regard him as yours while you're here. He's a reliable old nag if one treats him nice. He recognizes you!' Another wicked grin brought out the dimple at the side of his mouth.

Scarlet flags of colour unfurled on the girl's cheeks as she realized it was the horse of her dramatic ride with Scott. She held out the sugar lump in a tentative hand. Frost took it delicately between strong teeth, lifting his lips in a wicked grin that matched his master's!

Melinda climbed on to the rails and Theresa put a protective arm around her, not only for the purpose of safe-guarding the child but to hide and overcome an alarming, feathery feeling that coursed down her spine as Scott kept his gaze on her, a look that darkened as it moved to the child and then back to the girl with the shining honey hair. He turned back, almost as if it were an effort, to answer Dan's questions on his next cattle-drive. They discussed this im-portant matter while Mary, Theresa and Melinda started walking back to the house.

Vera Smith was crooning to a very discontented baby, and sighed in relief when they appeared. The house-boy wanted to know if the visitors would have coffee, but Mary negatived the suggestion. It was time to leave as the baby's bath-time was due and she was already becoming fretful.

Scott held the car door for Theresa. 'We haven't had our talk. You needn't come until next Sunday, that will give you a few more days with Mary and Dan. Vera will be leaving tomorrow week. I'll be over during the week to discuss finance and anything else you would like to know. Are you still agreeable?'

'Yes, Scott, and thank you for the respite. I like your Melinda,' Theresa said quietly.

'Good, that's half the battle won, and your feeling is evi-dently reciprocated by – my girl.'

'But not by you, Mr. Milward,' she thought as they drove off, 'judging by the dark depths in those grey eyes, I've been weighed and found wanting!' Well, he had a week in which to change his mind about employing her, but if he decided to stick to the arrangement, she would show him her capa-bilities or die in the effort! Not all women should be judged by the fecklessness of a minor few.

Theresa watched the miles of orange orchards pass by and the sweet smell of their blossoms impacted her nostrils and senses like a physical blow and intensified a sudden pain in the region of her heart.

CHAPTER FOUR

THE girl in the garden, hair and linen hat damp with perspiration, looked up from her hot, absorbing task as a shadow fell across the flower-bed and the next moment Scott Milward was down on his heels helping to pull out the tough weeds. Stubborn with her, yet they slipped out of the ground at his first tug, roots and all.

'Hello, Theresa. Hard at it, I see. Weeds are always sturdier than flowers or veg. People wouldn't use the term "a weed of a man" to denote weakness if they could work amongst our resistant vegetation for one day only!' His khaki sleeves were rolled up and a tanned arm inadvertently brushed against her bare elbow.

The sudden vibrating shock of contact coupled with his equally sudden appearance brought swift colour to cheeks already flushed from sun and exertion. Theresa was inarticulate for moments and Scott finally turned from his chore to look at her with sharp eyes.

'No talkie today, ma'am? Velly solly, missee, humble self will letleat—'

'Of course I can talk – if I want to. And don't speak so silly!' She spoke in irritation, more with herself than at the teasing, sing-song intonation. Standing up from her cramped position, she took off her hat and brushed the earth off her brown jeans. The darned man must be wired with electricity, statics or what-have-you!

'Well, kindly "want to", if you please. I came over especially to talk terms regarding our arrangement.' His voice was curt and abrupt, but softened as he also stood up and scrutinized her face.

'Hell, don't you know not to work outside in this heat? Your face is very flushed . . . and dirty. Go and have a quick wash, I'll wait and have tea with you. Go on, girl, you're not hypnotized, or has the sun got you?'

'I thought you were in a hurry—' she began indignantly.

'I am, but will contain my haste long enough to cure your

45

hypnosis—' he stepped closer and brought his face down. The startled girl took a step backwards. '—with a cup of tea, if you'll play hostess. Run along, lass,' Scott finished, and shot out his hand to flip strands of her hair across her face.

He watched her walk away, her slender shoulders stiff with inner fury, and called out clearly yet softly: 'Don't hate me so actively, honey, it gives a most provoking swing to your – er – posterior!

Provoking indeed! And the nerve to call her honey, who did he think he was, king of all he surveys? And telling her to wash her face, like a – a child!

This was all hissed at her reflection in the bathroom mirror. The dust-smeared girl hissed back at her and suddenly Theresa saw the funny side of it and started a hysterical giggle. Her reflection giggled back and she turned away in disgust to rinse her face and hands in the cool water. She ran a comb through her hair hastily. She must not keep the arrogant man waiting, he was quite capable of opening the door and demanding explanations.

Dan and family were away on a shopping trip to the village, so she would have to be the polite hostess to Scott. Theresa had declined to go with them, meaning to have a quiet rest, as she had been out riding the day before and her posterior, as Scott called it, was still smarting from unfamiliar exertions. Becoming restless later, she had wandered out to the garden and, spying the weeds, decided she would work a little for her keep. So Scott had found her.

He was sprawled out in a low deck-chair when Theresa returned, dark head resting back and eyes closed. She came close over the grass and studied the thick smudge of eyelashes fanned over dark, tanned cheeks, the reposed, well-cut mouth.

'Handsome guy, hmm, Theresa?' He spoke without opening his eyes.

She turned away and busied herself with the tea things. 'Handsome is as handsome does,' she quoted satirically.

'Hmm, so they say.' Scott opened his eyes. 'What does that mean, exactly? I don't mean your satire but the words of that silly quote. If handsome does, is handsome is? You said it, so elucidate, please.'

46

'Quite candidly, I don't know.' Theresa considered gravely. 'I guess it means if you think you're handsome then you are, and if you think what you do is handsome, then it is, even though others don't reckon so. Skin-deep vanity, in fact,' she stated with aforesaid (handsome) sagacity.

'Wisely and shrewdly put, dear nymph, sweet Theresa.'

He had never foreshortened her Christian name and it rolled on his tongue smoothly, almost caressingly. Prickles tingled her scalp every time he said it, and yet she would not have it any other way. It sounded so right – especially with the endearment attached. She caught herself up and asked primly, 'Sugar, Scott?'

'Two, thanks.' He sat up and took the proffered cup. 'We have Cleo, Melinda's coloured nanny, to give you a hand when necessary, so if you want time off to visit she's quite capable of taking over until you return, but only while I or my white manager are in the offing. I've never left Melinda in sole charge of coloured servants. That's very important; definite arrangements must be made if you go out.'

'Of course, I understand, and will make arrangements accordingly,' she answered.

'They are fairly reliable, but – call it a fad – fairly reliable is not good enough for me, not with my daughter's welfare at stake.' Scott lifted his cup and drained the contents. 'Now, about your salary. May I know what your dole was at the hospital?'

Theresa told him and he exclaimed in astonishment, 'A mere pittance! How could you live on it?'

She shrugged her shoulders. 'We get by. After all, our uniforms are free and if one lives in it's not too bad. Living out is only possible if you share a flat and expenses.'

'You still have an income from your father's estate?'

'Most of that has gone for my training, but there's still enough to last a year or so, depending on how I handle it,' she stated candidly. 'It's a good thing there aren't any flicks close by with dashing Westerns. My pocket money will be saved!'

Scott laughed suddenly, delightedly. 'Thanks be for a sense of humour, otherwise I would be in the dog-box right now! Forgive me, but that situation was irresistible. It happened to be one of my tamest bulls and they're all most amiable. You certainly turned the escapade neatly. I was shamed to the depths.' His laughter was infectious and Theresa joined him.

He then named a salary that she protestingly declared too generous. Scott insisted that she accept it. 'It's worth that to me if Melinda is kept happy and healthy.'

'Well, if I find that my services and the work entailed doesn't demand so high a salary, I shall refuse to accept it,' Theresa said flatly.

Scott stood up and smiled. 'We'll fight about that another day. Did Mary tell you about a dance and barbecue in the village, on Saturday evening?'

'Yes, they did. We're going. I believe a room is cleared at the club for the children and infants and one or two women offer free services as baby-sitters, while everybody else chokes outside in smelly smoke, downs great draughts of beer and dances into the early hours.'

Scott hitched his trousers in a decisive gesture. 'I'll have the pleasure of escorting you and Melinda to said bingo.'

'Oh, will you? It's the first I've heard. Do Mary and Dan know of this – decision?'

'No. But they'll be informed very shortly.'

Theresa felt exasperation rise. 'The correct procedure is to, firstly, request the pleasure from the lady of your choice. Secondly—'

Scott looked over her head. 'Will you come with Melinda and me?'

'—Secondly it's not seemly for an employer to escort his child's nurse to bing – dances and other entertainments,' she finished determinedly.

Scott's gaze fastened on her face. 'To hell with seemliness, will you come with me? On Saturday I'm still not your damned employer.'

Ungrammatical but reasonable. Theresa forced calm on a wild impulse that she wanted to go with this man and his daughter. Well, why not . . .?

'I accept your very polite invitation, Mr. Milward – perhaps only because somebody will have to stopper Melinda's young ears against profane language.'

A long silence ensued while they studied each other, he

48

with a sardonically lifted eyebrow and she with candid blue eyes.

Scott broke it at last. 'I seem to spend my life apologizing to you. Till Saturday, about six o'clock, then? au revoir, mademoiselle, my fondest to the Rourkes.' He tipped his hat at a dangerous angle and strode off.

Theresa waited until she heard the clatter of hooves and then walked slowly towards the house.

At supper table Theresa told Mary and Dan of Scott's visit and the subsequent invitation. 'He didn't even discuss it, simply informed me that he would be taking me.'

'Just like him to do that. Scott seldom discusses, he makes statements. I'm surprised at him, though, he rarely attends the local functions. He's keen on polo. We have quite a good polo field, and he turns up for that fairly regularly. Must have taken a shine to you, my girl.'

'Shine my foot!' Theresa exclaimed. 'He has some ulterior motive, I'll bet.'

'You're a very attractive damsel, why shouldn't he get cracking first before the other chaps monopolize you? I think that's a superior, not an ulterior motive,' Mary put in.

'Vera Smith's fiancé is coming on Saturday. He'll spend the week-end at Scott's place and take his bride-to-be back on Monday,' Dan told them.

Theresa looked darkly at her companions. 'Ah, the solution comes! He wants my presence in case Melinda becomes unmanageable or catches her finger in the door.'

Dan laughed. 'Well, be that as may be, Scott Milward is actually coming to our do. That does show he's getting over carrying a torch for Elaine.'

'Why did she leave, Dan? It can't have been only her dislike of surroundings. You have a social club, other entertainments, and Salisbury is barely a day's drive away. Is she very beautiful?' Theresa asked tentatively, a strange constriction in her chest as she waited for his answer.

'Yes, she was – is rather lovely, in a slightly flamboyant way. Gorgeous, dark red hair, green eyes and a figure that stops the traffic. Scott doesn't talk about it, but I think something happened in Salisbury—' Dan stopped.

49

Mary leaned her arms on the table. 'Scott went away for a week, on business, to Umtali and came back sooner than expected. In his absence Elaine took herself and Melinda off to Salisbury and he followed her. He came back with only Melinda. What transpired is anybody's guess, but Elaine never came back. Scott clammed up and not one of us could get a word out of him on that subject.'

'That was close on two years ago,' Dan remarked. 'He has occasionally taken other girls out, but spends most of his time on the ranch. Lately he's been going to Salisbury fairly often, whether it's *amour* or business I can't say.'

'You'll enjoy the dance on Saturday, Terry. Our friends are all agog to see and meet you, so put on your best bib and tucker, and wow them.'

'With Scott Milward looking on superciliously, I presume?' Theresa retorted, and pushed her chair back.

'Envy, I predict,' Dan chuckled as they walked to the verandah.

The next morning Theresa strolled down to the gate that led to the main highway. The postal bus was due today, she had offered to meet it. The gate was a good quarter of a mile from the homestead and the overhang of tall trees made her walk cool and pleasant. She opened the large metal box attached to a post and looked inside. No post as yet, so she settled down on a log to wait for the bus.

Five minutes had passed when she heard the drumming of hooves and a rider appeared in a cloud of dust. The girl on the horse stopped with superb horsemanship as she spied Theresa and swung out of her saddle to face her.

Her dark, windblown hair was held back with a rubber band in a rough ponytail and she wore washed-out blue jeans, a grubby denim shirt and worn-out tennis shoes. 'Are you the nurse?' she asked without any formality. At Theresa's nod of assent she continued abruptly, 'Will you come with me? My sister is in a bad way.'

Equally abrupt, Theresa demanded, 'Explain as quickly as you can. Where do you live, and what's wrong with your sister?'

'About three miles from here. Her husband, Sam de Wet, works for Mr. Milward. I'm Georgia Masters. Lily's baby was only due in a fortnight, but I think it's coming now.'

'Isn't there a doctor in the village—?' Theresa began.

Georgie Masters cut in angrily, her voice staccato with anxiety. 'I've been up to the big house to phone, but the doctor is away on a call. I left a message at his surgery – he may be too late. Are you coming?'

'I'll climb up behind you on your horse. Have you a medical cupboard at home, cotttonwool, disinfectant, etc.?' Theresa asked tersely as she prepared to mount behind the other girl, who was already back in the saddle.

'Yes, let's go!'

She hung on to the slender waist of Georgie as the horse was turned and put to a reckless gallop.

Legs shaky from the mad ride, Theresa entered the cottage that nestled in a grove of orange trees. A deep crimson bougainvillea almost obscured the front porch. Georgie pushed past her to lead the way to her sister's bedroom. A swift look at the woman on the bed and her training told her that the time was imminent.

Theresa smiled with steady eyes at Lily de Wet as she started rolling her sleeves. 'I'm Theresa Stanton and I'm going to help you. Have you a clean overall for me?'

Georgie ran to the wardrobe and snatched a light blue overall off a hanger. Theresa thanked her. 'Go to the kitchen, find your largest saucepans and kettles and get the water boiling. I'll find the bathroom.' She slipped into the large, sleeveless garment and tied it tightly at the waist. In the bathroom she scanned the medicine cabinet and sorted out what would be needed. Thank heaven it was well stocked!

'I'm Sam de Wet, nurse, and very grateful that you're here.' The tall, gangling man stood in the doorway twisting his hat in nervous hands. 'I was in the lands when Mr. Milward's piccanin brought the message from Georgie. Lily – will she – is she—?'

'She is, Mr. de Wet, and don't worry. Everything is going to be all right,' Theresa smiled confidently, hiding her own anxiety beneath a cheerful manner. She dumped the cottonwool and bottles into his arms. 'Put these things in the bedroom while I scrub. Tell Georgie you'll see to the hot water, so she can put on something clean and scrub her hands, in case I need her.'

On examination she found no signs of any complications and breathed a silent sigh of relief. Slipping a waterproof on to the bed, she turned the woman on her side and rubbed her back with comforting hands. 'Your baby is in a hurry, that's all, Lily. Not to worry, first babies are often that way.' A measure of peace came to the frightened woman when she felt the sure hands and confident words.

The next hour flew by on busy wings, with a dazed but dutiful Georgia Masters following Sister Stanton's orders. A car stopped outside, but a negative shake of her head answered Theresa's inquiring eyebrow. 'Not the doctor.'

In the kitchen Sam started up as he heard the angry wail of his new-born son.

'Sit down, old chap. When you're wanted they'll call you,' Scott grinned as he put a hand on the nervous father's shoulder. 'Congrats. It can only be a boy, with that lusty gruff voice. Sounds just like you when you're yelling at the stockboys.'

'*Magtig*, man, I am that glad the slip of a *meisie* turned up so promptly. I hope Lily is all right.' Sam started up as Georgie appeared in the doorway.

'Sam, he's lovely. Lily's fine, but Sister sent me to tell you to be patient a while longer, some more things to do,' she said importantly. A look of awe came into her face. 'She's absolutely wonderful, she knew just what to do and allowed me to help her too! Oh, Mr. Milward, her hands were so quick and gentle, and—' Georgie turned smartly as the voice called from the bedroom. 'Excuse me, I'm wanted.' Some time later she stuck her head around the doorway. 'You can come now, Sam.'

The poor man tripped over a chair in his hurried flight. Scott leaned against the window-sill and rubbed his chin reflectively. Had he acted just so, almost four years ago? He remembered the miracle of joy when a tiny bundle was placed into his eager arms, and shared for a brief instant the awe and wonder with Sam de Wet.

Theresa wiped perspiration off her face with a wet towel in the bathroom and took off the stained overall. She left her hair tied up in a topknot and walked into the kitchen.

The tall, rangy figure framed in the window straightened

up as she entered. 'Everything according to the books, Sister Stanton?'

'Yes, Scott – heavens, you startled me! When did you get here? One time I almost had a heart attack, when Lily disobeyed certain instructions. Whew, am I thirsty!'

A quick, firm movement of hands under her armpits and Scott had her sitting on the well-scrubbed table with her feet resting on a chair. 'Sit you down, honey, sustenance coming up in a jiffy.' He turned to the stove and lifted the coffee-pot. Seconds later Theresa accepted the large cup of coffee with a huge dollop of cream floating on top.

'This looks good. Georgia, take a cup for your sister, she needs it more than I do.' This to the girl standing hesitantly in the doorway. Georgie complied with alacrity.

Theresa sipped the coffee and glanced at the man standing so close to her. He was studying her topknot of hair.

'What's the matter, Scott?'

'You look like a prim little schoolmistress.' He lifted a hand and, before she could stop him, pulled the ribbon loose. Her hair cascaded on to her shoulders. 'That's better.' Scott ran his fingers through it and said, in wonder, 'It's so silky. Melinda's right, your hair is like sunbeams.'

'Rather damp sunbeams at the moment. I haven't done midwifery for ages and this one caught up on me so swiftly.' She laughed and buried her face in the large cup to cover her confusion at this unexpected action. A nerve tingled in her neck where his fingertips had brushed.

Doctor Lessing stopped his car and came bustling in. 'Hello, Scott. How's Lily and what's she up to, is it a false alarm? At least another fourteen days—' He put his bag on the table and looked long and hard at the girl seated on it. A whistle of appreciation formed on his mouth. 'I – er – I—' Scott made no move to introduce him. 'Well, what's going on here, anyway? The call was urgent.' With great difficulty Dr. Lessing removed his eyes from the girl and noticed the kettles on the stove. 'Good, I see somebody has prepared—'

Theresa lifted her feet off the chair and stood hurriedly to attention, professional etiquette to the fore. 'Good morning, Doctor. I'm Theresa Stanton. May I take you to the patient? This way, please.' She led the way with subdued formality, ignoring the amused eyes of Scott, to the bedroom and stood aside as she had been taught to do.

With a puzzled glance at her Dr. Lessing walked in and surveyed the contented mother, happy father, and then his eyes flew to the small cot.

Theresa spoke politely. 'An emergency case, doctor. I'm a nurse and, being available, did what I could. I trust everything is in order.' She motioned to Sam to leave the room.

Hugh Lessing stepped over to the cot and uncovered the new baby. A sharp scrutiny of eyes, ears, nose, mouth and umbilical cord assured him that all was well. He examined Lily while Theresa studied him unobtrusively – a man in his early thirties, brown hair and eyes, mouth widely generous, build slightly stocky and incredibly long, blunt-edged fingers. She liked what she saw. He replaced the quilt over a smiling woman and sat down at the foot-end of the bed, turning his attention to the silently dutiful girl.

'All's well, and a jolly good job you made of it. No complications?'

'None, doctor.'

'Hmm – Theresa Stanton? Yes, I recollect someone talking about the Rourkes' expected visitor. Are you on vacation?'

'No, doctor. I've resigned.'

'Why? In the course of duty or personal?' Hugh Lessing's scrutiny was sharp.

'Personal, sir. I'm still on the Nursing Register.' She quite understood the probing questions.

'Do you intend carrying on with your profession here in Rhodesia?'

'Maybe later. As from Sunday I'll be employed by Mr. Milward, as nurse and companion to his daughter.'

Hugh blew a long breath. 'I see. Well, Lily, everything is fine. You were very fortunate to have Sister Stanton within calling distance. I'll be out tomorrow, so take it easy. Maybe I can get Georgie to follow instructions as regards the baby, but she's such a tomboy, I'd better talk to Sam.' He congratulated Lily on her fine son, gave some medical advice and then walked into the passage. Theresa followed and put her hand on his arm as they reached the kitchen doorway. Scott, Sam and Georgia were still there. The doctor stopped and waited.

'Doctor, Georgia is a very capable girl, and I was very grateful for her help. I thought it worth mentioning.' Theresa looked at the girl and was startled to see a deep flush spreading across her face.

'Any simpleton could have done what I did, so don't bother with the kudos!' Georgie tilted her head angrily, dark eyes flashed for an instant at Hugh Lessing and then she stalked to the back door, flung it open and banged it shut as she went out.

'My, my, tantrums! When is the lass going to grow up?' Hugh shrugged his shoulders.

Scott spoke from his lazy posture against the window-ledge. 'She's nineteen, Hugh, and getting prettier by the day.'

'Is she?' Hugh looked puzzled for a moment. 'I'll take your word for it. Sam, I wish you all the best, he's a fine boy. Thank you, Miss Stanton, for helping out in a sticky spot. Are you sure you won't reconsider, about nursing? We desperately need nurses out here, and with your qualifications—'

Theresa broke in, suddenly very conscious of the tall man at the window. 'Thank you, doctor, but at present I'm perfectly content. If you wish, I'll attend Mrs. de Wet every morning until Saturday.'

The medical man looked so long and hard at her that she felt a warmth creeping into her cheeks. 'The name is Hugh — Hugh Lessing. Yes, I'll be glad if you would, one worry off my shoulders. I'll be around tomorrow, better push off now. 'Bye, Sister — 'bye, chaps.' He turned at the door and looked at Scott. 'You lucky dog, you!' and he was gone.

For the second time Theresa was startled to see a flush on someone's cheeks as, his grey eyes smouldering, Scott muttered, 'Silly old quack!'

They walked towards the front door and Theresa popped in to say good-bye to Lily, telling her she would be in to see her on the morrow. She walked out to the front garden. Scott was leaning against his car, talking to Sam. Georgia was not with them and Theresa started to walk around the house, but Scott's voice stopped her.

'Where is your horse, Theresa? Sam can bring him later, I'm taking you back in the car.'

'Well, I didn't come on my horse.'

Scott straightened abruptly from his laconic position. 'How the devil did you get here? You surely didn't walk all this way, in such a short time?'

'I think I was – hi-jacked.' Her answer was demure.

'Hi-jacked!' Both men spoke in unison.

'I'm beginning to think so. You see,' a chuckle rose in her throat at their expressions, 'I was sitting at the gate, waiting for the postal bus and minding my own business, when –' she snapped her fingers, 'just like that I was whisked on to a horse and woke up holding a baby in my arms!'

'Georgie?' Sam exclaimed. 'She didn't even give you time to let Mary know? *Magtig!* Mary must be having hysterics by this time, not knowing what's happened to her visitor.'

'And a good thing too, otherwise you would have been in a nice pickle, Mister Sam. I left my hat on the lone wayside rock so Mary will come to either of two conclusions – I've absconded with the bus-driver, or a lion has enjoyed a tasty breakfast.'

Scott laughed. 'The sooner I hi-jack you back, the better for that lady's peace of mind. Come.' He held the door open for her.

While Sam thanked her again, Scott climbed in and pressed the starter, revved the engine and they shot head-long down the dusty road.

'I'm not in that much of a hurry, Scott, or is this breakneck speed normal procedure?' Theresa asked dryly.

'Sorry, girl. There I go again, apologizing.' His glance appraised her swiftly, then his eyes went back to the road. She leaned her head on the back-rest, smiled secretively and closed her eyes. 'It's no crime to apologize, dear man, it's a sign of good manners.'

Scott did not reply and Theresa suddenly felt happy, in a contented way. He had his finer points and she felt fulfilled, somehow, by the work she had done this lovely morning. No word passed between them, she merely reminded him to stop at the gate for her hat and post. The silence lasted and she closed her eyes again, oblivious to the searching glances of her companion, to come abruptly from her dreaming cloud as he stopped the car with a jerk in the driveway. Before Theresa had completely collected herself Scott was out and had the door open for her.

'Will you come in, Scott—' she began, and was stopped by the same dark flame smouldering in his eyes that had been there in the de Wets' kitchen.

He closed the door, walked round to his side. 'No, thanks, I'll see you.' He slid into the seat and whirled away in a cloud of dust.

What now? Theresa thought amazedly. Is he mad because he had to bring me back? Whatever was wrong with the man? So much for finer points and contented clouds! 'Oh, what the hell!' Theresa spoke out loud and walked quickly up the verandah steps.

Fortunately for her peace of mind, Mary knew of the morning call to Lily's bedside. A passing stockboy had witnessed her flight with Georgia and Mary had phoned through to Scott's household. Vera Smith had been in such a dither when asked to help, so Georgia had tempestuously flung back on her horse and was on her way to Mary, only to accost Theresa at the gate.

Theresa briefed Mary on the latest bulletin, then walked to her room and flopped across the bed. Illogically, for no reason, she felt completely miserable and only pulled herself up when Mary tapped on the door to say lunch was ready. She did not feel hungry but forced herself to eat and converse normally with Dan and Mary.

The day passed somehow and, long after the lights were out, Theresa Stanton lay awake, battling with unfamiliar emotions brought on by a man's curt departure.

Theresa tucked the soft blanket neatly and placed the hungry baby into his mother's arms. This was the third morning she had come over to attend Lily; mother and baby were doing fine and Sam was as proud as a peacock.

She was puzzled about Georgia Masters. The girl was exceptionally gauche for her age and acted either brashly abrupt or like a startled fawn whenever Theresa approached her. A long talk was indicated, even if she had to lasso Georgia in order to do so. Her deep flush and defiant look at

57

Hugh Lessing, on that first morning, raised certain suspicions in Theresa's mind. At Hugh's consequent visits Georgia had made herself scarce and only yesterday, as he drove away, Theresa had noticed the girl leaning against a tree in the background, her attitude and face showing a strange yearning as she watched the receding car.

Georgia could be a very attractive girl if she took herself in hand, did something with her lovely hair and discarded the tatty jeans and shirts for neater, prettier clothes. Lily said she had tried to interest Georgia in pretty fripperies, to coax her to go out more, but her sister obstinately refused and seemed quite happy to roam around the countryside on her beloved horse, alone. She had been home with them for six months, having had her education at a college in Salisbury. At first eager to go back, being a qualified shorthand-typist, she had suddenly changed her mind and decided to stay on with her sister and Sam. Now Georgie seemed to have become a lone wolf and didn't care what she looked like!

Theresa walked out of the house, through rows of lush orange trees, and eventually found Georgia, who was busily grooming her horse. She sauntered up until she was standing next to the girl. Georgia looked up for a moment, gave a slight smile of recognition, then went on with her chore. Theresa found a curry-comb and casually drew it through the silky hair on the horse's tail. The two girls worked in silence, the sun hot on their backs.

Georgia stopped to push tangled hair, damp with perspiration, off her face. She fumbled in her pocket, pulled out a short length of tape and proceeded to tie the dark mass in a rough topknot.

Theresa also stopped and watched her critically, and then such a dreamy gaze came into her eyes that Georgia perforce had to speak. 'What gives? Why are you looking at me like that? My hair—'

'You know, Georgia, I have a magazine at home and there's a picture of a girl in it. She resembles you, the same shaped face – it's a "before and after" article.'

A flush suffused the girl's cheeks. 'Before and after? What exactly does that mean?'

'Well, this girl had just such lovely hair as yours. She

58

looked very nice, but her hair was quite unmanageable, so she had it cut short and styled. The "after" picture of her was most attractive, and the article tells how to shape the hair. I'm picturing you with a similar style.'

Georgia stood quite still while Theresa casually brushed her own chin with a silky tail-end. 'Georgia, I wonder if you could help me? I brought a couple of dress-lengths of the most gorgeous materials with me and I'm dying to make them up. Mary has a super machine, but I'm such a dumb bunny about sewing.' Crossing her fingers at this blatant lie, 'Do you know anything about patterns, cutting, and so on?' Theresa turned large, appealing blue eyes to her companion.

Brown eyes looked directly back at her. 'You can afford to be a dumb bunny about certain things, if you're so clever about other things – like nursing – the way you helped Lily. Who wants to sew if you can do all that? I did take a course on basic needlework at college—'

'Oh, goody, just the girl for me. I'm going to hi-jack you tomorrow, for the whole day! And don't heckle, because you owe it to me, in return for my services to your sister. Stop stiffening that pretty neck—' she hurried on before Georgia could protest, 'I'm going to have a go at that mop of hair. I'm not quite ignorant on hair-shaping, having to do a fair amount of it in the hospital on the patients. We'll follow the book instructions carefully – what say, Georgia M.?'

That young lady looked at the eager, vital face of her tormentor and a slight gleam of interest showed for an instant in her dark eyes before she dropped them, answering with feigned indifference. 'You can give me a Yul Brynner for all I care, it's cooler anyway and nobody would notice.'

'Are you referring to a particular nobody or just generalizing?' Theresa deliberately teased her.

'Of course n-not.' The sudden stammer and flush belied the quick retort.

'Well, a little bird tells me that one particular somebody in the medical world would certainly notice any change, if confronted—' Theresa was afraid she had jumped the gate too fast, for Georgia suddenly threw the brush on the ground and interrupted her.

'Don't be silly! As far as he's concerned I'm still in rompers!' She stalked off, calling over her shoulder, 'I'll help you with the sewing tomorrow!'

Theresa watched her and heaved a sigh. At least Georgia knew to whom she was referring when she spoke of a medical somebody. She was going to order Scott to take the girl with them to the barbecue, whether he liked it or not. If a certain doctor attended, he would be induced to join their party. She hoped to overcome Georgia's stiff-necked pride, to coax her to accept one of the dress-lengths for a party dress. Walking back to the jeep she pondered deeply on ways and means. Mary must be roped in to help. . . .

Mary was quite willing to help. The age-old urge to match-make bubbled in her motherly breast when Theresa told of the yearning look she had glimpsed in the young girl's eyes while she watched Hugh Lessing drive away from Sam's house.

The next day when Theresa had finished with Lily she found Georgia waiting for her at the jeep, dressed neatly for a change, in jeans and spotlessly clean shirt and hair tied in an awkward roll. She scowled self-consciously and climbed into the jeep with a muttered greeting. Theresa smiled back delightedly and started a gay, whistling tune as they bowled down the gravelled road. After a few sidelong glances of shy amusement Georgia suddenly joined in and Mary Rourke was startled out of her usual calm when she heard a squeal of brakes accompanied by 'Oh, what a beautiful morning' piercingly whistled in deafening crescendo!

Later, Mary watched in amazement as Theresa, a very good needlewoman, deliberately fumbled with the pinning of patterns. Only when Georgia took over with frustrated eagerness did she catch on. Theresa gave an exaggerated sigh of thanks and stepped out of the way, the solemnity of her face belied by twinkling violet eyes as she sent Mary a quick, warning glance.

Leaving the younger girl to her task, she slipped out of the room, to reappear after a short interval with a swathe of pure Thai silk, in burnt-orange colour, folded over her arm.

Georgia finished the last cutting line with the remark that the latest sheath dress fashions were so much simpler to make than full skirts and intricate tops. She caught sight of the material on Theresa's arms and an involuntary sigh of pure bliss escaped her lips. Her gentle fingers touched the silk reverently.

'Come to the mirror, Georgie.' Theresa propelled the fascinated girl and held the dress-length under her chin. Three pairs of eyes studied the reflection and Mary and Theresa nodded simultaneously. Georgia glanced up, a deep flush spreading across her face.

'Oh no, you don't—' she began, but Theresa had laid a cool gentle hand on her arm.

'Please, honey, it will give me great pleasure if you would accept it – as a birthday present. Oh, it does things for you that could never happen to me. . .!'

Georgia's eyes turned back to her stunned reflection, she stammered, 'Why, it could do things to any girl – the plainest, ugliest girl could achieve beauty – with this.' She turned suddenly. 'You don't even know when my birthday is – no, I can't accept it. You're only doing this to—'

'Because I would love to have you accept it in the spirit it's given, with pleasure and because it's you—' Theresa stopped as Scott's voice drawled lazily from the doorway:

'Flaming stars, Georgia girl, you're going to look smashing in that stuff! What is it anyway? Hopsack? Calico?'

Three feminine heads turned in indignation at this utter blasphemy! Theresa found her voice as sudden inspiration struck. 'Oh, Scott, I'm so glad, you've come just at the right time. We're all wearing new frocks to the barbecue-dance and Georgia won't have time to shop before Saturday. Now she's being silly about using this material, and who cares if it's not her birthday – after all, every day is another day nearer to one's birthday.' She stopped for breath and rooted him to the spot with large, hypnotic eyes. 'You did ask her to join us, as planned?' Whirling round to the astonished girl, 'Has he asked you, because if he hasn't I'll – I shall be – I was praying you would join us because I don't know – Melinda – very well and – well, have you or have you not, Scott Milward?' Flashing eyes turned back to the man.

That man straightened abruptly from his lounging position. A look of understanding crossed his face. He put a hand to his heart.

'You wound me to the heart, dear atom, with your suspicions. I've been chasing Georgie M. all over the countryside, but she's been too elusive for me to extend our – invitation. I extend it now, before you threat to do whatsoever—is carried out.' Scott smiled mockingly. 'What is it, anyway?'

Theresa drew a silent breath of relief. He had played it well, thanks be. She sent him a brilliant, condescending smile. 'Really, you men! It would have been simpler to send a note with Sam, instead of tiring your horse. As for my threat – well, you'll never know now, will you?'

Under his steady scrutiny she started to breathe hard to steady a sudden, suffocating turmoil in her breast. Scott's eyes left hers, dropped to a deliberate, slow study of the soft femininity of her silk blouse. The look in his smoky regard sent colour flying to her face and a strange, hot tingling started at her finger-tips. With an effort she turned back to Georgia, who still clutched the material in trembling hands.

'All right, let's get cracking, there isn't much time. Georgia, you cut. I'll help you and Mary can start sewing when we've finished, while I tackle your hair. Close your mouth, honey, you look like a fish caught on a hook! Where's that pattern you fancied so much, just the thing for this gorgeous silk.'

Georgia Masters still looked mesmerized and then a slow beatific smile spread across her face, and beauty was indeed achieved. Even Scott appeared to be enchanted, gazing in wonderment.

'Fish on a hook! The understatement of the year! We were all neatly hooked, with great cunning. Mary dear, you'd better close your mouth as well, there's a fly dangerously near to it. I actually dropped in for a cup of tea, but I'll forgo that pleasure. Hand me needle and cotton, I'll tack the split seams and crutch!'

Gales of laughter greeted this helpful offer as Scott lowered himself limply into an easy-chair. The laughter helped Theresa cover her inexplicable confusion. She was grateful for Scott's prescience, his quick understanding when she had shot her query at him. He could quite simply have denied knowledge of any invitation for Georgia to join them. Her eyes thanked him over her teacup and he acknowledged it with a mocking threat in his own.

Mary and Georgia became immersed in their work and Theresa walked with Scott as he took his leave.

He looked at her quizzically and there was a sardonic inflection in his voice. 'So you don't know Melinda very well? Hmm, could it be her father you're afraid of, hence Georgie's presence, for protection?'

'You know quite well that was trumped up on the spur of the moment. I'm not afraid of handling Melinda, or her father for that matter, but I do want Georgia to mix with other people. She's too young to become introspective, antisocial. Do you think Hugh Lessing will attend the do on Saturday?'

'Aha, now your quixotic impulses become clear. Matchmaking female!' He rubbed his chin reflectively. 'The unsuspecting doctor being the target, and I'll be cajoled into asking him to join us. Or does your own interest lie that way and Georgie gal is the sop to my ego? Not a bad idea at that. I've often wondered what makes the girl tick, maybe this is my chance to find out.'

'You've had ample time to do that, right here, and I strongly advise you not to cradle-snatch while she's in my care. Anyway, I think she likes Hugh, but he treats her like a child.' Theresa did not deign to contradict his version of her own interest in the doctor.

'To Hugh she's not a child, but where I'm concerned it's cradle-snatching? How ancient you make me feel!' A slight bitterness tinged his next words. 'Well, we're well matched, you and I. Our torn hearts know very well that love explodes or fizzles out quicker than a damp squib.'

A hot protest rose in her throat, but she willed it back and her reply came quick and light. 'Squibs are man-made, Mr. Milward, but the stars and sun will last an eternity. Maybe true love is not a flashing thing but an everyday occurrence that we know as friendship, companionship – and trust.' Theresa felt a sudden prickling behind her eyelids. 'I'm going to tackle Georgia's hair now, and I'm willing to bet that on Saturday not even an old man like you will be able to resist her. That girl's got possibilities. Thanks for playing along and inviting her, you're a honey.' She dashed up the steps before he could reply, turned to salute him palm upwards.

The sun was setting when at last Theresa stood back and surveyed her handiwork. Mary, putting the finishing touches to the silk dress, also looked critically, then approvingly at Georgia's hair. 'I didn't realize we had such a beauty in our midst.'

'I feel so light-headed – but I like it. It makes me look older, which is just fine.' Georgia spoke shyly.

'Heaven forbid any young girl wanting to look older than her years, precious years that pass on wings of speed!' mourned still young Theresa Stanton. 'Georgia Masters, you're going to wow the gentry tomorrow, make no mistake.'

'I really don't think—' the other girl began, but Theresa interrupted with distinct, definite emphasis on each word and syllable. 'You're not supposed to think as from now. You're to go home and not, I repeat *not*, clean the stables or any such unclean work. Here's the nail polish, bubble bath and gold sandals; where can I find a box for that ravishing dress? Thanks, Mary.' She changed her voice back to normal and impulsively hugged the strangely docile girl. 'You look delicious, honey. Between the three of us we'll wake up the little ole town, that's for sure!'

Georgia chuckled at her sparkling vitality and wondered briefly about the story of a broken engagement. . . . It did not seem to have touched Theresa too deeply. For then surely she would be pining away in a darkened room, mournfully refusing to eat any food or delicacies offered to her. That was what she, Georgie, would be doing if – someone – she loved did not love her back. . . . She suddenly felt very hungry indeed!

Theresa waited on the verandah and watched the approaching car lights. It would surely be Scott and Georgia at last! Mary, Dan and baby Glynis had long since departed, because Dan was on the committee and had to put in an early appearance. Scott was exceptionally late and she hoped he had not had trouble with Georgia. The car came to a standstill and the man at the wheel extricated long legs from the driver's seat.

64

The light on the verandah made a nimbus of the waiting girl's honey-blonde hair. Her slim dress of creamy linen outlined a silhouette of soft curves. Scott greeted her rather curtly and she, in turn, felt illogically disappointed when he made no comment on her appearance. . . . As if that mattered! After all, he was probably sated, used to glamour, having owned and possessed such beauty as his wife had – still had.

Theresa's greeting was equally stiff as he took her arm and led her to the car.

Georgia emerged from the front seat and Theresa gave her a swift scrutiny. An involuntary sigh of pleasure escaped her; at least *she* could be generous and open in admiration. 'You look absolutely divine, Georgia – doesn't she, Scott?'

'Absolutely, fantastically, unbelievably so,' Scott answered gravely, his wood-smoke glance on herself.

Georgia dived ungracefully on to the back seat while Scott's eyes commanded Theresa to take the front seat. A small voice piped from the back, 'Tresa, are you going to dance with my daddy?'

Melinda's gamin face pushed forward to gaze earnestly at her.

'Hello there, Melinda, what a lovely dress you have! Yes, I shall dance with your daddy if he asks me very politely.'

They shot off down the driveway. Melinda addressed her father. 'You will ask Tresa pitely, Daddy, will you, Daddy?'

'I shall, poppet, I shall.' Daddy spoke rather gruffly.

'Have you got a cold, Daddy? 'Cos if you have, Tresa is a nurse and she'll kiss it better.'

'In that case, even if I haven't, I shall develop one as fast as Timothy can blink an eye.'

'Timothy is my cat, Tresa, and he prob'ly blinks a lot.' Melinda passed on this information, her small hands hovering over Theresa's hair.

A mildly electric pause followed, broken by a sudden chuckle from the man behind the wheel. 'Apropos of this interesting conversation, Theresa, sorry I kept you waiting. One prize cow suddenly decided to drop her calf and your nursing experience will tell you that these things happen at awkward times. Normally we leave them be, but this one had slight difficulty and needed help.'

'Oh. Is the calf – is everything all right?'

'Fine, thanks.' Scott gave her a quizzical glance and smiled as Melinda ran her fingers through the shining hair. 'Don't do that, baggage. I know you're trying to catch moonbeams . . . leave it for another time.'

'Yes, Daddy. Tresa, have you smelt Georgie? She smells gorjus, can I smell you too?' The 'baggage' sniffed hard over the front seat. Georgia tickled her, she turned with a whoop and a general scramble ensued.

Scott spoke softly. 'I hope you will teach my daughter more ladylike manners and discretion.'

'She probably misses feminine company and is slightly overcome by the sudden influx—' Theresa bit hard on her lip.

'No need for embarrassment, young one, I have a heart of steel, and you're quite right. Vera Smith is hardly what I would call feminine, she scorns perfumes and all alluring jazz that goes to make a feminine world. Miss Melinda is going to appreciate the change. Be forewarned, though, keep that hank of hair out of her reach . . . and mine,' he added *sotto voce*, but she heard and glanced sharply at him. His face was bland and grey eyes were concentrated on the road, so she let it pass.

The lighted fires of the barbecue were now discernible and Melinda exclaimed delightedly at the festoons of coloured lights lacing the trees and buildings.

They alighted and Georgia hung back, clutching Melinda's small hand. Scott lifted the child and tucked a hand of each girl firmly under strong arms. 'Forward march, no retreats in this 'ere army!'

In no time they were in the midst of cheerful company. While Scott kept a watchful eye on Georgia, who looked ready to retreat ignominiously, Dan took Theresa's arm and gravely did the round of introductions. His smile was smug and proprietorial as admiring looks were cast at the attractive girl at his side.

Scott Milward's arm was resting casually round Georgia's shoulders when Dan and Theresa again joined them. Two nice-looking youths were in earnest conversation with him, although Theresa noticed with satisfaction that their eyes were on the girl in the circle of his protective arm. That young woman's eyes showed a sparkle of excitement. Was it caused by the two lads' interest or the tanned arm resting on her shoulders?

Theresa shivered suddenly as a thought feathered her mind; that arm looked so strong, gentle. . . . She brushed it ruthlessly from her mind and silly thoughts as she saw Hugh Lessing approach.

'Watch it, man, you're walking to your fate!' she silently warned the unsuspecting doctor. The stupid man walked right past his fate and took her own hand in a warm clasp, nodding to Scott and Georgia briefly.

'Miss Stanton, how nice to see you. I was hoping for miracles . . . lo and behold they came to pass! Hello, Scott, did you bring her?' Hugh's smiling glance rested on Georgia. 'Hi there, muggins, who lassoed you into coming? Some brave soul with little value for life, I'll bet!'

Theresa could have hit him then and there, with calculated pleasure. Not even a flicker of admiration or recognition of the change in the girl – some men were just too dense, even when their future was thrust right under their questing noses!

'It's my pleasure to escort three glamorous wenches tonight.' Scott's eyebrow tilted wickedly as Hugh continued to hold on to Theresa's hand. She jerked it free impulsively.

Melinda caused a diversion by calling for attention from her beloved doctor. Hugh swung her up and complimented extravagantly on her super party dress. Georgia bit her lip and tried to back away, but Scott's hand was firm on her shoulders.

'I hope you're not going to be greedy and hang on to all three. Even you, Casanova, will not manage that, and seeing you've already laid claim to the morsel at your side, I shall deem it a pleasure and honour to feed Miss Stanton – Theresa – may I?' Hugh bowed and offered his arm.

Theresa's eyes flew to Scott in appeal, but he merely quirked a challenged eyebrow. The flickering firelight danced across his face, highlighting strong cheekbones but leaving his expression utterly incomprehensible.

For the second time within minutes she could easily have hit a man! He was spoiling the whole show by keeping his arm so possessively around Georgia's shoulders. ... Maybe that was the way he wanted it? A slight lurch in the region of her heart was severely quelled as she allowed herself to be led away. She vowed that before the evening was through she would even things with that spoilsport. Hugh handed her a glass, she smiled at him and started her crusade.

'Georgia is a stunning girl, Hugh. She looks quite lovely tonight, don't you think so?'

'Yes, not bad at all, quite a surprise. You're a knockout yourself, honey.'

Theresa pointedly ignored the latter part. 'Well, why didn't you tell her so?'

Hugh raised surprised eyebrows. 'Should I have?'

'A girl likes a bit of flattery, and you did Melinda and me the honour.'

'That's the girl, showing up my manners, or lack of same! Anyway, Scott seemed to be fulfilling all her needs—' A frown puckered his forehead. 'Do you think there might be a slight romance starting? He's a bit old to—'

'Don't be silly, Scott could have started a romance long ago, if he so minded. He sees her often enough at the ranch. Georgia is a little like a scared fawn tonight and he's being protective.' Theresa found herself rather short of breath in her swift defence of Scott's intentions.

'Hmm. Maybe that's why Georgie girl disappears into the blue so often, on her horse. . . .'

Theresa interrupted furiously, 'That's a rotten thing to say, Hugh Lessing! Scott has – had a wife, if you remember. He doesn't strike me as that kind—'

'Whoa! Theresa, I apologize. I merely said that to get a rise out of you. Your eyes are as dark as a velvety night when you're angry and, at the moment, I'm very interested in the girl attached to those eyes. So why are we getting so wound up about Scott and his Georgie? Let's talk about ourselves, then we'll have tucker and I shall dance with you all night.' Hugh Lessing looked charmed at the thought.

Theresa sighed in exasperation and immediately became very conscious that someone was standing directly behind her. A certain, sure instinct came that it was Scott Milward.

'Mary sends greetings and will we *all* kindly join her at yonder table, loaded with goodies for our delectation.' While delivering this request he drew his forefinger down her bare back to where the low neckline started.

A shocking vibration through her body made Theresa gasp in surprise and she turned as though drawn by a magnetic quality, irresistibly inescapable. Scott was standing very close, a vibrant, smouldering anger in his eyes at variance with the half-smile on his lips.

With calculated coolness he continued, 'You are invited to join us, Hugh. Take my arm, Theresa, the ground is slightly uneven. Although if you fractured a limb I'm sure the doctor would be only too delighted to aid you in the course of duty.'

Hugh laughed delightedly as he fell into step beside them. 'You should have taken up my profession, old boy, you can be quite pompous at times and it has its compensations. Relax, Scott, I'll not devour this tasty morsel, much as I would like to. After all, she did me a good turn with Lily and I may need her future help again some time.'

The 'tasty morsel' was hardly conscious of his prattle, for she was trying very hard not to be so aware of the warm grip on her arm and wondering at the inexplicable anger in smoky eyes. . . .

Mary hailed them and, with gracious dexterity, led Hugh to the seat beside Georgia. Scott seated Theresa and swung long legs over the bench next to Melinda. Plates of sizzling mutton chops, sausages, T-bone steaks with salads, bread rolls and barbecue sauces were handed out in a spirit of general merriment. Brimming beer mugs made the rounds.

Scott and the Rourkes were evidently popular with the community and their table drew considerable attention besides having the added attraction of two pretty, eligible girls. Scott personally attended to Theresa's wants, but with a formal politeness strangely at variance in his warmth to others. A barnlike hall had been gaily decorated and now the band-boys could be heard tuning up amidst much hilarity.

Theresa walked with Mary to the rest rooms where three elderly ladies were preparing to baby-sit. Glynis went happily to sleep in her carry-cot and Melinda was soon busily engaged with crayons and colouring books. The dancing was in full swing when they returned.

She noted with satisfaction that Hugh was dancing with Georgia and an earnest conversation was in progress which seemed to hold the girl enthralled, judging from her expression.

Dan and Scott were still at the table, deep in shop-talk with three other men. At their approach the men stood up and Dan claimed Mary for a dance. Scott turned on the seat and leaned his elbows on the table as Theresa sat down next to him. The three men murmured apologies and wandered into the hall. Scott offered cigarettes and her hand shook slightly as he leaned forward, lighter in hand, for the small flame reflected a tiger-yellow echo in smoky eyes which held hers for a mesmerized eternity.

Highly annoyed with herself at this show of emotion, she forced her gaze away from hypnotic depths and followed his example of leaning her elbows on the table. They watched the dancing in silence until Scott suddenly stubbed his cigarette and stood up. 'I guess we should join the merrymakers. Are you ready?'

Theresa straightened up and he gripped her elbow in a hard hand, his face very close. 'Remember this, Miss Stanton, when I invite a female out, I don't expect her to hare off with some other man the moment we arrive. Is that clear?'

Her effort was sharp and quick. 'I can't remember you inviting me, I can only recall that you stated rather flatly that I was to accompany you! Your familiarity with Georgia probably led Hugh to think I was not your particular property. Which I'm not anyway.' She tried to shrug his hand off her elbow, but the grip became firmer.

'For tonight you are, spitfire, make no mistake, and stop splitting hairs about my invitation. Your devious ways with Georgia and Hugh might boomerang right back to your own pretty shoulders. He seems to be smitten with the wrong girl. When you throw that limpid gaze at a man he immediately forgets the world around him—'

'Do you feel that way too?' The question was out and she could have bitten her silly tongue.

Scott stopped in his stride, turned her towards him and the kindling anger faded to a deep calculated scrutiny.

'I've been bitten once too often to fall into that trap again, so rest assured, I shan't let the world fade for the sake of a pair of alluring eyes. Eyes that could be untrustworthy, as your ex-fiancé probably found, to his cost. As I did too. . . .'

The implication of his words hit her like a blow in the solar plexus. The pain in her voice spilled into darkened blue eyes as she looked directly at him. 'Are you merely judging the majority by your own experience with the minority, Mr. Milward, or have you official knowledge of my affairs?'

The hand on her arm became suddenly gentle and contrite. His mouth softened amazingly. 'By heavens, forgive me, Theresa. My own bitterness clouds my judgement sometimes. Knowing nothing whatsoever about your affairs, that was a vindictive remark, and I beg to apologize for my very bad manners.'

'Your apology is accepted, Scott. Just – just don't jump to hasty conclusions without a hearing from your victims.'

Scott looked at her gravely. 'I'm sorry. Maybe one day you might want to confide in me. Very often, to bare your feelings is to lighten them considerably.'

Theresa spoke softly, hesitantly. 'You speak words of wisdom but don't follow them yourself? Perhaps if you did so, the bitterness in your own heart will be washed away . . .?'

She sensed his body go taut for a moment, before he relaxed again and they started walking slowly. He did not speak until they entered the hall and his arms led her into a slow foxtrot.

'Shall we shelve both our past heartaches, and live just for the moment? I have a lovely girl in my arms, the night is beautiful, the music is hot and I want to dispel the pain of remembrance out of hyacinth eyes. Play along with me – Theresa?' Scott's voice was urgent and husky.

'Right you are, sir.' They merged into the happy crowd of dancers. A Paul Jones came next, but Scott held on to his partner throughout and smiled at the cries of 'spoilsport!'

His body, lithe and strongly firm against her, sent

strange vibrations through the girl. They seemed to emanate from the caressing quality of a sun-tanned hand resting gently on her bare back. Scott was a good dancer and the fluidity of movement made Theresa relax after a while, to enjoy the pleasure of being guided by him.

Georgia Masters was not allowed a moment of rest as the party geared to full-swing and Hugh Lessing cut in often, dividing his dancing mostly between the two girls. Scott did not participate every time, but kept a careful eye on Theresa while standing to one side, smoking and chatting to various men and women.

Theresa enjoyed herself as she swung from one pair of arms to another, but she was very conscious of the aura of his presence in the background and sensed his approach, to claim a dance, before she heard his voice. It troubled her inner stream of consciousness until she noticed that he was equally popular with either sex, so she put it down to a certain stimulating power that he obviously possessed. His charm was dangerously disarming!

Hugh had partnered her and he acquiesced with alacrity when the music stopped and Scott stepped up to announce, 'Time for a spot of fresh air. Join us outside, Hugh, there's a smog in here.' They relaxed into cushioned chairs and a coloured boy took Scott's order for three frosted, sparkling lemons.

Hugh spoke. 'You know, Terry, that youngster Georgie is a strange girl. I had my time cut out to make her say a few words, most exhausting—'

'She's rather shy, Hugh, and covers up with a veneer of stiff disinterest – and she's a young lady, so stop calling her youngster. You're only about five years older than Georgia, dear old sophisticate!'

Hugh looked thoughtful, then surprised. 'By jove, that is so. . . . Anyway, that stiff disinterest, as you call, it melted with astonishing swiftness when I, in desperation, reverted to "shop-talk" namely doctoring and nursing. She's mighty keen on nursing, but I don't think—'

'Well, don't. Georgia can think for herself. Let me tell you she was most capable with her help when I got stuck with Lily. Her tomboy exterior hides a very sensible and sensitive nature—'

'Crusader!' came softly from Scott.

Theresa shot him an indignant stare and continued defiantly, '—And I was going to ask you if something can be done about her, but I'll find out elsewhere if you're going to be superior and stupid about her youth!'

Scott grinned as Hugh looked flabbergasted. 'I warn you, doctor, this female's sweet exterior hides a snaky tongue. Be warned by one who knows.'

Sweet venom dripped while hot colour played in her cheeks. 'Certain people are so obtuse that sledge-hammers are sometimes indicated. Does Georgia look like a tomboy tonight? Does she now, Hugh Lessing? Look at her closely. There she is, surrounded by personable young men who surely consider her the epitome of beauty – of womanhood.' Theresa dropped a pointing finger in exaggerated despair. 'But of course, you're too old to appreciate extreme youth. . . .'

'I'm not too old to – by gad!' Hugh's mesmerized eyes tore away from the 'epitome of beauty' and settled on the 'crusader' who looked slightly breathless. 'Say, Scott, do you think she's taking the mickey out of me?'

'No doubt, old chap, no doubt.' Scott's voice was a lazy drawl of amusement.

'So are you going to ask her very nicely, in a decent adult way, to help you in your consulting rooms and also pay her well and not treat her like a – an office boy – but like a girl worthy of her occupation? Are you going to do that, Doctor Lessing?' Theresa ignored a mocking chuckle from Scott Milward and kept her eyes on the stunned medico.

Dr. Lessing swallowed hard and answered in a meek, subdued whisper, 'If you think it proper, Sister Stanton – if you think it in order—'

'I do.' The singular beauty of her smile caused two distinct intakes of breath. 'I thank you, Hugh. It will not be regretted,' Theresa finished simply.

The boy delivered the drinks and they sipped in quiet enjoyment. Still dazed, Hugh stood up and started to walk away, muttering, ' – Pay her well – office boy – occupational hazards—'

Theresa's voice stopped him. 'Did you come alone, Hugh?' He nodded apprehensively. 'Then I'm sure you won't mind taking Miss Masters home? Melinda will have to lie on the back seat, not much room, and Scott will be so grateful—?'

A slight hesitation, and Scott recovered. 'Oh yes, Hugh, I – er – would be.'

The other man's chin drew up belligerently, then sagged hopelessly. 'A pleasure, I assure you. Although—' a brief gleam of mischief showed in brown eyes, 'seeing as Georgie lives nearer to you, Scott, you could take her and I'll take – No! I might be further victimized by – I go now to my fate!' He squared his shoulders and walked away.

'Fate's the keyword to that jumble,' Theresa chuckled hysterically, and Scott smiled at her animated face.

'Do you often play this dangerous game of juggling other people's lives, *chérie*?'

The endearment gave her a sudden warm feeling deep inside. 'First time ever, Scott.'

'Aren't you rather rushing things? Hugh could easily shy off, for good.'

'Strike while the iron is hot. Give Georgia time to cool down and she'll retreat into her lonely shell again. Hugh can stop that now by asking her to fill the vacancy in his office. All businesslike and aboveboard, she won't suspect that romance might be included.'

'If you reckon so.' Scott spoke noncommittally. 'Would you like to go in again, or shall we make a move homewards? By the way, I didn't realize my car was so small.'

'That was what one calls strategy!' Theresa stretched her arms above her head. 'I'm ready to go and have had a heavenly time, Scott. Thank you for making it so.'

'It was a pleasure, ma'am.' He raised a servile finger to his forehead.

They rode swiftly through the velvety night, in a mood of silent empathy, and Theresa breathed deeply of the cool air coming through her window. Scott stopped on the front driveway. Melinda was sound asleep on the back seat.

'Would you care to come in for a cup of coffee?' Theresa invited him.

'Thank you, no. I want to have a look at that cow before I go to bed.'

Theresa put her hand on the door-knob, but he leaned

74

over suddenly, imprisoning her hand under his. Scott's face was very close to hers and she had an instinctive feeling that he was fighting some deep emotion. His glance clung and had a hot, embracing quality which brought precipitate colour to her cheeks. Was he about to kiss her? She closed her eyes involuntarily and braced herself. . . .

Moments passed while her heart beat against a hard shoulder. And then she opened her eyes to meet wood-smoke ones, dancing mockingly close. His breath was warm on her cheek as he spoke in satirical amusement.

'Something tells me that could have been easy and delightful. . . . But we will forgo the pleasure, another time perhaps? I merely wanted to know if you're still coming tomorrow?'

'You flatter yourself, Scott Milward, as you may have found if your so-called intuition had led you further. You have a distorted sense of your charms!' Theresa lashed words at him, to cover her own complex sense of frustration and fury. She had a brief moment of insight. This man had an insidious, physical attraction for her. . . .

He straightened up, opened his door and strode round the car to hold the door for her. She found a strange weakness in her legs as they faced each other. He broke the silence, to say woodenly, 'Do I come for you tomorrow?'

Theresa's back stiffened proudly. 'You may, after lunch, if it suits you.'

'Thanks, it does.' A brief goodnight, then she watched the tail lights of his car rapidly disappear down the drive.

Such a lovely evening and he had to spoil it all with arrogant, cynical remarks! Theresa's heart quailed as she thought of having to live in the same house as he. She was strong and would combat this fatal attraction, avoid him as much as possible. . . . Her chin jutted determinedly as she climbed into bed and within minutes she was asleep.

CHAPTER FIVE

It was with some trepidation that Theresa awaited the arrival of Scott Milward, the following day. Would it be in a friendly manner, or the hard, sarcastic mood of his departure the night before? She was puzzled by the many facets of his nature – tenacious, volatile, arrogant and at other times gentle, whimsical. It seemed that any adjective would suit him at any given time, according to his mood.

She felt a slight sympathy for the absent Elaine. To live with Scott must be very exhausting! He could, quite possibly, soar you to heaven or push one down into dungeons of despair. Why she should sense this, goodness knew, and Theresa mocked herself ruefully, now *she* was walking right into the lion's den. Well, she was not married to him, thanks be!

The Rourke family were sitting with her, under the cool of the trees, when they heard the deep purr of an approaching car. Sudden panic struck and Theresa wished she could fly into the surrounding thicket and hide, like a small animal, until the man had gone. She took pride in her serenity of face, while under her sky-blue shift-dress beat a floundering uncertainty.

The car door opened and a small volcano erupted, followed more slowly by its owner. Melinda was full of prattle about the lovely party and the fact that 'Tresa was coming to our house'. Scott lowered into the deckchair and extended long legs. 'She's been sitting in the car since after lunch. Vera has had the devil's own time with the minx.'

Long, frosted orange drinks were served and later, after many admonishments from Mary and Dan to visit often, Scott swung the car down the driveway. Theresa waved good-bye and felt small and lonely.

Scott had been very ordinary and noncommittal, for which she was grateful. It had stilled her own unrest.

Georgia waved frantically from the De Wets' gate and Scott trod hard on the brakes. She ran to Theresa's window and thrust in an eager face. Her hair was windblown, untidy, but, being shorter, did not look as scruffy as usual.

'Thanks for stopping. Mr. Milward. Nothing is wrong, everybody's fine. Terry, I just want to wish you luck, and here are some flowers for you, St. John Lilies.' She thrust three beautiful specimens on to the girl's lap. 'Also to tell you that Hugh – Dr. Lessing – has asked me to help in his office. I don't know what to do – Lily says it's wonderful – but I simply must talk to you. Can I come and see you tomorrow?'

'But of course, Georgia, I'm sure Scott won't mind—' Theresa looked at him hesitantly, suddenly realizing that he was now her employer.

He looked across her, to Georgia, warmth in his smile. 'Please do that, Georgie, come as often as you wish. No need to ask me.' His glance switched to the girl at his side. 'The more feminine company for Melinda the better, not so, Theresa?'

'Thanks. See you then, Terry. 'Bye, Melinda.' Georgia stood back and waved as they moved off.

A short silence prevailed. Theresa's eyes were on the lean hands manipulating the wheel with relaxed power in the blunt-edged long fingers.

Scott spoke quietly. 'Theresa, please don't contemplate asking my permission every time you have visitors. You have it, and also consider my house as yours, while you're there. By looking after Poppet you're doing me a great favour. I don't want you to think of me as your employer, rather as – a friend, and grateful father of your charge.'

'Thank you, Scott, I'll do that, and be circumspect in the amount and choice of friends who will visit.'

The smile turned to her illumined face, bringing a sparkling glint to imperious grey eyes. She turned quickly and became absorbed in the passing scenery, clutching the flowers in her hand harder than they deserved. A sudden thought came, of her own precious cache in an outcrop of rock, and she hoped fervently that Georgia had not raided that particular spot. It brought back memories of a hard body and strong arms holding her in a wild ride. . . .

Melinda showed her to her room while Scott busied himself with her luggage. The room was austerely furnished, but Theresa was standing in delighted admiration of the large

77

windows when he walked in with her bags. A rueful expression crossed his face as he put the cases down and studied the room.

'Heavens, I didn't realize what a dreary room this is. I'm seeing it now, through your eyes—'

'Oh, what a lovely window, just look at the view!'

Theresa drew back the heavy curtains as far as they would go, but, being heavy and thick, they obscured most of the light and view. Scott looked at them distastefully.

'Pull them down if you don't like them, and make a note of any alterations to suit your taste. I'll see to it.' He showed her an interleading door. 'Through here is Mel's room. The bathroom is two doors down the passage. When you're ready, we'll have tea on the terrace. Vera and fiancé must have taken a walk. The poor dope can't wait to carry off his bride-to-be.' Scott gave her a malicious grin as he walked out.

Melinda washed her own face and hands, imitating the older girl's every movement. When the little girl's hair was brushed Theresa ran a comb through her own silken mass. She dithered slightly about unpacking, then decided that tea would be kept waiting, so took Melinda's hand and walked to the terrace. Scott was chatting to Vera and her Dick.

Vera Smith stepped forward. 'Good afternoon, Miss Stanton, so sorry I wasn't here to show you to your room. Dick and I walked farther than we intended.' Her voice dropped to a lower note. 'Mr. Milward has been kind enough to let me leave right away, instead of tomorrow as planned. Dick likes to be at the garage early on Mondays, so if we push off as soon as possible we should be in Salisbury before midnight. Could you manage on your own? I mean Melinda's bath – her clothes – supper—' Her voice trailed anxiously.

'I am a nurse, remember?' Theresa answered brightly.

Vera tittered nervously. 'Of course, dear, nurses do have a knack of finding their way. . . . I've prepared a rice pudding for Melinda's supper.'

'Oh, do you prepare all her meals?'

'No – I just tell the cookboy or nanny what's needed, but I love making rice puddings.'

'And I hate them, Tresa!' Melinda piped forcefully.

'So do I,' thought Theresa as she assured Vera that she would cope quite well. She would find out about Melinda's likes and dislikes of her own accord.

An hour later the couple left, with Theresa and Scott's good wishes for a happy marriage, and Vera thanked the tall man again for his generous wedding cheque.

'Melinda, will you help me unpack? Pardon us, Scott, I want to get my bearings. Melinda can show me where everything is.'

Scott stood up politely and Melinda said in surprise, 'You needn't 'pologize to Daddy, Tresa. He lives here too.'

'It's polite to do so, honey, even though it's your daddy and you live together.'

' 'Scuse us, then, Daddy, we have so much to do.' The gamin face took on an air of gravity. Scott and Theresa exchanged quick, amused glances before the girl took a little hand in a tender clasp and led her away.

Scott watched them, an unreadable look deep in his grey eyes. His firm, generous mouth softened into sudden tenderness.

Much later, after her cases had been unpacked, Theresa wandered through the house with Melinda. The sun had set behind a rosy glow of clouds on the horizon. They looked for Scott because she wanted to find out about the child's bedtime procedure. He was not to be found, so she decided to bath and feed her charge, in case he wanted to play with his daughter before she went to bed.

Scott did not put in an appearance until she was about to leave Melinda's room. The night lamp was a soft glow as he walked past her and gazed down, touching the sleeping child's forehead with light fingertips. They left the room and he beckoned Theresa into the lounge.

'I usually have a bedtime chat with her, she doesn't normally go to bed so early,' he remarked as he busied himself with glasses and ice.

'This is normal bedtime for little girls and Melinda was really clapped. She worked hard at examining everything I unpacked, and then decided that every stick of furniture had to be dusted.' Theresa smiled at thoughts of the busy little bee.

Scott handed her a glass. 'Try this, it should give you the

extra stamina to cope. Melinda's nanny had the day off today, I completely forgot. So you had your hands full on your very first day here – I hope it won't frighten you off?'

'Don't be silly—' she began indignantly, and stopped as she realized that was not the way to address one's boss.

The 'boss' chuckled suddenly. 'That's right, have respect for the master of the house! Seriously though, Theresa (should I now address you as Sister?) don't take too much on your shoulders. Nanny, that's Cleo, does all the groundwork, bathing Melinda, washing and ironing clothes and making her meals. You will only supervise the jobs and concentrate more on Madam's health, soul and manners. That alone is a full-time job, believe me. Now polish off that sherry. Daniel has set a cold supper on the patio, so let's tuck in!'

Over a surprisingly delicious arrangement of cold meats and salads Theresa informed Scott that she would take her evening meals with Melinda in future.

'You'll do no such thing,' he returned sharply. 'Only if I'm not here may you share hers. Otherwise I expect you to dine with me. No arguments, please.'

She looked at the frown on his tanned forehead and thought he could be pretty grim and masterful, if he chose.

'If you wish it, sir,' she remarked primly, though a dimple lurked on a cool cheek.

'I do.' Scott looked suspiciously at the softly rounded cheek. 'I also want you to make a list of things you may need; curtaining for your room and Melinda's needs – er – clothing, etc. I'll leave it to you. I would also deem it a favour if you will help Daniel compile a list of foodstuffs needed. He's always running out of something or other and sulks if he can't make certain dishes, for lack of ingredients.'

'I'll do that, Scott. Where do you do your shopping?' He did not know it, but she was going to put white paint on top of the list, for Melinda's room. She hoped the store he patronized would have paint, and curtaining for hers *and* the child's rooms and some pretty murals, nursery ones? She would write it all down and hope for the best!

'I'm going to Umtali tomorrow afternoon and will be away for a day or two, depending on business matters. They have good shops there, and you're not to worry about the expense. My bank balance is fairly healthy. Sorry to leave you alone so soon after your arrival, but I have to go and I'm confident you'll cope on your own. Maybe you would like Georgie to stay with you?'

'I'll manage perfectly well, thank you, and would rather be on my own. I'll have the list ready for you tomorrow.' Theresa rose and hesitated. 'May I say good night now? It's late, and I'll take a bet Miss Melinda is an early riser.'

'For heaven's sake, girl, you don't have to ask my permission to go to bed, or for every little thing you want to do. Any major problems and I'm yours to command, but you're as free as the air otherwise.' The slender girl, standing in front of him, suddenly irritated him beyond measure. She looked so young, vulnerable and, illogically, against her polite request, he did not want her to leave him just yet.

Her cheeks flushed slightly at his evident irritation and she spoke stiffly. 'Politeness wouldn't be amiss all round, Scott. Thank you for a very nice supper. Good night.'

The slender back was uncompromisingly straight as she walked indoors. She was indeed going to have difficulty, trying to understand this baffling, moody man!

In the early morning Theresa met Cleopatra – buxom, dark-skinned, a gay red bandanna wing-knotted cheekily on the top of her dusky head.

'Ah done come from de banks of dat river Nile, so call me Cleo, eve'ybody does, ma'am,' she announced learnedly and gaily. 'That there Cleopatra must have bin some gal. Mister Scott done tol' me eve'ything. Fancy nursing *nyoka* dem snakes to youse bosom. . . . That pore reptile sure get lost in this Cleo's bosom – ha—!' Cleo stood, arms akimbo, and shook her generous front voluptuously, every white tooth on show with laughter. 'Come to brekfis, ma'am, Miss Melinda is waiting. Master Scott left with the horses, ver' early.'

Theresa battled manfully with the great breakfast spread before her on the table. 'Daniel, please, not so much for me! I'll have only toast, marmalade and tea in future.'

Cleo and Melinda helped to measure the windows for the shopping list. They studied the little girl's clothes, noting down what was needed. Theresa took a rough guess and ordered two gallons of white emulsion and one of gloss paint. Next to the nursery tiles she wrote, 'Leaving choice to Mr. Milward or assistant'. Daniel was then consulted and by the time the last item was listed it looked quite formidable, as if for a long siege! Theresa hoped Mr. M. would not think her extravagant as well as flighty. She would get in touch with Mary as regards the loan of her sewing machine.

The rest of the morning was passed on the patio, sorting out Melinda's books, of which there was a large and varied amount. While reading from *The Wild Swans* she became aware of thudding hooves and lifted her head to watch Scott cross the paddock. He rode easily, with perfect communion between horse and rider.

Theresa admired the lithe movement of limbs as he dismounted. Slim hips moved with supple grace and corduroy-clad legs paced with long, deceptively lazy strides towards them. Unaccountably, the girl's heart beat a little faster as Scott pushed the large-brimmed hat to the back of his head and his penetrating grey eyes surveyed the scene on his patio. Melinda flew to bear-hug his knees and he lifted her high.

'How's my girl, has she been good, Theresa?'

'Good morning, Scott.' The smile on Theresa's lips was reflected in them when she answered him. 'Melinda is a good girl and I'm proud of her. She helped to draw up this list for you—'

Scott fingered the fat envelope thoughtfully. Theresa felt the traitorous flush rise in her cheeks. 'Please don't let him open it now, and query the contents,' she prayed silently. She spoke hastily. 'If you open it at the store and decide that some items are unnecessary, please delete them, Scott.'

He quirked a knowing eyebrow. 'Right you are, ma'am, I'll use my discretion.' He tucked the sealed note into his pocket. 'I'm going for a bath and shave ... be a dear and help Daniel pack a grip for me. Enough for two days – don't forget my dinner suit.'

'But – but I've never—' she watched his receding back and finished, *sotto voce*, '—I've never packed a bag for a man in my life! Is this part of my duties, dear master?' There was no one to answer, so she shrugged her shoulders resignedly and went in search of Daniel.

They were putting the finishing touches to his bag when Scott walked in whistling, in Bermuda shorts and his towel slung over one shoulder. Damp, dark hair hung over one eye, making him look piratical, gay and sinister all at the same time. A sharp smell of sandalwood aftershave lotion emanated and Theresa's eyes were glued to the broad expanse of tanned chest. A strange feeling feathered across her scalp. She dropped her eyes with some difficulty to the open bag on the bed.

'I hope we've packed all your needs. I – er – I'm not used to – er—'

'Packing for a business gent like me? Well, are my socks in? Last time Daniel forgot and I had to rush round madly looking for an open store – most embarrassing, I assure you!'

'Yes, they're packed.' Theresa started to back out while Scott unbuttoned the white shirt Daniel had put out for him.

'Okay. Scram, will you – not that I mind if you stay,' he stated wickedly, 'but I'm afraid of maidenly blushes. We can have lunch, then I'll push off.'

Theresa 'scrammed', colour high in her cheeks.

Long after he had gone, a persistent picture of ludicrous floral shorts on long brown legs haunted her. Ludicrous, and yet so virile – manly.

Fortunately, Georgia turned up with her problems, pushing thoughts that were both besotted and silly back into unconscious regions.

They spent a pleasant afternoon discussing Georgia's future. An elderly cousin was reached by phone, being only too pleased to have the girl come and stay with her, for she was alone and her home was near to the consulting rooms. Georgia became too excited and shy to talk when Hugh Lessing was next contacted. She looked at the mouthpiece as if it would bite when she heard his voice, and shoved it into Theresa's hands. 'Hello, hello, who's calling?'

'Theresa Stanton here, Hugh.'

'Hello there, love, nice to hear your dulcet tones. What gives?'

'No one ill, Hugh, we're all in the best of health. I'm speaking on behalf of Georgia. She was called away when

83

this call came through. When do you want her to start? She's ready, able and willing.'

'Oh, she is, is she? Then why is she standing right beside you, breathing so heavily?' He laughed at the dumbstruck silence that ensued. 'All right, put her on. I won't bite. How's Scott?'

'He's gone to Umtali.'

'Good. Maybe I'll take a run out there this evening. Without his charm to distract you, my own charms may be appreciated.'

Theresa spoke hastily. 'We'd love to see you again, but not tonight, please. You know, my first day on the job, I'm having an early night. Thanks all the same, go spread your charm elsewhere. Good-bye now, here's Georgia.' She thrust the phone back at the trembling girl, walked hastily out of the room and stood in the passage where she could hear without being seen.

'Hello, Dr. Lessing.' Silence. 'Hello then, Hugh. . . . Yes, I have – yes, my cousin's house. . . . So soon? No, but . . . very well, Doctor – Hugh. No, Sam will – very well – er – thanks. Good-bye.'

Theresa came back and pried the receiver from still fingers, set it back in its cradle and gave the ring-off twist to the handle. 'So?' she inquired.

'He says I need only call him "Doctor" in the consulting room. He says to call him Hugh, as I've always done in the past. He says—' Georgia stopped.

'All right, he says all that. But what does he say about the job? When do you start, what is he paying you?'

A dazed look was cloudily focused. 'He said I was to start on Monday. Pay me? I forgot to ask, and he – forgot to say. He's coming for me on Sunday afternoon.'

'Oh, really, Georgia Masters, you'll have to pull up your socks if you're to work in a doctor's office. Vagueness won't get you anywhere,' Theresa said sternly.

Georgia recovered partly. 'Of course I'll pull up my doctor – I mean my socks, Terry. It's just that—'

Theresa dissolved into laughter. 'Oh, Georgie, you're priceless! Perhaps you're dithering because you're a little in love with your doctor?'

'Don't be absurd, Theresa Stanton. Now you're the one

84

that's talking rubbish. Why, I wouldn't be in love with that man. You're talking through your hat – I'm not in love with anyone—' An indignant flush was fast dispelling the dazed look in Georgia's eyes.

'Methinks the lady doth protest too much!' Theresa grinned at the girl and took both her hands. 'Come on, I was only teasing. Let's have tea. You look as if you could do with sustenance.'

Over tea they discussed pros and cons and Theresa offered Georgia three white nylon nurse's overalls she had brought with her. 'I have stacks of them, so won't run short myself. In any case I don't often wear them now.'

Georgia left, with fervent thanks for her help, promising to see her again before she started her new job.

After supper Theresa read to Melinda until her bedtime. The house was very quiet; outside, the night was velvety purple. She stood on the lawn, fascinated by a crescent moon rising in a sky studded with winking stars. The night seemed to tug at her heart and she knew a nameless longing, stirring deep inside her breast, for what or why she knew not.

The telephone aroused her and her steps were quick, light. Surely it would be Scott, to let her know he had arrived safely, to inquire in his deep voice if all was well at home.

A throb in the pulse of her throat subsided as Mary's voice inquired if all was well.

'Yes, thank you, Mary.' Theresa stammered slightly as she pushed down a wayward disappointment. After all, Scott could look after himself and he knew that all would be well at his house. So why should she expect a call from him?

'—And Dan will be helping with Scott's cattle round-up next week, so I shall spend a whole day with you. It's usual for the wives to help with the cooking at drive-time, the men are so hungry when they get back – are you there, Terry?'

'Yes – yes, Mary, I'm listening. That will be perfectly marvellous and sounds exciting. No, I haven't had time to arrange a day off yet. Not while Scott is away – no, I feel quite safe and happy. Melinda is a darling, so don't worry – how is Glynis?' She listened to a long rhapsody on baby's charms, and then her friend rang off with a warm good night.

There was a soft, sighing wind outside her open window. For a long time sleep eluded Theresa and the whispering wind seemed to coax her heart out of her body with a deep, velvety call. She punched her pillows and turned her back to the inviting night. 'You're getting soft, pal,' she chided herself scornfully, settling down at last.

Melinda was fretful and restless the next morning, quite obviously missing her father, for she kept asking when would he be back. Theresa concentrated on keeping her entertained and occupied, and after a mid-morning sleep the child awoke refreshed and in a better mood.

Lunch over, Theresa scratched through her own belongings and found a length of sprigged voile that was intended for a blouse, but which she now proceeded to cut and sew into tiny clothes for Melinda's lovely doll. The child was delighted and fascinated when she too was provided with threaded needle and a small square of material to hem, for a scarf.

Tenderness welled up as Theresa sewed and watched tiny clumsy hands work with laborious care, while a little rosy tongue was constantly in evidence. What an amazing feminine replica of her father! She felt an urgent need to take Melinda Milward in aching arms, to cuddle and comfort her with soft words of love and kiss away the sweet frown of concentration on a puckered forehead. This feeling was replaced by sudden fierce hatred for a mother who could forsake her child so ruthlessly — and bring such bitterness to a man's woodsmoke eyes. Her hands were still shaking when they started to dress the doll.

'Oh, Tresa!' Melinda's eyes were rapt as she held her 'baby'. She looked at it in long silence and then, with glistening lashes, climbed on to the older girl's lap and put chubby arms round her neck. 'Tresa, I do love you so much, I love you for ever 'n' ever. Don't go away, please!' and burst into tears.

Gently she was cuddled, murmured words of love, yearned for only moments ago, had their way, soothing and comforting two feminine hearts, with a promise from the older girl never to leave. 'Heart's promise?' 'Heart's promise, darling.' Tears were magically dispersed, Cleo and Daniel must be called to exclaim over the wonder of 'my boot'ful child'.

Later, Theresa sat on the patio and watched a solemn garden-boy and piccanin raise their hands in awed delight at the transformation of their beloved 'Nonny's' baby. Timothy, the cat, was honoured next and the watching girl smiled as a small imperious finger pointed to admonish him for lack of manners in yawning in a lady's face! 'Scuse him, Tresa, my daddy says he's just a tom-foolish cat.'

Sam dropped in to check if all was well after Melinda had gone to bed, her doll looking very snappy in new shortie pyjamas, and when he left Theresa settled under the reading lamp in the lounge to cut strips of white cardboard into one-inch widths by various lengths. She then printed simple everyday words on them. As from tomorrow, she was going to teach Melinda to sight-read, having heard about the new method of teaching the very young. Her thoughts wandered to Scott . . . what would he be doing, right now? Out with any particular cronies, or maybe some attractive girl, seeing a show, nightclubbing. She envisaged him, sleekly dark in black trousers and the snowy jacket which Daniel had so reverently packed.

Suddenly restless, she lit a cigarette and walked out to the darkening patio. The stars were so bright, they looked unreal. Maybe he was looking at them too, this very moment, an arm around his companion. Mutinously she forced her thoughts further south of the continent, to Derek. Would his suave, sophisticated arm possibly be resting on Sylvia's elegant shoulders? Theresa miraculously realized, after a moment of thought, that this picture which should have instantly raised her blood pressure left her strangely empty and cold. A maliciously insidious voice hoped that the gay widow had hooked her doctor – talk about just deserts! 'How mean can you get, Theresa Stanton?' her good spirit prevailed reproachfully, and the nurse-cum-ex-fiancée moodily pitched a half-smoked cigarette into the night, turned her back on the bright stars and walked indoors.

She was standing under a stinging shower when the sound of their telephone code-ring shrilled through. Turning the tap off, she listened as Cleo answered, but the conversation was indistinct and of a short duration. Cleo entered the bedroom soon after with a glass of hot Milo. 'Master Scott phoned, I tol' him the missy's in the shower and he say to give'm regards, he'll be back tomorrow. I brought this drink 'cos Master Scott he say to look well after you 'n little nonna. Everyt'hing is good and locked, so I'll wish you God bless 'n good night.'

'Thank you, Cleo, sleep well.'

So while she was having malicious thoughts Scott Milward was patiently waiting for his call to go through! Even though, when it did, he did not demand to speak to her personally . . . well, why should he? It was not imperative.

The next morning passed pleasantly. Melinda was an eager pupil and quick in absorbing the printed words. Her favourites were 'Daddy, Theresa, Melinda and Timothy' because they were the best 'shapes'. 'Daddy 'cause it reminds me of his long legs, Tresa looks like a soft bed and the other two 'cause them's are me 'n my cat!' Soft bed indeed? Theresa studied her own name long and hard.

CHAPTER SIX

THE hot sun had reached its zenith and moved with inexorable heat and unhaste to its allotted place to the west. Theresa found her eyes straying often to the ribbon of dusty road. No puffs of dust heralded an oncoming vehicle and eventually she dropped the book she was trying to read. Irritation at her lack of concentration made her sneer scornfully at herself, 'Stop it, you ass! Why so anxious for his return . . . do you expect a smile and a hug, like Melinda? What you'll get, old girl, is an arrogant turn of the head and a haughty inquiry after duties well done, and what in hell did I mean by giving such a ridiculous order and did I think I owned the place, by any queer misconception?'

Her thoughts brought forth a nervous giggle, and she decided to take Melinda for a walk before bathtime. The sun was much lower now, so it was not too hot and light remained long after sunset. So it happened that the two of them and a piccanin watchboy were some way from the house watching a gush of water flowing into the reservoir and listening to the slow regular beat of the pump when Melinda suddenly shouted, 'Daddy's come!' and tugged Theresa's hand frantically.

Reaching the house somewhat breathless, Melinda hurled herself at the tall man who was standing at the steps and directing unloading operations. He greeted his daughter with matching enthusiasm and turned a tired but smiling face to the quietly waiting girl. A fleeting, wondering expression sobered his smile for a moment and then it was back again as two warm brown hands enclosed hers. The strong, sensitive hands sent a sudden flare through her pulses and her eyes dilated.

'Hello, Theresa.'

'Hello, Scott.' Her reply came husky, soft.

Cleo broke the spell. 'Sure, Boss, but dem's a helluva . . . I mean dat's a lot of parcels. Dat long box, likely a new radio?' Her black face beamed expectantly.

'Who knows, inquisitive woman. Patience is good for the soul. A lot of parcels, you say? Well, whose fault is it?' He wiped his forehead with a handkerchief. 'It takes a woman to think up a list like the one I was handed. Snakes alive! I never want to go through that again.' His groaning chuckle was reproachful and resigned.

Theresa gave a slow sigh of relief. He was not going to storm and rant as she expected – not now anyway. 'Let me get you a long cool drink, Scott. I'm sure you must be parched.' She ran up the steps. 'I'll bring it out to the patio, would you like that?'

'Surely. I'll wash the grime off my face and hands. Come, Melinda, don't gawk so, I haven't forgotten your request. Daniel, that box can stay on the verandah, and that one, and that . . .' He ticked off the boxes for the kitchen, then went his way.

Ten minutes later, sitting with satisfied ease, Scott allowed Melinda to open her parcel and she squealed with delight at the miniature sewing-machine, complete with needles and thread, that actually worked, as a sample under the foot showed. A neat chain-stitch appeared when the handle on the wheel was turned.

Theresa almost followed suit with her cry of joy when lengths of curtaining were opened for her inspection – sun-filter in dove-grey for her room, cinnamon and yellow for Melinda's, complete with cottons, rufflette and rings, also exquisite nylon-net falls. Another box revealed soft rose bedspread for her and blue for Melinda, with matching scatter-cushions.

She held a cushion against her breast and looked at Scott, wordlessly. Not so Melinda. Chubby arms hugged him, kisses rained on his face. Through this he managed to splutter, 'I've bought the paint and brushes as well. I'm certainly going to absent myself for the next few days. Something is going to be whitewashed and it's not, I repeat, not going to be me!'

'Ah, Scott, you're an angel already, you don't need to be whitewashed . . . I mean. . . .' Colour flooded Theresa's cheeks as a sudden, quizzical gaze held hers, '. . . thank you so much. The colours are wonderful. I didn't think you had such taste for . . . I mean, they're beautiful. . . .'

'I get the message, ma'am. Now, before you collapse completely, let's open that large one.' He stood up and in a businesslike way snapped the packing wire with pliers, then stood back. 'Open up!'

Theresa stared in awe at the lovely table-model sewing machine, complete with handle and motor. Her conversation with Mary had been heard and noted! Dazedly she looked at him, trying to speak, but her tongue would not co-operate.

'Tresa, kiss Daddy thank you.' Melinda added excitedly, 'The cat's got her tongue, the cat's got her tongue, Daddy!'

'It sure has, pet. Shall I help her find it?' He came closer. The nymph's open mouth and the way she clutched that cushion as if it were a lifebelt made him burst into delighted laughter. He took her face between his hands and kissed her full on the mouth. The friendly caress became prolonged and she found herself incapable of drawing back while her heart reached top gear and raced madly.

Scott dropped his hands and drew back. His voice was brusque. 'Sorry, honey, but the invitation was irresistible. Have I annoyed you?'

'Not at all, Mr. Milward. I didn't find it annoying at all. I liked it, thank you?'

'Well then, let's be rational as from now. Here's the book with instructions for using all these gadgets. During the day you can use the handle and if you want to sew in the evenings our plant has the standard volts and amps, so we'll fix a plug wherever you want it.'

'You're very good to us, thanks. I can't wait to try it out. Come, Melinda, a quick bath and supper, then you can talk to Daddy again till bedtime.' Theresa wanted to get out of reach of his magnetic gaze as quickly as possible, otherwise she would start dithering like a silly schoolgirl with a crush.

It took her some time to calm an excited little girl, but eventually sleep claimed her and Theresa joined Scott for dinner. While they ate he was silent and answered in absent-minded manner when she spoke to him. She was rather relieved, for it gave her time to compose her own self. They moved to the patio with coffee and cigarettes. She persevered with small talk and had the satisfaction of drawing his attention on a subject which interested him greatly – local lore, fauna and flora.

Scott was certainly knowledgeable and spoke at length, holding her intense interest. She was surprised to learn that he was born in Australia and had come to Rhodesia with his father, as a young lad. The older Milward had worked hard to establish Windimount. Meanwhile Scott had attended university, qualifying as surveyor engineer. The death of his father was a terrible blow and he had finally come back to the ranch which now was his property. Scott omitted to mention the tale relating to his conference trip to America, where he met and married Elaine. Theresa felt this was deliberate and temerity forbade her curiosity to find tongue on a subject which was still too evidently raw and hurtful for this moody man to relate.

Finally he stood up and stretched long arms. 'Bed for me, I've had a hectic day. There's another parcel of under-clothes, etc., for Melinda. Thanks for giving sizes, it was a big help. If anything isn't right put it aside to be posted back for exchange.' He studied Theresa as she too arose. 'Are you settled, Theresa – more important still, are you happy here with Melinda?'

'I have no complaints sir. Melinda is a good child and responds like a kitten to affection. She's bright and has a quick brain, although she's slightly blasphemous at times.'

Scott caught her clear, direct gaze and smiled back sweetly, albeit a slight flush was noticeable across his fore-head. 'O.K., ma'am, I'll watch my tongue in future. You'll have us all ladylike very soon, with those violet eyes looking so sad and reproachful.' Playfully Scott grabbed her shoul-ders. 'Be still, you're in my power, woman. Dr. Jekyll was a healthy cousin of mine. I can be a worm, but I can also be cruel and savage and drink every drop of your heart's blood! That is, if you have a heart. A nip in the jugular vein is the usual procedure, I believe. . . .'

Theresa stood petrified, not in fear, but in the mes-merising aura of his close, vital presence. Scott looked at her for a moment, then loosened his hold on her shoulders. A brown hand flicked her hair and cheek carelessly as he stepped back, an impish glint flickering in smoky eyes.

'My word, you scare easily. I'll have to curb any – savage impulses – otherwise I'll find my golden nymph has flown the nest.'

'I'm not scared, Scott Milward,' she retorted, and retreated hurriedly to the door. 'I didn't realize my boss was quite demented, that's all!' Before he could speak she made her escape.

The following day was a busy day indeed! Theresa did not see Scott as he had breakfasted early and departed to the tobacco lands. She thanked the good mercies for that, being somewhat dubious of his reactions to her parting speech of the night before. Her sewing machine was proudly installed on a large table in a spare, sunny room which was duly dubbed as 'The Workhouse'. Melinda's tiny machine was screwed on at the opposite end of the table.

Georgia came visiting and was promptly roped in to tack curtain hems. The morning passed in a swirl of sewing and happy chatter. Scott did not appear for lunch and again Theresa felt a sense of reprieve. She could not pin down her feelings as regarded her boss. At certain times she hated him for his proud arrogance, then melted at his generosity. And now take last night . . . he was not above playing silly games! Then he would look at her in a certain way or come too close and she would instantly become aware of his physical attractions. Then again, coldly contemptuous, superior and distant . . . how on earth was she going to keep track of this complex man in order to meet his moods on equal ground? And above all, why couldn't she forget or disregard it all and enjoy her job? She loved her surroundings, was vastly intrigued with the ways of the Africans, and a mutually satisfying affection had developed between Melinda and herself. So forget about the man of the house whose moods probably stemmed from bitterness and disillusionment at his ex-wife's behaviour.

Theresa stopped and watched Melinda. That absorbed young lady was working on her tiny machine, sewing along the lines of pencilled flowers drawn on a square of linen. Not quite true yet, but she was getting the hang of it and her manipulations were dexterous, clever for her years.

93

'Let's stretch our legs and take fresh air, girls. My back's aching like the devil.'

They walked round to the cooler side of the house where a slight breeze cooled their brows. Georgia pointed in astonishment. 'Whatever is Scott doing at the swimming-pool? It's been dry and neglected ever since Elai— for a long time.' The three girls hurried over and watched three Africans diligently scrubbing the walls and floor of the tiled pool.

Scott tipped his hat back. 'Hello, girls, feel like pitching in to help, seeing as you're all loafing?'

'Daddy! We working very hard all day. Tresa and Georgie have done the curtains and my baby's quilt is almost done.' Melinda could look very indignant.

'Pardon me, such diligence, I do declare!'

'Goodness, Terry, you've made a difference here, but fast. Mr. Scott is waking up to feminine needs. Er – may I come over for a swim – when will it be full? Did you choose all that lovely curtaining and bedspreads all by yourself, Scott? They're gorgeous!'

'You may swim, and I'm fully aware of female needs *and* I chose everything myself. That's the second time someone has queried my good taste. I am a sophisticated man of the world and have acquired discrimination by my contacts with many distinguished, beautiful dolls. Furthermore—'

'And what does all that mean, Daddy?' piped a small voice from the vicinity of his knees.

'It means that Daddy has seen the light,' ventured Georgia.

'What exactly are you insinuating by that dubious remark, Miss Masters?' His tone was haughty and Theresa rushed to the rescue.

'It simply means that we're going to have gorgeous swims and – er – gorgeous curtains and – er lovely beds.'

'Very well put, Theresa, your perspicacity is fantastic Such intuition or prescience is rare in golden nymphs. The species are fast becoming obsolete—'

'Come off it do, Professor, please! Your boys can't work when they can't follow the conversation. Look at them gawping. Come on, girls, back to the workhouse, we've had all the rarified air we can take.' Theresa marched off and the other two followed rather reluctantly.

After dinner she politely excused herself and climbed into bed, very pleasantly tired and with hopes of tackling the painting on the morrow.

Stepping back to survey her handiwork, Theresa wiped her hands on a paraffin cloth. What a change glossy white paint made to Melinda's bed, dresser and stool! Gone was that drab uninteresting brown. The dressing-table had quaint white enamel knobs with hand-painted forget-me-nots, and now they added an elegant touch to the finished effect.

The ceiling was white and clean so all that was needed was a coat of soft, eggshell blue on the walls, a nauseous green at present, and, with the sun-filter curtains hung, it would be a dream room fit for a princess. The floor could be sanded and scrubbed to remove the dark polish revealing the natural golden wood.

Her own room had a similar floor; the suite was light oak, so she would leave it and paint the walls white. Theresa curbed her desire to pull the dark curtains down and hang the dove-grey ones which were hemmed and ready. Scott had glanced in while she was painting the furniture and she stifled his protest that it was not a job for girls by requesting help in scraping the walls prior to painting them.

Her request was met and a boy was even now busy in Melinda's room. Watching him, she thought it should be ready to paint the following day. A bed had been moved to her room to accommodate Melinda until this room was complete. That lass, supplied with a small tin of yellow paint and brush, was carefully painting her doll's cot. The floor of the side verandah was covered with newspapers to prevent any mess and the newly painted furniture glistened in the strong light.

Later that night the reading lamp cast a soft halo on Theresa's hair as she sat reading in the lounge. Scott was seated at the writing-desk across the room, writing in his ledgers. The desk-lamp brought into relief his strong, brown hands and cast emphasis on high cheekbones. A now familiar gesture of running his hands through his hair had ruffled it and an unruly lock hung over his forehead. Theresa, glancing at him, had a sudden urge to smooth it back with her hands. Scott raised his eyes and intercepted her gaze.

Confusion brought colour to her cheeks. She lowered her head and fumbled with the book on her lap. There was a long silence while she was very conscious of his appraisal of her.

'You look very cosy in that chair, Theresa, with the lamplight shining on your hair. Almost as though you – you belonged.' His deep voice quietened.

'I am comfortable – it's so peaceful here,' she stammered. 'Just listen to that nightbird calling outside.'

Scott turned his head towards the window. 'Rather a plaintive call, don't you think? When he eventually finds his mate (she plays hard to get) the call becomes more joyous, masterful, and nature comes into its own.'

Theresa considered this. 'Nature is cruel yet wonderful. One seems to be more aware of it here than in the cities.'

'Oh, definitely. In densely populated areas there's so much of the rat-race that fundamental nature is obscured by greed, lust and pecuniary gains. Don't you feel a slight longing for the bright lights sometimes, Theresa?'

Laughter bubbled up. 'Shades of lust, greed and lolly! Honestly, Scott, I haven't had time nor the inclination up to the present. Stop worrying about my gay spirit wanting that sort of outlet. When you see me climbing the walls, then you can start a panic. I'm going to do that tomorrow, but only to paint 'em.'

'You'll do no such thing. The boy I sent to help you knows what to do. He only needs supervision, he's apt to get lazy on his own. Like the great Sherlock Holmes I shall examine the wall through my spy-glass every night, and if I discover dainty footmarks, then forsooth, I shall know the time has come to send you back to civilization – especially if they're on the ceiling!' Scott smiled wickedly at some unseen vista.

Theresa closed her book with a snap and stood up. 'Do you get like this every night? Anyway, until that time comes, we'll say no more. 'Night, boss.'

'Just a moment, please, Theresa.' She stopped at the doorway and faced him inquiringly. 'I'm going to Salisbury at the end of this month. I want you and Melinda to accompany me. Tobacco and cattle sales – we'll be there approximately four days. During the day you and Poppet can explore the town and surroundings and in the evenings we can visit night spots. They sport a very good theatre and the lights are satisfyingly bright as well.'

'Oh, Scott, you don't have to worry. We'll be quite content to stay here. There's no need to drag us—'

He retorted sharply, 'I don't intend to drag you. I'm merely stating that it's my wish that you come with me. I have good friends in Salisbury where I usually dump Melinda and Cleo, while I go about my business. Cleo can come with us as chaperone, if you're feeling prim and jittery. Dave and Val would feel most annoyed if I didn't put up at their house as I usually do. You'll like them, they're good company.'

Theresa answered mildly enough although, unaccountably, her heart started hammering in her throat. 'As you wish, Scott. I would like the trip very much, thank you.'

'My pleasure, ma'am. Goodnight, and pleasant dreams.'

Excitement boiled strangely with a queer foreboding in her breast as she prepared for bed. Excitement at the forthcoming trip, that she could understand, but the other feeling was beyond comprehension and troubled her greatly.

Rain fell softly throughout the night and dawn came, sparkling fresh and bright, giving no warning of the upheaval which was to come later and cause Theresa's world to streak beyond heaven's delight and then to the very depths of despair, alternately and ruthlessly.

A boxed parcel arrived on the postal bus, containing four nursery mural tiles. Theresa and Melinda were delighted; they were just what the little girl's room needed, for the finishing touch. Theresa had presumed that item on her list had been ignored, but now it was evident that the shops did not stock them, so Scott had ordered the tiles, to be sent by post.

A serious discussion started between Cleo, Daniel, Melinda and herself as to where the murals must hang. It was Nonna's room, so she had first choice. Unerring taste in so small a being showed in her final selection. 'These three must hang on that wall opposite my bed so that I can see them when I wake up, 'n this one—' pointing to a picture of two big-eyed kittens watching a fluffy yellow chicken, '—this one must hang over Beth's cot, 'cos then she won't feel lonely when she wakes up.' (Baby doll duly named Beth.) Against the newly painted wall the three pictures were hung and Beth declared she was ' 'liriously happy with her special one, thank you.'

Melinda and Theresa lunched alone and after the child had her afternoon nap they settled under a shady tree with picture-books. An hour later Cleo called Theresa to the telephone. It was Mary, to inform her that they would be over that evening in order to discuss the coming cattle round-up.

'How are you, girl? I hear you've been busy with the rooms. Have you tackled the lounge?' Mary chuckled knowingly.

'Good heavens, no! I'm dead scared to ask Scott for anything more after that last lot, although he didn't blast me. I'll give him time to recover and then insinuate—' she broke off as Cleo suddenly appeared in the passage. Her dark skin was a queer grey colour and she was extremely agitated. 'What's wrong, Cleo?'

English was forgotten, two terse words choked out. '*Nyoka! – Nonna!*'

As the dreaded word left her lips, the receiver was slammed down. The girl streaked past her and ran down the front steps. Daniel stopped her head-long rush and pointed. Her blood ran cold, she beheld Melinda, absorbed in her book, quite unconscious of the ugly head reared within four yards of her small, vulnerable back!

With cold calculation Theresa took the spade from Daniel's nerveless fingers, praying silently, devoutly, that the child would not look up or move. She approached the evil reptile from the rear and, as it sensed her presence, some inner spring uncoiled in the girl to a forward leap that buried the spade edge cleanly into the writhing neck and ground.

Simultaneously, Scott stopped the jeep with a squeal of brakes, was beside her in seconds.

'Good girl!' He moved to take the spade, but she clung to

98

it with hands that were white-knuckled, stiffly paralysed.

'*Bulala yena!*' Daniel recovered his wits, sprang to beat the shining flat head to a pulp with a rock he had found. Melinda jumped up, alarmed and white-faced. A jittering Cleo scooped her to an ample bosom and carried her to the house with babbling endearments pouring from thick, shaking lips.

'You can let go now, darling ... that was very brave of you. ... God, that was a close shave!' Scott stood behind the rigid girl, his arms encircling her waist, brown hands gently massaging white fingers that would not, could not open. 'It's all right now, love, it's quite dead.'

Theresa let the spade drop from sudden lax fingers and found her vocal chords. 'Melinda – it was going to strike her, it – dear God—' A white fist clenched against her lips and the man turned her round and held her close.

'Relax, my dear. It hasn't struck her, thanks to your quick action ... thank heaven she didn't move. I've never seen a human being uncoil and leap the way you did! Stop trembling, honey ... it's reaction. Daniel, fetch a glass of water with three teaspoons of sugar, chop chop!' Scott stroked damp hair and her stiff back with sensitive fingers.

Quite suddenly, Theresa was no longer trembling with fear. Another terror ... mixed with delight ... had taken hold of her senses. Nothing mattered in the world but the feel of this strong body against hers, those wonderfully gentle hands and the beautiful words of endearment that pierced her shock-clouded brain. 'Darling, love, honey' – surely they were the most beautiful words in the world? The heavenly feeling deepened as his hands cupped her face and he kissed her gently on her mouth.

Scott let her go rather suddenly and she had the strange sensation of bones becoming fluid, melting. She closed her eyes in a supreme effort to still the wild fluttering of her heart. His hands moved to her shoulders.

'Sit down, Theresa. Daniel has brought a chair. Drink this – you certainly are numb with shock – a delayed reaction.' She was firmly pressed down and a glass held to her lips.

Theresa sipped the water, her thoughts in hysterical confusion; of course that was her name, Theresa. Not darling or love or honey. Just Theresa, the girl who had killed a snake that was dangerously near his child (had there been danger – why had the spade stuck to her hands?). She must see Melinda – oh yes, Theresa was the girl who needed soft words to calm her shock. Anodyne for hysteria. And with that came the quite hopeless realization that she, Theresa Stanton, had fallen utterly, desperately in love with Scott Milward, her boss. Who was still in love with his ex-wife.

Warm hands were chafing her cold ones and she opened her eyes, to meet his darkened, smoky ones, very close as he bent in front of her, speaking softly. Her eyes were drawn to his mouth and longing filled her so that she scarcely heard the words, but watched his lips in fascination.

'Good, you're looking better now, there's more colour in your cheeks and lips. For a moment I thought you were going to faint. Do you know, I feel like kissing you again. I'm very grateful for your quick action, Theresa.'

Her smile was watery. Grateful kisses, that's all, dear Theresa. Remember that.

Scott did not kiss her but looked at her, long and searchingly, drew a deep breath and straightened up as Melinda came running across the lawn. He held her closely in his arms as she chattered excitedly about the ' 'orrible weptile' while the girl in the chair wished achingly that she could also creep into that warm, loving embrace. She stood up and found that her legs could hold her after all. The stiffening aid of pride helped her to toss back unruly hair, to speak with quiet composure.

'That 'orrible reptile has had it, for sure. If that spade had gone any deeper it would probably have frightened the life out of some poor wombat down under. If I'd had a revolver and could shoot, then I needn't have come so close to the – to the—' Words failed as she met penetrating eyes again and she turned quickly, almost stumbling, to walk away, calling over her shoulder, 'Lashings of tea, that's what we need!'

The man lowered his daughter into the chair, but his gaze lingered on the slender, retreating figure. Tenderness gleamed for an instant, then was blotted out by lowering lids.

During the course of the day and evening, Theresa hugged her new-found, dangerous knowledge close to her heart and it fed on small things, like the quirk of an eyebrow above dark lashes, the turn of a high cheekbone, lithe movement as Scott poured drinks for Mary and Dan. Sweet torment, listening to his husky, compelling voice. They played Canasta, Dan partnering her. Normally a good player, she now needed superb concentration to keep her mind on the cards, to stop it from veering away at the sound of that soft arrogant and always slightly mocking tone.

Theresa took pride in her deceptive outer calm; no one guessed at the tormenting emotions surging beneath her cool exterior. Scott remarked at one time on her prolonged contemplation of the cards in her hand. 'You're concentrating with such devout severity, dear Theresa. Like those women who read your future in the cards. What do you hold, a fifty-joker or an ace of hearts? Be careful you're not caught with it, points against you, love.'

Sudden poignant resentment at his easy use of endearment made her voice sharp as she retorted, 'That's for my partner to groan about, if it happens. And it's not going to happen, partner, may I play out?' To Dan's nod of delight, she played out, catching Mary and Scott with full hands.

'Proper witch, she be! Painting, sewing, slaughtering dragons, cheating at cards, and she be turning the world topsy-turvy next and that's a fact!' Scott grimaced ruefully.

Amidst laughter, Theresa stacked the cards while her heart repeated, You've turned my world topsy-turvy, Scott Milward. That is an irrefutable fact, beloved.

She stood with him in the velvety night, watching the receding lights of Dan's car. He put a friendly arm across her shoulders. Tension shot through her arms and she shrugged irritably, almost physically sick with the violence of recent emotions.

He stepped back immediately, sardonic mockery in his voice. 'So sorry, ma'am. Shall we adjourn to the lounge? You in your small corner, I in mine? I have no grim intentions, so don't snap and snarl. Were you going to do that?'

'Of course not – I guess I'm tired.'

'You've been through a lot today, Theresa.' 'The understatement of the year, if you only knew!' she thought. 'And if you'll creep into bed, I'll whip up a glass of hot milk. I have very good pills, tranquillizers, and will bring it to you. No arguments now, I'll give you ten minutes to retire and look proper.' Scott moved down the passage.

Theresa looked desperately into the night for guidance, but none was forthcoming. She turned away and walked to her room. The bedside lamp glimmered softly, Melinda slept peacefully in her small bed in the far corner. Scarcely had she time to compose herself under the bedclothes when Scott whistled a warning and walked in. He placed the glass of milk in her hand, fumbled in his shirt pocket and handed her a pill. Silently he watched as she swallowed it and drank the milk.

'Goodnight, girl, sleep well.' At the doorway he turned, looked at his daughter and then again at the older girl. The door closed softly.

Theresa was grateful for the ensuing busy time which started on the following morning and lasted for three very hectic days. Mary, Lily, Georgia and another neighbour, Mrs. Henning, came over with their menfolk. Horses were saddled and the male party set off to comb the nearby gullies and scrub, for stray calves and steers. The next day they would ride further afield.

Great activity prevailed in the kitchen as the women baked joints of meat, bread and large saucepans of sweet-sour beans – sous-boontjies, Aletta Henning informed them. Hungry riders would be back for the midday meal and supper. The following days would be spent in the open as the round-up took them farther into the hills and valleys, so enough food had to be cooked and packed into saddlebags to satisfy vast appetites away from home base.

No time at all to brood on the sudden awakening of her love for Scott Milward. Georgia took charge of the small fry while she helped in the kitchen. At noon the men returned and clattered on to the verandah where a long trestle table, loaded with food, awaited them. Healthy badinage was exchanged amongst them and Scott joined them, flinging his hat on a chair. All were dusty, from hat sweatbands down into the open necks of khaki shirts. Having washed dirty hands at the tub outside, there was not time enough for further niceties before mealtimes.

Theresa inadvertently brushed Scott's arm as she replaced his plate and he raised shocked eyebrows as she stepped back hastily.

'Scared of a bit of honest dust, lass? Hmm, may I tell you, there's a luverly smudge of flour across your pert nose? Sam, remind me to buy some face powder for the desperate girl. No wonder there's a mighty depletion of same in the larder!'

Indignation coloured her cheeks, and then she joined the laughter that followed as her natural sense of humour was restored.

The ladies sat down to a leisurely lunch after the men had left. Lily's baby was admired and Melinda was in her element, having two babies to croon over. Aletta Henning, pregnant with her first baby, hoped fervently that Theresa would be around in case of emergency! Lily was full of praise at the expert handling of her own case.

Melinda's room, ready for occupation, came in for inspection. Lily helped Theresa to hang the curtains while Mary smoothed the bedspread. She stood back to admire the effect. 'I can't believe it, the transformation is terrific. How far are you with your room, Terry?'

'The boy is scraping the walls.'

'Well, tomorrow won't be quite so hectic. Aletta can watch the children and we'll help you to paint while the men are away.'

'That will be great. I love the team-work that goes on here. Do you – er – all sleep here?' Theresa asked tentatively while visions of sheets, pillows and rooms swam before her.

Mary laughed. 'Of course not, dear. We can all steer a wheel.'

They trooped to the lounge. Lily looked around thoughtfully and her gaze finally rested on the fair-haired girl. Intercepting her thoughts, Mary and Theresa burst into convulsive laughter. 'Oh, so already there's a conspiracy in the air! Yes, it certainly needs a woman's touch.' Four pairs of eyes swivelled in accord, and Theresa became the focus of attention!

She blushed furiously. 'I simply can't go around changing Scott Milward's house as if – as if I owned it!'

Aletta studied her intently. 'As if you owned it – you've

got something there, *meisie.* Maybe you could—'

'What are you getting at?' Theresa became speechless.

'Well, he's good-looking and – er – eligible, and no one else has got this far about altering the house. Elaine did damn all while she was here. Melinda is fond of you, you're a very attractive girl. Any man with sense—' Aletta's voice trailed off as she met the full glare of Mary Rourke's angry eyes.

For Theresa's friend had glimpsed, and read rightly, the sudden deep pain and love that showed in her eyes, moments before she dropped a curtain of dark lashes. 'Oh, my God!' she thought amazedly. 'She's gone and fallen for Scott. And his heart is buried beneath an avalanche of disillusioned love for Elaine. What now?' Her glare took in everybody. 'Stop acting like a lot of matchmaking biddies. Terry will find her own way without the desperate means of – marrying – the wretched man, just to get her way in his house. Come on, you bloody lot of conspirators, we've still got that batch of scones to bake.' She softened her harsh words with a smile. 'Take you a bet mine'll be lightest and bestest!'

Standing aside, she waited while they trooped out; only Theresa was still standing, petrified, at the window. 'Fetch Glynis's bottle, please, Terry dear. I left it in the bathroom.' On this blatant lie Mary turned and followed the others.

In the bathroom, Theresa gazed around unseeingly. What was she looking for – oh yes – the bottle. What a funny place for Mary to leave it anyway. Dawning realization came when she failed to find it. Mary could always read her like a book, had sent her here to recover. Dear heaven, was it so obvious, had anyone else noticed? Dan? Or Scott himself? Oh no, no, that couldn't happen! Then she would have to leave, very soon – no, this place had become so dear to her. What of her promise to Melinda never to leave her? Could she possibly stay, with an aching love that would never be reciprocated, while Scott's heart belonged to Elaine – and could she keep it hidden? Already Mary knew, and Scott was quick, perceptive. Her emotions could slip. The scorn in his eyes, the thoughts in his mind: 'Fickle, hardly out of sight of the old love and on with the new!'

The feeling she had had for Derek Mann paled into insignificance beside this love, physical and spiritual, that had awakened within her. Could she stifle her feelings, knowing the poignant joy of being near to him, or would it be far better to leave, soon, before making a bigger fool of herself?

Theresa dashed cold water on her face, emerged from the bathroom looking cool and placid. She smiled at Mary's quick, anxious gaze. 'Bottle's not there, Mary,' and had that woman wondering if she had misread the signs. Otherwise her friend was only a superb actress.

With a sense of satisfied weariness, the families took their leave at dusk. The hot bath Theresa wallowed in produced a sort of protective, languid miasma. No one was more surprised than she when sleep claimed her the moment her head touched the pillow.

Two more days passed in bustling, busy activity. The men returned, tired, dusty but triumphant, and there was a great bawling and lowing behind the cattle rails when, on the last day, dipping and tallying was done. Theresa was amazed at the great number of cattle which Scott possessed. There seemed to be miles of white faces milling around the men as they shouted in the dust-laden air.

Meantime, her room was completed and she revelled in its beauty and freshness. Sweeter was the torment as well, as with aching heart she watched a tall rangy man slap on his big-brimmed hat and stride away, brimful of vitality.

CHAPTER SEVEN

'SOMETHING wrong, Theresa?' Scott noted the white face and queer attitude of the girl as she stood at the window, a letter clenched in her hand. She turned dazedly and sank into a deep armchair.

'Well, what is it?' the commanding voice repeated.

Theresa looked at the letter in her hand. 'A letter from – from Derek.' She swallowed painfully.

'Derek – your fiancé?'

'Yes, ex-fiancé. He's in Salisbury and wants to come here, to apologize for his behaviour – wants to know if my friends could put him up for a day or two.'

'So?' Scott's question was curt.

'So Sylvia finally overplayed her hand, and the great man wants to apologize – and carry on where we left off. Just like that.'

Scott regarded her in silence for a few moments, then voiced mockingly, 'So that's why you're so pale! Excited at the thought of seeing him again—'

'No!' she exploded. 'I don't even hate his guts for being so gullible, but I'm revolted at his certainty that I would fall into his arms so readily. "All is forgiven, dear heart. I shall die without you" – Bother him and his man's conceit!'

'And all is forgiven?' the query fell softly.

'Forgiven?' Candid blue eyes were raised to his. 'Why, I've even forgot, now that—' She stopped abruptly.

'Now that—?'

'I mean – he means nothing to me. I couldn't have really loved him, after all. My pride was hurt and his distrust was hard to take. I don't want to see him ever again.'

'Well, what are you panicking about? Write to him, tell him just that.'

'He's not the sort to take note of a letter. Derek believes his presence is more convincing and – his charms will make one capitulate instantly. He can be most charming.'

'Would you capitulate?'

Theresa answered with grave finality. 'No. For reasons of

my own, I could never go back to Derek. Aside from his weak loyalty I simply have no feeling left – for him.'

'I'm not in full cognizance of your affairs, but why not prove it by inviting your doctor here?'

'He'll probably come, with complete disregard of my letter. What should I do, Scott, if he won't take no for an answer?' Her reliance and trust in his wisdom was sweetly naïve.

Scott drew out a letter from his own pocket and said slowly, 'I have a proposition to make, Theresa.'

'Yes, Scott?'

'I have here a letter from Elaine. No, don't say anything, hear me out. She's coming here to pick up some personal things which she has suddenly discovered she needs. She's in Salisbury. Could be the thin edge of the wedge if she wants to come back—'

Theresa could only stare at him, shock curling down her back. His jaw was steel as he continued, 'I don't want her back here. Aside from anything I may still feel for her, she can't come back here. So, until we both know exactly what we want, I suggest we protect each other.'

'How do we do that?' The rigid shiver up her spine frightened her.

'By becoming engaged – to each other.'

'Are you joking?' Theresa stared at him, appalled.

'I was never more serious in my life.'

She stood up in agitation. 'I couldn't possibly agree to such a – cold-blooded arrangement!'

'My dear girl, it's merely a protective arrangement.'

'But l-love is part of an engagement—'

'As I've mentioned before—' the sarcasm was back, '—love explodes and fizzles out. You should know that. Where's the love you thought you had for Derek?'

'That wasn't true love.'

'What is true love, then? Describe it!' he taunted.

Theresa was silent, while she yearned to shout, 'What I have for you, my disbelieving beloved.'

The unconscious 'beloved' asked cynically, 'You'll recognize it, I suppose? The all-powerful and everlasting Love, spelt with a capital L—'

'Scott! Don't let your own experience make you cynical

and disbelieving. There is such a thing.'

'I'll take your word for it. Now, Miss Stanton, will you kindly become engaged to me? For mutual protection only, I assure you. Advantages will not be taken. Also, it will be broken at such a time when either of us feel there's no longer need for protection.'

Her chin tilted defiantly. 'I'm sure you'll not take advantage, and I'm not in such dire need of your protection. On the other hand, being engaged to someone else would be the surest way to impress Derek that all was over, finally. As for you, if you're so weak that you need my help while making up your own mind, well then, I accept your proposal!'

Flame flashed deep in woodsmoke as he returned her gaze. With calculated candour, he spoke at last.

'Thank you, my dear. I may look strong, but where my emotions are concerned, I'm – awfully weak. Let's break the seal on a bottle and celebrate?'

'Yes, let's,' Theresa agreed.

Trying hard to examine the situation dispassionately, while Scott was out of the room, her mind was so chaotic, the only solid thought to be pinned down was of Melinda. What had Scott told the child about her mother's absence, how would she react if Elaine suddenly turned up here? Theresa stifled her own feelings relentlessly. She must not think about that aspect and how it would affect herself. Had Scott really meant it, that he did not want his wife back? According to Mary and Dan she was very beautiful and had the advantage of being Melinda's mother. All that, plus her proximity, would surely make Scott change his mind, forgive her for whatever she had done and welcome her back.

An engagement that Elaine would see through, right away, if she was determined to stay. Unless Theresa and Scott played it to the hilt, pretending to be very much in love. It would be no pretence on her part. Could the man play with sincerity in front of the woman he had loved, or still loved deeply?

Scott came in with bottle, ice and glasses. While he busied himself at the sideboard she walked over and watched him in silence. She accepted the frosted glass and asked tentatively, 'Scott, what about Melinda?'

He leaned back against the sideboard, studied his glass. 'Melinda? Hmm, that's my biggest problem. She has only a vague memory of her mother. To her question on the lack of a "mommy" I simply said she had gone away. It satisfied her then. Now she's older, if Elaine comes here—' a world of pained experience shadowed his eyes and his fist thudded against the top of the table, 'I will not allow her to come here and upset my daughter! No. I'll ring her in Salisbury, take a list of what she wants and send it to her.'

'You'll not want to see her yourself?' Theresa's heart wept at the sudden clouding of his grey eyes.

'Perhaps it would be best, more polite anyway. We'll take her things on our trip to Salisbury and confront her with you, my fiancée. That will convince her that I have no wish to take her back – if she had those intentions.' A clenched fist showed white at the knuckles.

'And Melinda?' The question came inexorably.

'My child will be kept out of the way. Her mother forfeited any right to see her, long ago.'

'She's the child's mother, Scott. Maybe she did something dreadfully wrong, but surely there's still some mother love—' Theresa could not stop flagellating herself – and him.

Scott's face became set, grim. 'Not knowing the circumstances of our last meeting, would you kindly stop this – persecution – and take my word, Elaine is not fit to be a mother to any child nor a faithful wife to any man.'

Restrained contempt hardened his voice to such an extent that the girl was perplexed, almost afraid. How very much he must have loved her, and how terrible to be so disillusioned, to let this awful, implacable scorn replace the feeling he once had for this woman. Theresa walked to the window and stared out into the clear, star-studded night. Soon she felt his presence near and then he cupped her elbow lightly.

'This should be a gay celebration, my dear. Let's smile and wish each other luck and may our hearts' desires come true. Look at me, Theresa.'

She turned her head and the fathomless look was back in her eyes. The man's heart missed a beat as he tried, unsuccessfully, to pierce the obscuring mist. He raised his glass. 'To our future, honey, and may it be a lovely engagement.'

'While it lasts!' She smiled sweetly and the misty allure enthralled, enchanted him, made him ask huskily, 'Can we seal it with a kiss?'

'We can, we will.' Theresa lifted her lips.

The kiss was fatherly, gentle. He lifted his head and the slow smile set her pulses on fire. With an effort she restrained herself from leaning forward to beg for more.

Scott turned abruptly and drained his glass. 'You'd better be off to bed before I forget that this engagement has no advantages. You're rather beautifully provoking and I'm only human. Go, before baser instincts overcome me.'

Theresa thrilled to the husky tones and could not have cared less if his instincts were physical or spiritual. She wanted his arms around her. But the back turned to her was uncompromisingly straight and forbidding. A sigh of regret and frustration escaped her as she murmured a low 'Goodnight' and left him.

She lay awake for a long time, her arms pillowing her head. Scott *was* attracted to a certain extent, even though he did not love her. He was hard, but presumably still capable of reactions to a woman, when that woman was enticingly close and alluring. Theresa knew, without being vain, that she was attractive, though probably not a patch on his ex-wife. If they could overcome the hurdle of meeting Elaine and Scott found that he really did not want her back, that his love was ashes after all, then perhaps he would soften towards her, Theresa. She could not expect love to blossom immediately on his side but would hide her own feelings, offering him only calm, warm friendship. Melinda was a slender bond between them and that bond plus understanding companionship could strengthen, in time, to something deeper. Her love must kindle an answering spark eventually. But – that but loomed large and terrifying – Elaine Milward must be confronted first. She sighed deeply. Of such hopeful, flimsy stuff are dreams made.

On Saturday morning Scott ordered her to pack an overnight bag. 'I'm taking you to Mary's. You're off duty until tomorrow night – about time too, you've been working too hard and you're looking pale and peaky.'

'What about Melinda? Who will see to her?'

'I am. I've done so fairly often and Cleo is here. I know what you're going to suggest and the answer is no, you're not taking her with you. A complete break is needed however much you're attached to my girl. I'll drop you at the Rourkes' after lunch. Mel and I are spending the night with friends in the village.'

Theresa welcomed the idea of visiting Mary and Dan. The tension of being on her guard with Scott could be relaxed for a few blissful hours.

'Are we going to announce our engagement?' he asked, a humorous twist to his mouth.

'Is it necessary? The Rourke family will see through the farce quickly enough. Would you mind if we simply explained the position?'

'And let them know I'm hiding behind your brief little skirts?' he asked sarcastically.

'Don't forget I'm doing likewise behind your – er—'

'Natty slacks?' Scott began to smile mischievously. 'No, we will have to act madly in love to convince those two! So we'll forgo that torture and you can relax for the week-end. We shall suddenly announce the thrilling news before our trip to Salisbury. That will give respite from prying questions and exclamations of joy; the ladies out here give tea-parties and kitchen-teas at the drop of a hat!'

His grin was contagious, and Theresa found herself chuckling. 'Oh dear, I can foresee a lot of complications arising out of this unholy alliance!'

'Is it so unholy, after all? We're fairly companionable, there are no upsetting heights of emotion to contend with. All right, I'll shut up, knowing your views on Love (with capitals) but, Theresa,' his voice was suddenly low and urgent, 'it need not be unholy. You and I could be happy and content. Melinda likes you and your presence here pleases me—'

'Oh, it does, does it?' she retorted hotly, completely forgetting her vow to win him with friendship. 'Comfy, very comfy, but I don't believe in milk-water half measures, Scott Milward. We will stay engaged just as long as it remains convenient. After that—' she faltered, could not continue.

'What then, Theresa Stanton? You look lovely when you're angry. Do you reckon hyacinths will grow here?'

Bewilderment replaced her anger. 'Hyacinths? Y-yes, I think so. In the shade – why do you ask?' Theresa looked at him suspiciously. 'Are you trying to change the subject?'

'Not at all. I want to compare the colour of your eyes with the blooms, especially after a fall of rain.'

'Oh, you're impossible!' She flushed and her hair swung out as she turned sharply away. Even so, a small sliver of joy entered her heart. He was taking notice of her, and if only Elaine could be consigned to the other end of the earth she, Theresa Stanton, had a slender thread of hope.

So her presence pleased him, did it? A bone for a hungry dog. He sounded like a – a rajah, complimenting his dancing girl–'Dear Salome, your presence pleases me. I will clap my hands when I need you. Run along now and send in my first wife as you pass!'

She found herself outside, grabbed the small fork out of an amazed piccanin's hand and, through a haze of tears, weeded furiously. 'Oh, darling beloved rajah, you can throw every bone you possess to this hungry dog-girl. I will hoard them like gold, precious beyond belief. You stupid, stupid fool, why did you get yourself into this silly state – I'm talking to me, not to you, my beloved rajah Milward—'

A sedately composed young woman was safely deposited on Mary's doorstep. Theresa waved airily as Scott and Melinda drove away and kept her inner feelings so superbly hidden that in the course of the day and evening, Mary Rourke wondered again if she had been wrong in her diagnosis. She did not notice that the girl often subsided into long far-away silences and her volatile spirit was not at its best, while blue eyes had strange new depths. All this could be attributed to the Derek affair, however.

On Sunday morning Theresa told her two friends of the letter she had received from Derek. Her manner was so noncommittal that they were assured her only worry was that he would turn up and embarrass them by asking to be accommodated.

'There's a perfectly good little hotel in the village, I shall tell him so,' Dan declared, but his wife hushed him. 'We can't be so inhospitable, Dan. I have no liking for him especially now, but he's going to be a very disappointed man, we can afford to be generous for one night only.'

'Thank you, Mary. I've written to him, stating in definite terms that I haven't the slightest wish to see him again, so his journey would be quite unnecessary. So the chances are he won't even turn up unless he chooses to disregard my letter. Now, my friends, if you have no objection I'm going for a ride on my favourite horse. I have a secret cache of jewels to be inspected and gloated over.' Theresa shook her head at their puzzled queries.

Stepping carefully across the stones in the river, she approached 'her' rocky outcrop and scrambled up. Oh, glory be, they were still there! More blooms had opened and shone radiantly scarlet against the sun-drenched rocks. The recent rain had brought out clusters of sword and maidenhair ferns. Theresa sat down and leaned back carefully, not wanting to bruise the delicate fronds. An overhang of rock shaded the upper part of her body. Her hat was discarded, the ponytail of silky hair was loosened and spread in wild confusion by slim fingers. It had grown appreciably longer since her arrival in this land of the flame-lily.

She dug her fingers into the soft pockets of soil. Her land, where she had found affinity. Not only the land but love as well had fastened claws of velvet around her heart and she was a willing prisoner. If only her stern jailer would cooperate by reciprocating that love.

Theresa gave dreamy thought to that mad, wild ride when Scott was still an unknown factor. He should have pointed the nose of his steed in the opposite direction, they would still be travelling, fast as the untrammelled wind. Free as the air – of course detouring just long enough to gather up Melinda, who would have her own fast little steed. Theresa would stay where she was, firmly held in strong arms, her flying hair kissing his cheek – the girl closed her eyes, sleep claimed her, but fantasy still circled in dreams and there was an infinitely tender curve to her lips when Scott Milward walked up softly and looked down at her.

Very quietly he sat down and waited. Her dream became horror as she found herself tied to a stake in the blazing sun,

Scott and Melinda were laughing madly as they rode away from her. She opened her eyes in a mist of tears and his face swam close to hers.

'Oh, Scott, I'm so very glad you didn't leave me!' Theresa sat up, looked around her and sanity, reality returned joltingly.

'What makes you think I would leave you?' Scott spoke softly, for she was still halfway in a dream-world.

She stammered, 'I had a – lovely dream, but it changed. What are you doing here?'

'Melinda and I thought you might be missing us, so we came back early. We were right, or you wouldn't be dreaming such silly things,' he was teasingly gentle, 'things that bring raindrops into your eyes.'

Theresa coloured deeply with the thought; how right can you get? Aloud she wondered, 'How late is it? Have we missed lunch? How did you find me?'

Scott raised three fingers and ticked off. 'It's too late, I've brought lunch, and I found you by following my nose.'

'Do I smell that strong? Why did you bring lunch? Are you going to have yours here as well?'

Up came three fingers. 'The first I'll not answer, the third answers the second. The thought crossed my clever mind that it would be fun to lunch wherever I found you. Good lady Mary obliged by packing a basket and promising to mind Melinda. My turn for questions; why have you chosen this spot to sleep and dream, and what jewel cache are you hiding?'

Theresa promptly held up two fingers. 'This is my special dream-spot, and here are the jewels.' She indicated the flowers and ferns.

Scott held an imaginary eyeglass to inspect them. 'You have perfect taste, nymph, they are indeed a hundred per cent.' He looked around. 'Isn't this the place where I rescued – er—'

'Yes, and this is the place where you're going to feed me, before I die of starvation.'

They fed each other drumsticks and other morsels. Scott held his glass of iced lime to her lips and she did likewise with hers, spilling some on his shirt in the process. Her hand had trembled unaccountably.

'You're getting tipsy!' he accused her.

Theresa laughed. 'This nectar is highly potent, sah.'

Hunger satisfied, they both lay back and smoked contentedly. She thought; he can be such fun. I could spend my life like this, like a rock rabbit—

'Like two stuffed pigs,' Scott remarked languidly.

Now there was another memory jewel to hide. Theresa raised her hands, scooped the air and buried it beneath the fern fronds.

'What the devil are you doing, nymph?' Scott wanted enlightenment.

'Mind your own business, rajah.' She experimented the word aloud.

'Hah, I've been promoted. For that, you may use my arm as head-rest.' He drew closer and slipped his arm under her neck. 'Relax, I'm not going to strangle you.'

Very cautiously Theresa relaxed, while Scott put his other arm across his eyes.

'We should be walking, to work off all those calories.'

'Should we, nymph? If you start I'll follow.' His reply was muffled.

Her own eyelids started to droop and the last thing she heard was a muffled snore. Very much later, she woke up with the late sun in her eyes and sat up stiffly.

Scott opened his eyes. 'Thank heavens you're awake, for the last ten minutes I've been tortured by pins and needles.'

'Why didn't you wake me?'

'You were giggling in your sleep. At least I think it was a giggle.' He yawned and sat up.

'And you snored,' Theresa retorted, standing to dust her jeans.

He laughed. 'Now that we've slept together and know each other's secrets we'd better be engaged, or else!'

'Scott! That sounds awfully – indecent.'

'It sounds frightfully delicious, my sweet. Pity it only sounds so and not—'

'That's enough, you're a wicked man!' Theresa interrupted hastily, 'Lift your lazy bones, let's go. Mary will be thinking of police and search-parties again.'

Scott straightened sinuously. 'Yeah, I guess so. Oh well, all idylls must end, more's the pity. Come, nymph, to our horses, I'll race you.' He grabbed her hand and stepped out.

Slim legs stretched their utmost to keep up with him. If he had ordered her, just then, to jump off a cliff, she would have obliged blindly. She was happy because he looked happy; at least he had said it was idyllic, so he must feel that way too. Perhaps – perhaps—?

The wind whistled through her hair as they raced across the veld. Scott graciously held back the speed of his mount to keep pace with her effort and they stopped neck to neck at the paddock gates. He slid easily off and held up his arms to help the girl, holding her for moments longer than was strictly necessary. Abruptly he let go, the smile disappeared and he turned back to his horse, speaking curtly over his shoulder.

'Don't try racing so recklessly when you're on your own. Mishaps come very suddenly. I'll attend to the saddles, tell Mary we'll be glad of a cup of tea before leaving for home.'

Theresa walked quickly, a stinging behind her eyelids. Must be dust in her eyes – why, oh, why did he treat her so wonderfully, teasing and friendly, to change suddenly into this ... arrogant martinet? 'I hate him!' she told herself furiously. 'Scott Milward is just an irritating egotist, that's what he is, and I can't stand him!'

Scott's expression was blandly disengaged as he answered the Rourkes' teasing queries about the afternoon's outing. His glance flicked to the girl sitting on the grass with Glynis and Melinda. She was intently examining the baby's tiny fingernails, but a flush on smooth cheeks gave evidence that she was listening.

Mary laughed softly. 'Sleeping, hmmm? One way of passing a Sunday afternoon. Next time Terry visits, I shall lock her up. After all she sees enough of you, so stop hogging all her time.'

'So sorry, sweet one. I'll keep away in future,' he answered shortly, and turned to Dan to discuss ranch affairs.

Hugh Lessing and Georgia stopped by for a hasty greeting on their way to Chindi. The girl looked quite pale with excitement and extracted promises from all and sundry to come for a visit whenever expedient. The doctor grinned at them. 'I'd swear that she's being kidnapped and taken to the East, judging by her manner. Do I look the sort, think you? The sooner I deposit her with the aunts the better for her virginal little heart – and my nerves!'

The ride back to Scott's house passed in silence. Melinda was tired and subdued, Scott kept his eyes on the road and Theresa gazed out of the window, her mind curiously blank and eyes unseeing. Daniel had prepared a light cold supper and it was Cleo's day off, so Theresa welcomed the tasks which kept her busy when they arrived. She bathed and sat with her charge, coaxing her to eat and lingered in the bedroom when Melinda was sleeping peacefully. She decided to forgo supper, informing Daniel when he came to call her that she was not hungry.

Theresa fully expected him to come back with an imperious demand from Scott that she attend the evening meal. None was forthcoming, so she went to her room, had a bath and crawled into bed. She tried to read, but the book might as well have been blank; words and sentences did not penetrate her consciousness. Sleep came eventually, uneasy and troubled by vague, nebulous dreams.

The days passed in a cocoon of withdrawal on her part, made easier by Scott's apparent indifference to her presence. She seldom saw him other than at mealtimes and concluded that he was also deliberately avoiding her; perhaps he had sensed her feelings on that balmy Sunday afternoon and this was his way of taking steps to disillusion her of any serious participation on his part, fun and flirting being all very well, but only when he was in the mood; it must be kept in bounds. He had not mentioned the engagement again and was probably regretting the hasty proposition!

Theresa dearly wished she could recall the letter to Derek, telling of her engagement to another man, in order to change the reason for not wishing to see him again. It was too late however, and anyway, it would not affect Scott if Derek took it at face value and consequently did not come. He was far away, there would be no contact unless he became awkward and appeared on the scene. She hoped not, for then

Scott would have to acknowledge the engagement; she was sure he would not humiliate her to the extent of disclaiming the situation. He had proposed it, so if there were embarrassing repercussions, he could jolly well bear the brunt and stave them off to the best of his ability. In her heart she knew he would be courteous and circumspect; for all his autocratic ways Scott was yet gentlemanly and considerate.

A wail of pain sent Theresa flying out of the work-room to where Melinda lay sprawled on the gravelled drive. She lifted her up, murmuring softly while inspecting grazed little knees. 'All right, my love, Theresa will fix the hurt.' She carried the sobbing child to the bathroom and sat her on the washing-machine. 'I'll sponge off the nasty dirt, don't cry, love, that's a good girl.' Tears stopped, a small voice asked, 'Will it hurt, Tresa?'

She was aware of Scott's presence in the doorway as she answered firmly, 'No, my sweetie, it will sting a bit and then it will be better.'

The small girl met her steady gaze, and trembling lips tightened, while threatening tears were defeated with quick blinking of her eyelids. Melinda spied her father and spoke bravely. 'Tresa will fix it, Daddy, you can watch.'

Scott's smile was full of loving compassion and his daughter responded with a watery grin. Theresa sponged the tiny knees, with quick, sensitive fingers she picked out several pieces of grit. The dressing applied, she spoke cheerfully. 'There you are, it's all over. Look, Daddy has brought Beth. She had a fall too, so let's attend to her as well.'

She turned to take the doll and it was suddenly disconcerting to meet his bright gaze so close in the confined space. He came closer, his tone low and caressing, but he was addressing the child. 'My, but you are a brave little soldier! Your knees look funny all painted pink. Do you reckon our nurse would paint mine too? Ah, here's Beth all nice and clean again – thank you, Theresa.'

Her heart turned over at the soft quality stressed on her name. Dear heaven, how she loved him! It was unbearable to be so burningly aware, when she had, or thought she had, mastered her feelings down to a slow dull ache. It was there all the time, just waiting to be sparked off again at the merest glance or sign of gentleness. Or the proximity of his lean, lithe body, smelling of dust and horses. The physical magnetism and nearness was like an explosion on her own senses, making her realize the dangerous capabilities of her unexplored but ardent nature.

Scott lifted Melinda and waited for Theresa to precede him. She did so, her heart thudding almost painfully. They went on to the verandah, he lowered the child into a chair and straightened up.

'Theresa.' He spoke to her back.

She turned slowly, emotions finally under control, to meet his direct gaze. An inexplicable awareness of her thoughts and feelings must have touched him, for smoky eyes glinted with strange lights of a puzzled near-discovery.

'Yes, Scott?' Dark lashes fanned her cheeks as she dropped her eyes from his searching gaze.

'Do you consider it unconventional, living here in my house, without another European to allay suspicious minds?'

Her eyes flew to his. 'Why, I – I've never given it a thought. Has – has someone—?'

'Someone has,' he remarked grimly. 'Friend of mine warned me that it might damage your reputation, even though you are in my employ.' He smiled cryptically at her outraged gasp. 'You may well gasp. People are the same all over, even though said friend implied he trusted me implicitly, especially after I almost blasted him off his horse. The thing is, how do you feel about it?'

Her eyes were a wide, angry blue. 'I've never thought of it. I mean, what others would think. It's downright silly – old-fashioned!'

'Do you trust me, Theresa? Would I be the sort to – hmm, sully your nice reputation?'

'You don't have to be sarcastic, Scott Milward. If you're getting a dig at me concerning Derek's distrust, then I think it's rather demeaning—' She was not allowed to finish.

Scott had stepped forward and taken her wrist in a grip of steel, his face a tight mask of anger. 'You dare to think that was my implication? I trust I can recognize honesty and integrity when faced with it. You're right off the beam, girl. Think again.' He dropped her wrist as though it were red-hot and stepped back. 'Well?'

'Sorry, I'm still rather touchy on that subject. I should have known better. I trust you, Scott, with my life.'

He smiled sardonically. 'That's not what I meant either. Let it go. ... I'm not allowing any talk about you, and to blast every gossiping biddy won't help any. I appreciate your trust in me, however. Nevertheless, I'm putting a call through to Salisbury, to a very dear old lady who used to do battle with me when I was very young. She lives alone and would be delighted to play chaperone to the wicked, such as you and I. She disliked Elaine and left here soon after I brought my – wife – home.'

'Oh, I see.' Theresa still felt speechless from the blaze of anger he had displayed.

'Talkative lass, you be. Well, if Miss Matilda is willing, she can return with us. By the way, be ready to leave as early as possible tomorrow morning. It's a long ride.'

'Tomorrow morning? But—'

'Tomorrow morning!' Scott mimicked. 'Oh, but, Mr. Milward, I haven't packed, I haven't a thing to wear! All the better, just toothbrushes and something for Poppet. A nice fat cheque is due anyway, you can have a delightful time in the shops.' He patted her shoulder and started for the steps. 'We can choose your engagement ring as well.'

Dumbstruck, Theresa Stanton watched his receding back. 'But—' came a belated, inane whisper.

'Can I walk now, Tresa? I'se better,' Melinda implored.

She whirled. 'Of course, honey. We'd better start packing pronto. Such short notice and I haven't a thing—' She bit her lip sharply.

Some time later, Cleo came into her room with a pile of sorted clothes for Melinda, to find Theresa muttering to herself, 'Early tomorrow – what does that mean, the crack o'dawn, before that or after breakfast? Oh, Cleo, what time is early?'

'Ask the master at dinner tonight, ma'am,' Cleo sensibly advised. 'I'll pack missy's clothes.'

'Daddy 'n me usually go ver' early and the birdies are still asleep and then the sun looks like my red balloon,' Melinda confided.

Daniel had rung the dinner-bell when Theresa finally emerged from her room. A quick shower helped her to look cool and fresh. Her dress was a pale yellow dacron, brown belted around the slim waist, and her hair hung loose and silken from a vigorous shampooing.

Scott kept glancing at her while they dined and she eventually became so self-conscious that she was forced to ask if something troubled him.

'Not troubled so much as disturbed. You're looking so sweetly young and vulnerable, I'm beginning to think that tongues have a right to wag about the dire results of being solely in my charge, under my bachelor roof.'

'But of course you know better, differently,' Theresa retorted, with sweet venom. 'I'm not so young and vulnerable at all. Quite the contrary, and you're every inch the cultured gentleman, so why be disturbed?'

'Because by rights you should look the part – a prim tight bun of hair, stern-featured visage, corseted waist, black stockings and Mother's cameo locket. Slight difference, by jingo!'

Theresa sighed, despairing. 'You're old-fashioned, Mr. Milward; *that* female went out, with corsets, years ago. The flightier, fluffier we are today, the better chances we have of landing a job. Witness mine. I bet if I'd looked like that, you wouldn't have glanced my way, so it stands to reason—' She stopped, for Scott was laughing delightedly.

'My, my, the vainglorious female! So it was your looks that landed this job, Miss S.? Well, you have something there, but I actually succumbed to the defiant tilt of your stubborn chin, and the slight alarm, when I agreed, that clinched the deal.'

Her reply was succinct. 'Also the fact that you were in desperate need! I well remember the disparaging conversation on the station. Think of the effect on Melinda of such an individual as you've described, poor mite.' She put an end to this leading interchange, became businesslike. 'What time are we leaving in the morning?'

He was amused at her abrupt change. 'Early.'

'What's early, crack o' dawn or after breakfast?'

'It's rather nice to be on the road when the dawn breaks. The world is hushed and God's hand of peace is felt. To see the sun rise gives one a feeling of awe-inspiring humility . . .' Scott came down to earth, asked matter-of-factly, 'Can you make it?'

Theresa assimilated this new facet of his character as she, equally laconically, replied, 'I'll make it.'

'Let's take a stroll, it's stuffy in here,' he invited.

His thumbs were hitched into trouser pockets as they strolled across the lawns. The night was still, there came only faint chirrupings from unseen birds nesting in the trees. The moon hid behind slivers of cloud and bright stars winked from their heavenly heights. An asbestos bench loomed white and Scott motioned her to sit down. Pipe in hand, an eyebrow was lifted for permission to smoke. The flame of his match burned briefly and he leaned back in contentment. Wafts of self-grown tobacco drifted to her nostrils and she savoured the aroma.

Imagination soared; so heavenly if they were a contented married couple sitting here. She, nestled in the crook of a strong brown arm, not at least three feet away as now. Presently they would retire, first to peep in at Melinda while their eyes met in perfect harmony. Then – then she would change into a flimsy nightie, brush her teeth. He would be in bed, both arms under his head and smiling admiringly as she walked in. She would sit on the bed and he would hold out his arms invitingly. . . . Her mind jibbed at further flights of fancy and she stood up abruptly, then stooped to retrieve a forgotten toy of Melinda's that gleamed palely in the starlight.

The silence was suddenly painful. 'I'm going in. Sleep is needed if we're to leave early.'

Scott knocked the ash out of his pipe and did not speak. There was a closed look to his face, as if his thoughts too were deep and secretive. As they reached the steps he touched her arm. 'Theresa?'

She stood at the soft inflection and waited.

'Theresa, I feel there's something – I want to ask—' the proud voice was unaccountably hesitant and she waited, heart in her mouth. 'I – I guess it can wait. Please don't be troubled about this fake engagement of ours. I won't make a fool of you under any circumstances – please believe me?'

'I do believe you, thanks. I'm not troubled at all. Good-night, Scott.' Her head held high, Theresa walked steadily up the steps to her room. For a single moment her heart had beaten with tense hope. Would she ever learn, ever find out what he had been about to say? Or had second, cautious thoughts warned against committing himself before the coming trip, before his meeting with Elaine? Well, she thought hopelessly, time would tell whether her heart had hoped in vain.

The telephone rang and she stood inside her doorway to listen. Scott answered the summons.

'Yes? I'll hold on – hello, love, it's grand to hear your voice–of course I've missed you. Why?–well, I'll tell you—' Theresa closed her door quickly and leaned against it. For all the grim insistence, that was a very intimate greeting. From her window she heard the soft knock on her door and hurriedly slipped into her gown as Scott's voice came.

She opened the door and faced him, a dull, thudding ache in her breast. 'What do you want?'

'The call was from Miss Matilda. She's delighted at the prospect of coming back with us and is looking forward to meeting you.'

'That's charming of her, thank you.' The mist of apprehension cleared and left her eyes looking more like rain-drenched hyacinths than ever.

'You do seem pleased. She's good company, bit of a tartar, but her mind is quite lucid and humorous. I – ah – took the liberty of declaring our engagement, to explain the position – predicament we're in.'

'Oh?' Theresa looked at him woodenly.

Scott leaned laconically against the door frame. 'She was thrilled and sends heartfelt congratulations. In her own words: high time I settled down with a nice girl and glad that I've stopped pining for "that witch" – no punches barred with Matilda girl!'

'There was no need to complicate things so soon by telling her. I wouldn't have minded if you had explained about the gossip.'

'I do mind, so we'll say no more. She'll be ready and willing to come back with us.'

The girl studied him curiously. 'How is she to know I'm a "nice" girl anyway? After all, your first – experience – was not a success, so how can she, not knowing me, conclude that I'm suitably nice for you?' Scepticism dripped.

A derisive quirk twisted the well-cut mouth. 'Naturally, having chosen without success the first time, I'm not expected to do any better the second? You may have forgotten that this is only a temporary arrangement, so the implication of a second faulty choice doesn't arise.'

'I haven't forgotten, but how do you intend breaking our fake alliance, if and when you discover that Elaine is not for you and Derek not for me?'

Woodsmoke eyes held captive devils. 'I rather go for that "fake alliance" stuff, it sounds devilishly mediaeval. We'll cross that hurdle when we come to it. I'll knock on your door if you're still asleep in the morning. 'Night, fiancée, pleasant dreams.' Tall, lithe and brown, he turned and walked away.

It was indeed wonderful to be out before daybreak. The only sound to be heard was the purr of the car's high-powered engine, in the soft hush of pre-dawn. Melinda had fallen asleep on the back seat with Theresa's promise to wake her when the 'red balloon' came up. Scott was quiet and preoccupied, his strong brown hands skilfully direct as they sped along the dusty ribbon of road that gleamed in the powerful headlamps. His passenger breathed deeply of the refreshingly cool air that breezed through her window.

Theresa had accepted this trip as the ultimate test. Either the culmination of her dreams or ... relinquishing of all heart's desires. A blanket of indifference, like an anaesthetic, had been forced down on emotions. *Che sara sara*. Nothing must mar her enjoyment of this trip, every moment would be savoured, until the final showdown.

Melinda awoke of her own accord, and the two girls' awed wonder grew as a pearly-pink flush coloured the horizon while the red-gold rim of the morning sun grew ever larger, rising above its misty mountain nest. Pink candy clouds feathered teasingly above and one felt you could reach out quite easily to bounce this heavenly balloon along the blue hilltops. . . . All too soon, the pink haze disappeared, turning to a yellow brightness that dazzled the naked eye.

Scott stopped the car under a spreading wild mimosa tree. The breakfast hamper revealed individual bowls of pawpaw salad, hot crunchy rolls and steaming coffee in a flask. They tucked in with gusto and then Theresa took the small girl for an urgent walk behind a convenient jut of anthills. As far as the eye could see was wild, beautiful country; they were suspended in a world of their own, with a ribbon of road the only sign of civilization.

Back on the road Scott became more loquacious and his descriptive summaries of the far-reaching surroundings of his beloved country kept his companions entrancingly fascinated.

'You must visit the Zimbabwe ruins, they're quite fantastic. Then the Kariba Dam, one of the greatest man-made wonders of the present generation. Victoria Falls must be seen to be believed . . . the rain forest. . . .'

The powerful car ate up the miles and the sun was setting when they finally drew up alongside an imposing white-porticoed dwelling on the outskirts of Salisbury. Shade-giving flamboyant trees, covered in bright scarlet clusters, lined the driveway and lawns – the home of David and Valerie Martin, friends of Scott.

Val, a petite, vivacious brunette, was waiting on the steps to welcome her guests. Scott swung her up as she darted down wide steps and kissed her soundly on her mouth. Free of him, she hugged the little girl and then faced Theresa, a smile of welcome brightening her pixie face. A swift scrutiny circled the figure that stood so quietly to one side and Valerie Martin instantly liked what she saw, clasped the slender fingers as Scott introduced them.

'Come in, do, you must all be feeling hot, sticky and weary after that long trek. Dave will be with us in a jiffy, he's cleaning up.' Val led the way into a large, airy lounge, then popped her head through the inner doorway to call someone to handle the baggage. 'I've been on absolute edge all day awaiting your arrival. Did you have a good trip? Oh, it's grand to see you again, and just look at our poppet, quite the young lady. Miss Stanton . . . Theresa, may I? I'm so excited and slightly dizzy—'

'So excitedly dizzy that I was dashed off to the bathroom,

ordered to clean and make myself respectable for our visitors. Mark this, I wasn't dirty, not even a speck!' A deep voice interrupted her chatter and David Martin clasped Scott's outstretched hand warmly. One large hand on Melinda's head, the fair, rugged man now surveyed Theresa. 'Wow! It was worth the effort after all.'

Scott walked across the room and seated himself on the arm of the chair on which Theresa was sitting rather primly, and rested his hand on her shoulder. The hand tightened slightly as he remarked laconically, 'This "wow" belongs to me, old chap. Be warned, take heed, she's engaged to me.'

His action and words fell on a dumbstruck silence. Theresa stiffened involuntarily, to feel his hand, reassuringly, tighten still more. In the act of sitting down, Valerie became frozen and her husband's mouth went slack.

David recovered first. 'Unwind, Val, you look awfully silly. Scott, you sly devil, you sure caught us by surprise. Congrats, and all that jazz.' He clamped a hand on his friend's shoulder and leaned over the girl. 'A kiss is quite in order. Trust Scott to spring surprises, a passing thought for the joy of our bachelors has now promptly been nipped in the bud!' He kissed her soundly.

'You naughty man, you didn't even warn us in your letter, only to state that you were bringing Melinda's nurse-companion. When did this happen? Come on, give with the gen.' Val kissed Theresa and continued before either of them could form an answer, 'Blissful heaven! This is going to rock a certain madam on her stiletto heels. You do know she's here, Scott?' Suddenly uncertain if she had made a *faux pas*, Val looked anxious.

Scott said blandly, 'It's all right, Val, you don't have to sink out of sight. My Theresa knows all – and I'm perfectly aware that Elaine is in Salisbury. I shall contact her, concerning some personal belongings.'

A thought stampeded unwillingly into Theresa's head; are you going to be added, thrown with those personal belongings; are you, Scott Milward?

'Oh.' Val was relieved. 'Well, come along to your rooms, girls. Sorry I'm such a bad hostess, but you sure shocked me into forgetting my manners. A fresh-up before sundowners is indicated. Dave, tend to Scott.'

The bedroom was tastefully cool in autumn shades, with Melinda's room leading off it. Theresa bathed the tired youngster and put her into shortie pyjamas. Val offered to feed Melinda while the other girl freshened herself. Theresa showered and slipped into a slim dress patterned in pale blue paisley. She brushed her hair and rolled it into a chignon, low on the back of her neck. Her mind could not deny a certain phrase, repeating it endlessly: 'My Theresa – my Theresa—'

The two men stood up as she entered the lounge. Scott met her halfway and took her arm courteously. His back to the others, he flashed her a wicked conspiratorial wink. 'You look lovely, darling. Who would ever guess that you've travelled so far!' Himself looked coolly suave in a cream silk shirt, blue cravat and tight-hipped tan trousers.

Theresa smiled sweetly back at him, and if there was a certain venom in the sweetness, no one but he noticed it.

David Martin raised his glass. 'I drink to Theresa and Scott, to your future happiness. Have you set a date?'

'A date?' Scott looked blank.

'The wedding date, dear man.' Val looked curiously at the tongue-tied girl by his side.

'The wedding date? Oh, that ... good heavens, we haven't even bought the engagement ring. Don't rush us, dear friends!' Scott touched the fair head so close to his chest. 'We must take time out tomorrow, to choose your ring, darling.'

His touch, the nearness of him made her breathless and impeded vocal cords. Speech formulated with difficulty, making her answer rather short and submissive. 'Yes, Scott.'

David said, 'You both sound in the clouds – to be expected, I reckon. Sit down, honey, here's your glass.'

Theresa sat and Scott again settled on the arm of her chair, drink in hand.

David continued, 'I contacted Mannering, in connection with the sales, and he's coming after dinner with the other agent chap. You'll be busy with them, so what shall we do with the girls?' He raised an inquiring eyebrow at them. 'Any plans?'

Val looked uncertainly at the other girl. Scott's free hand lightly fingered Theresa's neck, below her chignon.

She sat forward with an instinctive, reflex movement, out of reach of electrifying fingertips. 'May I beg an early night, please, Val – that is, if you haven't made any specific plans? I'd rather – I'm rather tired.'

Val smiled. 'As you wish. We'll desert them after dinner, have a good natter in your room and you can boot me out when necessary. I'm simply eaten up with curiosity, so be warned, I shall worm out everything – how you met, how and why did you fall in love with that lug, actually hook him. It's useless to frown so forbiddingly, David Martin, I shall be impossible to live with, if I'm not humoured.'

Theresa felt Scott's eyes on her. He asked whimsically, 'Do you remember how we met, love? I'm dashed if I can.'

Her cheeks went hot even as her eyes were drawn irresistibly to meet the impact of deep-lashed grey eyes, so very close. She knew perfectly well he was remembering, not the brief encounter at the station, but their wild ride over the veld. With a heart beating uncomfortably fast, she replied serenely enough, emphasizing the adjective. 'How dashing of you – I remember only too well. Do I have to divulge everything, expose your devious ways?'

The upward quirk of her mouth brought Scott to his feet suddenly, away from temptation. 'Tell whatever you wish, just don't besmirch my character too much,' he dared her.

'Only if you behave yourself, as you promised. No embarrassing display of emotions – in public. Our pact, remember?' Theresa mocked, unconscious of the extraordinary appeal of her upturned face.

A pulse started an irrational count in the hollow of his throat, but he spoke with sly solicitude. 'I keep forgetting that you're shy of public demonstrations, honey, and promise to try and confine them within the bounds of – privacy.'

David cleared his throat. He and his wife had watched this by-play in delighted silence. 'Don't mind us, please. We're not "public". Val and I don't care a damn if other people notice that we love each other. Never be shy to show your love, Theresa. We revel in it, especially as it's directed at the one man we thought had forgotten he possesses a heart.'

Scott looked at Theresa in silent derision. Sudden agitation at David's perception brought her upright and her hand shook as she helped herself to a cigarette out of the box on the table. Scott held his lighter, the tiny flame reflected in pools of grey as he looked at her.

'Dave is right, nymph, don't be shy. I appreciate that to you it's rather a fresh, new experience, something to get used to. I'll curb my impulses, however.'

She knew he was mocking her and a thrill of freezing resentment flooded her body. Her voice was icy. 'They're rather exuberant at times, darling. Shall we change the subject lest we bore present company?'

Val was surprised at the man's sudden change of expression. Scott's eyes narrowed with some inexplicable anger. Then he chuckled softly, '*Touché!*'

The dinner gong sounded, and although Theresa still simmered with resentment, she found herself surprisingly hungry. She enjoyed the succulent pickled beef, new potatoes and avocado salad with peach melba as dessert. Scott's business associates arrived while they were drinking tiny cups of black coffee in the lounge. One was a large South African and the other a dapper Portuguese. Scott introduced Theresa, not adding that she was his fiancée. She thought: he's not going to let personal issues interfere with business, and that suited her just fine. The whole thing was already getting out of hand, the fewer who knew the better!

The men were eager to get down to business, so she and Val left them, to take a leisurely walk in the garden. Later, she sat at the dressing-table in her room, brushing her hair while Val lounged on the bed asking eager questions about Scott's ranch and Melinda. The Martins had visited there some time back, had met and liked Mary and Dan. Theresa told her as much as she knew and then the questions became more personal.

She skirted the details and only outlined the fact that she had disagreed with her former fiancé, come on a visit to Mary Rourke, met Scott there and ended up by being employed to look after Melinda. She became silent, and Val exclaimed, 'You've left out the most important part, your engagement to Scott. Come on, give, girl, give!'

Confusion threatened again and Theresa fiddled with her brush and comb while she sought composure.

'You don't have to tell me, Theresa. I was only joking when I said I would worm it out of you. It is your own personal affair, my dear – please, I didn't mean to upset you.' Val was distressed and apologetic, yet slightly puzzled at the girl's evident reluctance to disclose confidences.

Theresa turned to speak, then hesitated. It just was not fair to mislead these good people. She sensed the high regard for Scott Milward, and now he was deliberately deceiving them . . . with her connivance. She felt a quick sense of repulsion at the thought of their joint deceit. Far better to have explained, at the outset, the why and wherefore of the bogus arrangement. Val would have understood and aided them; she obviously did not care for Elaine.

Now it was too late. Scott had already chosen the way and she could only follow his lead, short of making fools of them both. Especially Scott; she suspected he would not take kindly to being exposed at this stage.

She said, 'Val, there really is nothing more to add. We decided to become engaged, so – we did –' her voice petered out, but she managed a bright smile.

Val snapped her fingers. 'Just like that? Crikey, what price romance! Yet Melinda adores you, Scott dotes on you and there's no doubt that you're very much in love with him.'

Theresa stammered, aghast, 'Isn't there, Val? Is it so evident?'

'But of course, don't look so astonished. It shines on your face, any woman can recognize that look. Men are more obtuse—'

'Thank goodness for that!' The exclamation came with great fervour, for the mere thought that Scott might read and interpret 'that' look sent a violent perturbation coursing through her entire body.

Val looked astonished at this outburst. 'Whatever for? Oh, you are a little prude, why shouldn't the man see you're in love with him? It's a glorious feeling, and you should feel proud to show it, especially when it's reciprocated by the man of your choice.'

Misery engulfed her at the utter untruth of Val's closing statement. Scott was an excellent actor if he could make his closest friends believe that he loved Theresa Stanton. She knew differently. . . .

Theresa made a gallant effort to curb the fast array of emotions, and partially succeeded. 'I'm not a prude, and it *is* a glorious feeling, only . . . it's rather new . . .'

'And you would rather hug it to yourself for a while longer?' Val laughed and stood up. 'Very selfish, but quite illogically logical. I know how you feel and promise not to probe any deeper.' She stretched sensuously. 'I'm for bed. What's on the agenda for tomorrow?'

'Melinda and I want to explore, see all we can in the laziest possible manner.'

'Good. I shall accompany you, as guide. Then I'll discreetly whisk the little one away while you and Scott choose the ring.'

Theresa said cautiously, 'Yes, the ring. It's very kind of you, offering to be our guide. So much easier to be with someone who knows the layout.'

'I can't figure you out somehow, Theresa . . . you're being rather carefully polite, and I'm almost certain it's not your normal nature. You look as if you're hiding a vital, spontaneous joy under a matter-of-fact exterior. Cut it, girl, you can be natural with me . . . you can do handsprings and walk across the ceiling, and I wouldn't turn a hair. Crikey, I want to be present when you crackle your chrysalis and take wing. Oh, yes indeed! Good night, angel, I'm glad Scott chose you.' Val left, shutting the door gently behind her.

CHAPTER EIGHT

THERESA wished she could attend the auction sales of
tobacco and cattle, having heard so much about them, but
she did not have the courage to speak up and Scott did not
invite her. After breakfast, as he and Dave were leaving, he
turned at the doorway. 'Theresa, I'll meet you at one o'clock
on Jameson Avenue. Val knows the place, please be prompt
as I won't have very much time to spare. My car is at your
service, so use it for your shopping and sightseeing, as Dave
is taking me. You can drive me back to the sales this afternoon after we've had lunch in town. 'Bye.'

Val chuckled over her coffee cup. 'Takes some getting
used to, hmm, that lofty manner? But he is an absolute
sweetie really, under that autocratic exterior. He took your
threat seriously, I notice . . . didn't even kiss you good-bye,
the so-and-so!' She chattered on while the other girl
gathered together her wits and self-control (a battle which
was becoming monotonously familiar). 'Shall we visit the
Gardens and Art Gallery this morning, or would you rather
do the shops? Later you can dump Melinda and me back
here, and still be on time for Scott and your lunch date. I'll
point out the jewellers, they stock the most fabulous
rings.'

Theresa plumped for the Parks, greatly to Melinda's
satisfaction. Nervously dubious about driving Scott's big
car, she found it an easy pleasure once they started off. Val
directing, they finally stopped under a magnificent avenue
of trees and walked through imposing gates. The gardens
were cleverly landscaped in a natural setting. An Art and
Sculpture exhibition was in progress and they spent two
happy hours wandering through the collection. Val was ex-
pertly knowledgeable about such things and Theresa came
away happy and enlightened.

After an enjoyable tea at the restaurant they walked down
to the lake and sat on incredibly green grass to feed the
swans. Melinda was highly intrigued at one stately black
swan who seemed to lord it over the others.

Theresa remarked, caustically, 'He must be an Arabian swan – just look at all his wives and the way they bow meek, graceful necks when he sputters and pecks at them!' She studied him closely and said *sotto-voce*, 'He reminds me of Scott.'

Val heard and laughed delightedly. 'That I'm going to repeat to the poor man! My imagination boggles at the spectacle of six or seven wives fluttering around Scott Milward!'

Theresa joined her laughter. 'He would be quite capable of mounting his steed and dispersing them with flying hooves, trampling them into the dust and—'

'Theresa,' Val interrupted softly. She was staring over the girl's shoulder. 'Elaine has just come out of the restaurant.'

Theresa's eyes flew to where Melinda was sitting at the edge of the water, her back to them, still watching the swans. A shiver shot up her spine, she spoke quickly and quietly. 'Turn your back so that she won't recognize you, Val. Is she coming this way?'

Val turned away, throwing a sidelong glance. 'No-o, I don't think so – she's wearing a large picture hat which may obscure her view of us.'

'For goodness' sake make yourself inconspicuous, Val. Scott doesn't want her to see Melinda or upset her.' She prayed that the swans would occupy the child's interest for just a while longer.

Val whipped the scarf she was holding over her hair and replaced her dark glasses, trying to appear as nonchalant as possible as she turned her head for another look. 'They're coming down the cement walk, behind us, which leads to another exit gate. If they stick to it, we won't be noticed; there are quite a few people between them and us.'

They waited in a tense silence.

'Those swans look ducky, let's feed them, Elaine.' A woman's voice came clearly. A silence ensued that taxed the girls' nerves to their utmost, and then the answer, with insolent languor. 'Be your age, Madeline, there are enough trippers around to stop them from starving. It's so hot, all I crave for is a cool, cool shower, having been dragged for simply miles—' The drawling voice died away as they walked on.

'Relax, Theresa.' Val slumped her own tense body.

Theresa turned and watched as Elaine Milward walked away with her friends. All she saw was the back of a slim figure, clad in a grey sheath dress, smart grey shoes to match and a very fashionable wide-brimmed hat. Light laughter floated on the air.

Voices and laughter, which settled into her stream of consciousness, never to be forgotten. A woman had just, unknowingly, walked past her own daughter. Melinda ran to Theresa and she took her tiny hand in a trembling clasp. 'I think we'd better get back, Val.' She spoke huskily.

'Whew, yes!' They started to walk and Val continued urgently, 'You're bound to run across her some time, Theresa. It's inevitable . . . what then?'

Candid blue eyes held troubled depths, but she replied in a low, controlled way. 'I know, but I'm not troubled about that. Scott is adamant about keeping—' she indicated the child, '—away from her. Don't ask me if he's doing the right thing. Oh, lord, if she'd recognized you, seen Poppet, she would know – she expects Scott and knows you and Dave are his friends.' Appalled at the thought of Scott's anger, their close shave, her consternation almost overcame her.

'Don't panic now, honey, it didn't happen . . . does she know about you? Not that it matters one scrap, she doesn't own him any more – but I have a queer feeling she would like to. Elaine treated Scott abominably and treacherously, maybe only Dave and I know how badly, for Scott is too reticent and chivalrous to talk about her. He was badly hurt and disillusioned. He became hard and cynical to cover the hurt, but I'm convinced that what hit him hardest was the way she ignored and abandoned the infant. Has he spoken to you?'

'Just the bare details, we haven't known each other very long. I don't really want to know, it's enough to judge by the way she simply left M., without a care. I don't even know if Scott has written or phoned her – about us.'

'Well, I guess he knows what to do. I'm only glad that he has someone like you, to soften him, make him come alive again. He's a normal, vital person, not cut out to be an ascetic. The bitterness bit deeply, that's why Dave and I are so pleased—'

Theresa cut in hurriedly, being deeply ashamed of the deceit. Scott's heart was still bitter, certainly not melting because of her. Face to face with his ex-wife, he might discover he loved her enough to forgive everything. She wished desperately that she could confide in this girl at her side. She would be kind, compassionate and understanding.

'Please, Val, let's not talk about it now, I have a nasty taste in my mouth. Must have been the fright I had, about Melinda.' A shaky laugh followed her words.

Val studied her watch and thought, there is something I can't quite put my finger on; all is not as it should be. The only certainty was that Theresa Stanton loved Scott Milward very deeply. Aloud she said, 'You can take us home now and freshen up for your date with Scott. I can't picture him waiting very patiently if you happen to be late!' On the way home she pointed out the place where Theresa was to meet him.

Driving there later, pride began building up her resentment to a pitch of mutinous rebellion against her invidious position. She found parking right in front of the imposing building which housed the jewellers. Scott was not there, so she waited in the car. Five minutes later Dave stopped on the opposite side and Scott stepped out.

He came over, was about to open the door for her, but she stopped him. 'I want to talk to you, it will only be a minute, please, Scott.'

He walked round and eased into the seat beside her, smiled and said, 'Hello there, fire away.'

Theresa clenched hard on the wheel. 'Scott, I really don't think it's necessary to go this far – to buy a ring. Surely it's enough just to say we're engaged. Nowadays, couples aren't forced to show a ring to prove they're affianced, people take their word. And this is only fake, after all.'

Scott offered her a cigarette. She refused and he took his time about lighting one for himself. 'I intend to make this look genuine. We're going to choose a ring,' he stated flatly.

She became angry. 'It's unnecessary, I tell you. Apart from that, they cost a great deal of money. Think of that and the waste of it. Val and Dave accepted our, or rather, your declaration without looking for proof, so why shouldn't your Elaine?'

'My Elaine – you said it – needs visible proof. I'm not exactly penurious, so if I wish you to have a ring, you shall have a ring.' His face remained inscrutable, but the grey eyes darkened and narrowed.

'What must I do with it afterwards? You may decide to take her back . . . and even if you don't, it will still be redundant, for then the silly alliance becomes null – void. What then?' Theresa challenged, anger still bolstering a sinking sensation in the pit of her stomach.

'A diamond never loses its value, honey. You may keep it for a souvenir or throw it on the carpet, at my feet, in the good old traditional manner. It's immaterial – the point is, I don't want to be swayed by an alluring ex-wife to do something I may regret, and you promised protection against such a happening. Your Derek has evidently been put off by your letter, so you don't need my side of the bargain, but I would most certainly have kept it and I hold you to said bargain. We're wasting time, my beautiful fiancée; look happy and radiant.' Scott stubbed out his cigarette, opened the door and stepped out.

Theresa sat woodenly for moments, then got out reluctantly while Scott patiently held her door open.

They were greeted ceremoniously at the door by a courteously suave gentleman. The next half-hour was passed somehow, with a rising desire in the girl to kick somebody, hard – Scott mostly, the salesman coming in a close second. She agreed to every ring that was held up for her inspection until Scott lost patience, finally selecting one to his own satisfaction.

She gave an involuntary gasp at the beauty of stone and setting, her heart wishing forlornly that everything could have been different, real. That this lovely ring would join Scott and her in true, joyous love. . . .

The man attending them evidently mistook her manner for shyness. The price was not mentioned, that would be discreetly handled later, but she was certain it was fabulously high. Scott remained unconcerned. They were escorted to a private room where the proud man could slip the ring on to his sweetheart's precious finger, and kiss her to their hearts' content, in perfect privacy.

The door closed softly and Scott took the ring out of its velvet box. He lifted her hand and began to slide the gleaming circle gently on to her finger.

Theresa felt tears prickle under her eyelids and with sudden frustrated, angry longing, snatched her hand away and jammed the ring further into place. 'Let's not be hypocritical about it. There, we're engaged, it's a beautiful ring and I'm duly impressed. Shall we go?'

'We shall not. I promised not to take advantages, but that man has charmed me into a kissing mood and you're very beautiful and my resistance is low. Now show me how impressed you are.' Scott had his arms around her.

She pushed furiously against his chest. He waited, compelling her by his very magnetism, until she stopped at last and met his eyes in mute, desperate appeal. Only then did he bring his head down and claim her mouth.

The kiss started casually, but seemed to get out of hand, and when he finally released her, it was with a savagely suppressed violence. He breathed heavily and flickers of flame danced in his eyes.

Theresa stood motionless, pale and powerless, afraid to lift her eyes lest he see the truth in them. Her heart was beating like the wings of an imprisoned bird, while a queer, almost shamed wonder at the spontaneous response of her body prickled through her veins.

Scott regarded the down-bent head for a long while, then slowly put the back of one hand under her chin and brushed the hair from her cheek with the other. 'I'm not going to insult you by apologizing for kissing you, only for losing my head and not stopping when I should have – and for shocking your sense of propriety so badly. You're very pale, Theresa. Can I bring you a glass of water? Come and sit down. I'm an insensitive brute.'

'I'm perfectly all right, Scott, just slightly dizzy from your rib-cracking hold.' Not for worlds would she let him know the truth – a million glasses of water could not help her sickness! He did not have to be in love with her to kiss like that, it did not mean as much to him as it did to her. For then surely he would declare his love in words? She was convinced of that when she finally raised her head and looked at him. Scott was perfectly at ease, his mouth a trifle austere, showing only slight anxiety for her 'dizzy spell'.

A sudden image of water being forced down her throat by the gallon restored her natural sense of humour, helped her as nothing else could have, at that moment. She looked for her bag, a whimsical curl to her lips. 'Water won't help a cracked rib.'

'Is that all it meant, for you?' His question hung in the air expectantly, sounding urgent, imperative.

Theresa lied, not wanting to embarrass him with any declarations of undying love at this stage. 'Excepting the pain in my rib, a slight dizziness, it was fun – but I would be fearful of being the recipient when you become serious!'

Scott regarded her, his jaw stony. 'Then try not looking so outrageously seductive in broad daylight. No wonder Derek was jealous and distrustful! Had I been in his place you'd be under lock and key. Did you respond to his kisses as you did to mine, and then laugh them off in the same way?'

Theresa said quietly, 'Shall we leave now? They probably need this room for the next couple's blissful tryst. It's only your hurt pride hurling insults, so I forgive you.' She walked to the door and waited politely for him to open it.

Her dignity was unassailable. Scott acknowledged it silently and they left, with the salesman's best wishes falling on deaf ears.

They walked towards the car and his hand on her arm held her back. 'I've ordered a table at the hotel. It would be silly to forgo our lunch and their cuisine is good.' A tantalizing smile played on well-defined lips.

'Thank you, I'd like that,' Teresa said steadily, determined to play it as coolly as he. The dining-room was large and airy, one entire wall being sliding glass doors which were opened wide to a view of shady trees and smooth lawns.

While they ate she was very conscious of the ring on her finger. Its many facets sparkled every time she moved her hand. Scott's quick eyes noticed her interest and she was vexed at the sudden heat that flooded her face. His smile was without guile, sincere and charming.

'It looks fabulous, just right for your pretty hands, Theresa. I'm proud and honoured to be the man who put it there, even though it's only temporary and done in such a clumsy way. Am I forgiven for my clumsy tongue?'

'Yes, Scott, I told you that I understood a man's pride.' Theresa looked down as his hand covered hers.

'To be quite honest with you, it was not my pride, it was a streak of sheer jealousy that made me say what I did. Jealousy at the thought of another man having the right to kiss you and your possible response to his ardour.'

'Jealousy?' The blue of her eyes deepened in disbelief.

'Oh hell, I know I had no right to feel that way, but there it was – a raging streak of jealousy. I know you're still feeling pretty raw about Derek and it was brutal of me. As for kissing you – well, I've told you before that I'm weak, you looked so irresistible, beating your little fists against my chest, some inner compulsion led me further than I intended. Will you be a dear, blot out that little episode and let's be friends again, with no hard feelings?' His hand tightened over hers, his voice deeply urgent.

Theresa gazed down at the brown hand while her heart, that a moment ago had flared with hope, died down despairingly. It was just an episode, a flare of jealousy that was already gone . . . to him.

'Well, Theresa, are we friends?'

Turning her hand under the warm clasp, she laid her palm against his. Sweet torment came with the action, but she answered coolly, 'My hand on our friendship, Scott.'

'That's my girl!' Scott held her hand a moment longer and then removed his to look at his watch. 'I must get back. You'll have to deliver me to my destination and then I suggest you go back to Val and have a good rest while it's so hot. Dave and I have plans for you girls, we're taking you to a posh new club tonight.'

'It sounds great, but what about Melinda?'

'Pity we didn't bring Cleo, but with Miss Matilda coming back with us, it would have been rather a squash having the fat Cleo taking up air space. Dave said he would phone Val to ask their neighbour's teenage daughter to baby-sit. I'll be free tomorrow morning, so we can have tea with the old girl and you can make her acquaintance.'

Theresa acquiesced, silently wondering when he would

contact Elaine – or had he already done so? No, he would surely have shown some sign of the meeting or told her in his inimitable way. Hard on this thought came another; she had not told him of the almost disastrous encounter in the park, when Elaine had almost met up with his (and her) child. Well, nothing had come of it, so she would not arouse his anger by mentioning it, and Val would keep mum as well.

Aside from voicing directions Scott was silently pre-occupied as she drove a few miles out of town to where the great auction sheds sprawled, dusty and hot in the shimmering afternoon sun. A salutory 'thanks' and he strode off, indolently long-legged, brown and tall.

She sat listening to the sounds of one-pitched and droning auctioneers' tones with a background of unintelligible voices and, not being able to see or hear properly from where she sat, felt frustrated so she turned the car and headed for the Martin home.

That evening, she surveyed herself in the bedroom mirror. Dalene of Johannesburg had assured her that this was an exclusive model from their salon. The price had lowered her bank balance considerably, but it was worth the extravagance – purest white Thai silk, sheathed to fit her slender body with alluring perfection, the neckline high in front and slashed down daringly almost to her waist in the back. The cutaway sleeves emphasized smoothly moulded arms and shoulders that had acquired a delightful tan from the hot sun of Rhodesia. Her hair, brushed to a shining gloss, hung shoulder-length with the ends flicked slightly out and up. A soft pink on her lips, blue eye-shadow and the shimmer of her dress gave her an attractive, ethereal look.

Theresa slipped into silver sandals as Val put her head in at the doorway, to exclaim admiringly, 'You look stunning, honey! Scott will have his time cut out tonight. The wolves are going to howl!'

Val was dressed in black chiffon, tight in the bodice and swirling from her waist. Shimmering pearls glowed round her neck. Theresa smiled, picked up her soft stole. 'There'll be an awful din when they see you as well.'

They walked to the lounge where the two men were having a leisurely drink. Theresa's eyes were drawn to

Scott, he looked incredibly debonair and handsome in black trousers and a white tuxedo. David was equally distinguished in similar dress. A dead silence prevailed as the two girls were critically studied.

David said softly, 'I vote we stay right here tonight, old boy.'

'I second that vote, old man.' Scott followed instantly, his grey eyes resting on a vision in white. He put a glass in Theresa's hand, raised his own to touch rims. 'I drink to a goddess.'

Val and her husband exchanged glances and followed the action. 'Drink to Love and lovely, romantic males!' Val sighed voluptuously. 'And now, despite your vote, let's go!'

In the general exodus and laughter nobody seemed to notice that Theresa had remained silent. Her love for Scott, love for his way with her tonight, fired an ache in her breast that was almost unbearable, leaving her too tongue-tied to join in the gay badinage.

A wide, screened verandah encircled the rambling building that was the Sporting Club. The dancing would take place on the outdoor floor, owing to the heat, and the diners could watch from their tables which were set out on one side of the spacious verandah. Lights were strung at intervals amongst the trees and glowed invitingly.

The dinner was superb, music from the band floated in the air and gaiety was the keynote of the evening. Theresa relaxed and gave herself up to enjoyment and good company. They settled in the lounge for liqueurs. David and Scott were well known and soon their party augmented alarmingly. Male eyes, drawn to the new and attractive girl in their midst, looked hard and their owners hovered expectantly. Brothers Victor and Gerry Belmont waited with polite impatience until David noticed and introduced them, then lost no time in drawing up chairs as close as possible, nearest Theresa. They vied for her attention.

Scott had excused himself in order to chat to an elderly couple who were seated in a far corner. He returned to find his chair occupied. Theresa felt his presence, looked up to see grey eyes behind curling cigarette smoke watching her quizzically. His smile was cynically charming as he put the cigarette in the ashtray and spoke formally. 'May we dance?'

She extricated herself from the boyish ardour of the two brothers and walked with Scott down the wide steps. The soft music and the encircling feel of hard, strong arms quietened an erratically beating heart and she yielded to the languor of rhythm. Oh, to be held thus, for ever, into infinity. ... 'Don't ever let me go, beloved,' she pleaded silently. A soft touch on the top of her head as Scott rubbed his chin against her hair and she could almost believe that he had heard her plea – and answered.

The dance ended all too soon. The man's hand cupped her elbow and remained there when they had stepped aside on to the lawn. The next number started while they watched and Scott's eyes were drawn to the honeyed hair, so close to his shoulder, where stardust entangled to make a silvery sheen. Unconscious of darkening smoky eyes above her, Theresa watched the dancers. The sudden halt in mid-step of one couple drew her attention and she looked straight into the startled eyes of her ex-fiancé!

Shock made her step closer to the man at her side, seeking protection instinctively. He sensed her sudden agitation, followed the direction of her eyes and they both watched as the couple left the floor and approached.

'Is he Dr. Mann, Theresa?'

Her 'yes' was husky and muffled.

'Well, don't let it show. Your feelings, girl – keep it covered, and straighten that backbone!' Peremptory and urgent came the order.

No time to protest that it was not love, but shock, that had shaken her. Derek Mann was standing in front of her.

'Terry, how nice to see you! I got the surprise of my life when I spotted you just now.' He held out his hand.

A pressure on her arm forced her paralysed hand into his. 'Derek! I was surprised too. How are you?' The stilted phrases sounded formal.

Dr. Mann turned to the girl at his side. 'My pardon, Mary, for stopping so abruptly in the middle of that dance. Miss Stanton and I were – old friends – in Pretoria. Terry, meet Mary Bolton. Theresa Stanton. . . .' He hesitated, eyes on the man at her side.

'How do you do, Miss Bolton. Scott, this is Dr. Mann . . . Mr. Milward . . . Miss Bolton.' Pride held her stiff and haughty.

Scott acknowledged the introductions in a level, casual way, his hand still firm on her arm.

Derek's eyes dropped to the sparkling gleam on Theresa's finger. He said, 'In her letter, Terry didn't mention a name. May I presume you are the one she referred to?'

Scott replied evenly, although Theresa detected a hint of malice in his tones. 'I lay claim to that privilege. Theresa has honoured me with her love – and trust.' A deliberate emphasis on the final word.

The girl felt a thrust of pride at Scott's superb acting, more so when she observed its effect on Derek. The thrust had found its mark, for the doctor's austere features showed a certain amount of comprehensive embarrassment, before a cold smile replaced it.

'In that case, may I extend my congratulations? You're a very fortunate man, Mr. Milward. She deserves every happiness . . . and trust plays its own part towards that goal.' This oblique apology for his own lack was not lost on either of them. 'May I have the pleasure of one dance, Terry – that is, if your fiancé won't mind?'

Scott dropped his hand from her arm. 'Not at all, it's good to see old friends, eh, Theresa? Miss Bolton, may I?' An arm was held politely and a slightly puzzled Mary Bolton smiled her consent.

'Well, Terry, although I'm somewhat shaken, I'm glad that your heart found solace so quickly and unexpectedly. I had hopes—'

'Did you now? Still the complete egotist, dear Derek!' Theresa was cool and distant as they circled the floor.

The doctor's arm tightened. 'After all, circumstances were against you, my dear. How could I guess that silly bitch had inveigled her brother to compromise you in order to play on my sympathies and honour? I found out quickly enough what her game was, one evening, when she visited my house—'

'Spare me the sordid details, please. I haven't the remotest interest. I found out soon enough, as you remarked, that my heart was not affected at all, merely my pride. I hope, if your heart ever breaks, you'll find solace as quickly as I did.' Theresa spoke lightly; she felt wholly free of this man. Mary Bolton was dancing with a complete stranger – the girl seemed destined not to finish a dance in one pair of arms – and she wondered what had happened to Scott.

Derek put her wise as his voice seeped into her consciousness. 'And I was knocked for a loop when you introduced Scott Milward as your fiancé. I've heard of him, quite a big man in these parts. Strange to say, I've met his former wife – there he is, speaking to her, right now.'

Theresa caught a glimpse of coppery hair under the lights before her vision was obscured by dancing couples. Derek was asking, 'Have you met her? I'm rather bewildered, as I got the impression that she was looking forward to a reconciliation.'

Theresa rejoined tartly, 'That's the trouble with you, Derek Mann. You're too easily swayed by outward impressions. Granted, you're a good doctor, but in many other ways you're very obtuse.'

The apprehension she felt was superbly concealed. They looked so intimate, another quick look told her; the tall man's interest was fully concentrated on the quite lovely woman facing him. Even as the band stopped she saw them walk towards the clubhouse.

Miss Bolton and her companion joined Derek and Theresa. 'Mr. Milward apologized for not dancing with me. It seems the lady had urgent business to discuss. Anyway, I know her escort and he took over. Donald, meet Theresa and Derek. A drink is indicated, let's go, folks.' Mary chattered on and Theresa dazedly allowed herself to accompany them up the steps of the club.

Following the contract of their engagement, was she now supposed to follow Scott and wrest him from the lure of the woman (he had gone with her willingly enough) or would he be angry if she interfered? After all, it was for this very purpose that their alliance had been concocted by Scott.

The dilemma was taken out of her hands the moment they entered the lounge. Dave, Val and the Belmont brothers were still there. Elaine Milward had joined them, was smiling up at Scott who was in the act of lighting her cigarette. He slid the lighter into his pocket and stepped forward as they entered. 'Enjoying yourself, honey?' He gave Theresa a secret smile, put his hand under her elbow and led her forward. She smiled back dazzlingly, acutely aware of the insolent scrutiny of the woman lounging in the armchair.

Scott said casually, 'I see you've met Donald, that's Elaine—'

'Don't tell me, dear man, she can be none other than the captivating Theresa Stanton,' Elaine drawled nonchalantly, but Theresa caught the pure hatred that flared for an instant in amber eyes before they were hooded by white eyelids. 'My dear, I can quite see why Scott waxed enthusiastic. Such fair charm must be so refreshing, after—' she left the unfinished sentence to hang suggestively in the air, then continued roguishly, 'I had high hopes of lighting smouldering fires, but it seems I prevaricated too long.' A sorrowing sigh followed.

'How unfortunate for you and lucky for me, Mrs. Milward. Do I address you rightly, or have you reverted to your maiden name?' Theresa looked formally interested.

Obviously Elaine was not accustomed to, or did not expect such a direct thrust, and she stiffened perceptibly. Exhaling smoke through her nostrils, she snapped, 'I have retained the title. After all, it's quite distinguished and observation has proved that the name carries power. To my benefit.' She smiled sweetly at Scott.

'Admittedly, very convenient for you, at present. But later – slightly confusing—' Theresa put a bored hand to her lips, terminating the conversation, and turned to David Martin, 'Lazybones, when are you going to dance with your wife? Come on, stop vegetating and breathe the glamour of the night. It's much fresher outside.'

The whole party had listened to this interchange and various expressions now changed perceptibly. David gave a distinct 'thumbs up' before taking his wife's hand to help her from her chair. Derek's party moved to the bar, Val smiled sweet venom at Elaine while Donald Somebody yanked that lady, from whom the sweetness had slipped somehow, unceremoniously to her feet and said, 'Come, sweetie, your slip is showing.'

Through it all, Scott had stood, still and unmoving, with

his arm round Theresa's waist. She had felt him tense at her first words, but not by any movement had he indicated displeasure or otherwise at her cool reception of Elaine's insolence.

Her legs weakened with a sudden reaction as she looked up at him. His expression was closed, enigmatic, but glinting depths in grey eyes denoted some unknown emotion. He waited until she was seated, then followed suit. The two Belmont boys had joined the general exodus, they were alone except for an unobtrusive, red-fezzed waiter in the background.

Scott watched Theresa while she leaned back against the high-backed chair and closed her eyes. 'Quite some little protector you were.' His voice came deep.

'Did I perhaps overdo it, then?' Eyes still closed, her question was lazily forced, she daren't lift eyelids to read possible disapproval in his.

'You were superb, young woman. I didn't realize you had the spunk ... but I think you have acquired an enemy. Elaine won't like being "hoist with her own petard".'

'Did you approve, Scott, or did I mess up any chances of reconciliation?' Theresa asked levelly.

'My fault if you did, nymph, you did exactly what I asked for when I proposed the protective arrangement.' The oblique answer skirted her question; she still did not know if he cared or approved.

'It was rather hard on you, to have to play up like that with your ex-lover at your elbow.' Blue eyes flew open to meet amused grey ones. 'Or does he know all and is the romance palpably on, or still off?'

His cynical manner and her outraged senses decided Theresa to pay him back as obliquely as he had done. 'Your malicious taunt about trust was equally superb. But they do say that love knows no barriers, least of all taunts and words. Shall we say we've each done our duty, as contracted? As for inspiring Elaine's enmity, I couldn't care less!'

Scott said with harsh finality, 'I care, for it can quite easily boomerang back to my daughter. The whole object is to keep Elaine from Melinda. Whether I care for her or not is beside the point. I repeat, I do not want any contact between my former wife and my daughter.'

Theresa's cool exterior disintegrated, she stammered 'Wouldn't it be better, then, if I quietly disappeared from the scene? Then there would be no object in her becoming — venomous — towards Melinda, because of me. This business is becoming too complicated — I mean, she's never troubled about her daughter, so why now? Perhaps Elaine has learnt her lesson, will be a good mother — and wife — if you give her another chance?'

'I don't choose to do that—'

'Don't be so hard, Scott!' Oh, why was she fighting Elaine's cause when her heart cried out for him to declare that he was no longer interested?

Scott looked at her with sudden, hard speculation. 'Have you found your affections are still with the doctor, that this is your way out, to force Elaine back on me? Rest your busy mind, such lengths will not be necessary. We will, however, carry out our agreement until such time as it suits me to break it up. And it doesn't suit, as yet. Let your man dangle a while longer, before you crawl back to him. I'll safeguard Melinda against any animosity.' He sat back, lit a cigarette and studied her derisively as furious rage flooded her cheeks.

Val and Dave were coming back, so Theresa clenched her teeth and whispered sibilantly, 'You're a wretched, arrogant monster and I hate your guts!'

Scott leaned forward, took her hands and said lovingly, 'Language, your language, darling! Don't look so frustrated—' as Val sat down he was smiling admiringly, '—don't you think my girl looks lovely when she blushes? Love makes her ravishing.'

David bowed formally. 'And now I'm going to take her away from your charm, it's time she sampled some of mine.'

Reluctantly Scott released the trembling hand, and Theresa could have hugged David, for rescuing her from further indignities.

She stayed outside for a long time. Victor and Gerry claimed their respective dances and then a succession of keen males vied for that pleasure. Scott never appeared and she realized that Elaine was not in evidence either.

Derek came to her to ask if she would have tea with him

147

the following morning. Rather absently she informed him
that her day was fully booked. He looked at her curiously as
he said good night, adding, 'I'm leaving for the Republic the
day after tomorrow. Be happy, Terry, and know that for one
man there will always be a regret that he didn't trust
enough.'

He leaned forward and kissed her cheek just as Scott
halted a few feet away. Theresa met his eyes squarely as
Derek left, and then she turned on her heel and walked up
the steps in the direction of the cloakrooms.

Inside, she sat down and stared at her reflection, feeling
somehow numb and exhausted. Let the man make what he
could of that kiss of Derek's. She had known him a long
time, bore him no animosity, and a farewell kiss on the
cheek was nobody's affair but hers!

The door opened, a familiar voice drawled, 'Ah, the fair
charmer in person!' Elaine seated herself and also scrutinized her own reflection. 'Heavens, some men can be masterful, just look at the dishevelled state of my hair!' Deft
movements tidied the copper red mass, and Theresa wondered in sudden misery if she referred to her escort, or Scott.

Elaine Milward's casual question came like a blow in her
solar plexus. 'How's my daughter Melinda? She must be
quite a girl now. Does she look like me?'

Theresa managed woodenly, 'She's the image of her
father.'

'Poor child.' Elaine outlined her lips. 'I do hope, for her
sake, you have a chaperone. I believe you're living in the
house with Scott.' The innuendo was maliciously evil.

'That's my concern, I believe.' Theresa went to the basin
and started washing her hands.

'Your reputation is your concern, darling, but you see, I'm
thinking of Melinda. Just think what such an immoral situation can do to her.'

'Your own behaviour doesn't warrant any sudden concern
for your daughter, Mrs. Milward. I'm referring to the desertion of a baby, not to any personal behaviour on your
part.' The fair hair fell forward as she inspected her
hands.

Venom dripped. 'How sweetly pious! But it does warrant
thought, dear, for if the Welfare were notified of any signs

148

of – shall we be cosy and say lax morals? – on the part of a parent, well, they waste no time here in looking after the characters of dear little susceptible girls.'

'Meaning Melinda? Your own morals separated you from your daughter.'

Elaine laughed. 'Dear, righteous Scott may well find himself separated from his beloved child!'

The sheer spite in her declaration made Theresa quake inwardly with rage ... and fear. She straightened up proudly and faced the hate in amber eyes.

'That will never happen. Miss Matilda has been a most correct chaperone!' She hoped desperately that Elaine had had no contact with that innocent lady, while the second lie fell from stiff lips. 'Also, did Scott tell you, we're to be married while we're here.'

Theresa knew then that it was not Scott who had mussed that lovely hair, for Elaine would have immediately called her a liar to her face, on that fantastic statement!

Instead, the older woman's face whitened, she looked suddenly tired ... and older. 'That old witch could chaperone the very devil into behaving. Spans of luck with Scott Milward, you'll need it!'

Theresa's heart was filled with sudden compassion for this one who had thrown away a mother's love, and the love of a man like Scott, so lightly. The smile she bestowed on Elaine was sweetly compassionate and left its mark on a stony heart. There was nothing more to say. Theresa quietly walked out.

Her fair head was held high, but she felt absolutely wretched inside, fearing the consequences of her lies. She would have to confess, sooner or later. Not too late either, for Scott must be given time to leash his anger, to warn Miss Matilda. If he decided to conspire in her lie. ... What that unknown old lady would think of Theresa's devious ways, she dare not even think about.

As for her rash statement about getting married ...! Well, they could pretend to have one hell of a row, shattering that fallacy.

Theresa danced once more with Scott, her body and mind tensed against his attraction while the voice of conscience clamoured in her head. She was also downright terrified that Elaine might join them again and mention the chaperone or their supposed marriage!

Scott sensed her withdrawal, wrongly attributing it to her encounter with Derek. Green fire smouldered in grey eyes as he envisaged again that picture of the doctor leaning over her so tenderly, kissing her. . . .

Theresa was immensely relieved when he suggested rather brusquely that they should leave and David agreed. Back at the house, sitting relaxed and sipping coffee, she decided to put off the moment of confession. Scott was taking her to meet Miss Matilda in the morning. She would tell him on their way.

A restless night followed and, at the breakfast table, Val remarked on her wan and hollow-eyed appearance. Scott's quick scrutiny made her flush and choke on her toast. Her throat was grittily dry and she felt headachy from the heat that could already be felt; also from the ordeal that lay before her.

The time came for the trip to the old lady. Theresa wore a cool blue dress with low-heeled tan sandals. Her hair was brushed up in a high pony-tail. As he drove off Scott thought she looked absurdly young and nervous. They approached an avenue of tall trees and she turned quickly to him before her courage ebbed completely.

'Scott, please stop here for a moment. I have something very important to tell you before we arrive.'

His face grew grim and austere. He stopped the car and gazed straight ahead. 'Go ahead, confess.'

Confess? So he knew! She could have sworn he had not contacted Elaine before they left the club. Breathlessness impeded her speech. 'Please believe me, Scott. I only said it to protect you and Melinda.' She waited for the onslaught.

Scott turned his head and regarded her. 'Go on.'

'Well, she did say that the Welfare Officer wouldn't take kindly – wouldn't be kindly disposed – to you and me being in the same – house. So I made up those rash lies – on the spur of the moment. For Melinda's protection, so that they wouldn't take her from you.' Theresa stopped, for the grim man at her side had drawn a deep, ragged breath and settled further down in his seat.

'Welfare Officer ... lies ... take Melinda from me? Kindly elaborate.'

'But I thought you knew. You ordered me to confess!'

Scott's eyes darkened. 'Just an expression, nymph. Your distressed manner told me you had something on your mind. Now start from the beginning.'

Hesitantly, Theresa related her encounter with Elaine in the cloakroom. She did not tell of the hate and venom, sticking only to the bare facts. Her voice became silent.

The silence grew and she lifted her eyes, to see Scott studying his hands as they rested on the wheel. He spoke at last. 'How vindictive can one get? A sullied mind will always find dirt where none is to be found. Miss Matilda will be glad to conspire, to nullify any mudslinging. Not that a Welfare Officer would take much notice of complaints from a – oh, never mind. Theresa, will you marry me? Within the next two days?'

She looked at him incredulously. 'You must be mad!'

'Perfectly sane, I assure you,' Scott answered levelly.

'You don't have to be chivalrous on my account, Scott.'

'Chivalry was not intended. Will you, Theresa?'

Her blue eyes narrowed. 'You're not so clever, after all. You should have asked me in front of witnesses, then my refusal would be noted and your conscience clear. My rash lie last night, to Elaine, would be—'

Her arms were gripped in steel. 'For that you shall be held to our contract and little old Matilda will have the joy of being the first to hear of our marriage, to take place the day after tomorrow!'

'Let me go, Scott Milward!' She struggled futilely.

Scott's voice continued inexorably. 'Of course you're quite right. If we're married, there'll be no cause to feel that Melinda might possibly be removed from our care. You are now committed to honour your declaration.'

'You're crazy, I tell you! There'll be no problem if I just walk out on you, disappear from your horizon.' An avalanche of emotions threatened to choke her. She had longed for a proposal from him, and here she was, fighting it tooth and nail!

'And leave poor me in the nasty position of being the

151

jilted one? Oh no, my ego won't stand for it, much too humiliating. Besides, who's going to look after Melinda?' The derisive note was back.

Theresa tilted her chin scornfully. 'I'm not afraid of being jilted – again, I'm used to it. You need a housekeeper, not a wife. Let me go, please, Scott!'

He released her. 'Good, it's settled. You'll stay on as Melinda's protector, and my salaried, married housekeeper. Married to me. Tongues won't wag. Jolly arangement.' His finger pressed the starter and they shot away.

Theresa stared straight ahead, her mutinous chin high He need not think she would play along, she would refute every inch of the way. She was not prepared to argue now, for vague fires were dancing along her veins at the very thought of being married to Scott Milward. Fires of fury, she thought, that must be relentlessly controlled, and extinguished. This time his high-handed manner had gone too far, and would have to be grounded down to sane levels.

Matilda Todmore was typically 'ye olde English', small, spirited, pink and white. One wondered how she could have survived her years under the tropical climate of the Rhodesias. Blue, beguiling eyes still sparkled with life as they frankly summed up 'Scott's girl'. She was delighted at their announcement and her eyes grew moist at the thought that she was needed. Scott should have sent for her long ago, she would have come now that the hussy was out of the way. Now her boy could settle down sensibly and have sons and a wee sister for Melinda.

Thus the old lady chattered on while, under amused grey eyes, Theresa felt hot and uncomfortable. She waited tensely while Scott explained the necessity of her compliance with their deceiving of Elaine, that she had been at Windimount during the past few weeks. Miss Matilda was suitably indignant, quite sure that her Scott would never be underhanded, and, although she did not connive with lies openly, to this one she would make her presence felt without opening her lips!

Scott did not carry out his threat to inform Miss Matilda of his marriage plans. Tea was served while the old lady reminisced about his childhood. Theresa became highly intrigued at anecdotes that emphasized Scott's young days and teenage pranks. An embarrassed man eventually put an end to it.

'Look you, Matilda love, that's enough, your stories are getting too personal for this girl's tender ears. We've dallied long enough. By the way, we're not leaving tomorrow as planned, but the following day—' Theresa held her breath, steadied for a firm contradiction, ' – as early as possible, so can you be ready? Walk to the gate with us.'

Finally they were in the car, ready to leave. A relieved girl smiled at the little woman by the gate. Her companion's words penetrated too late.

'Matilda, I didn't tell you inside, for fear of too much dithering and – explosions. Be a dear and don your best rags tomorrow at three o'clock. Val will call for you,' his grin was wicked. 'Got that? You're being invited to a wedding, Theresa's and mine. 'Bye now!'

Scott shot forward, leaving a bewildered but joyous old lady behind him. At his side a young lady was shockingly aware of a paralysis that had attacked her vocal chords!

The monster smiled, captive devils in his eyes 'Thanks for not contradicting me. I may take your silence as consent?'

Paralysis passed swiftly. 'I wasn't given much chance, was I? That poor deluded woman's illusions about your not being underhanded is sadly unfounded.' Theresa turned her head, stared out of the window and spoke quietly. 'You can't force me, Scott.'

'Is the thought of marriage to me so odious to your fastidious mind?'

'A marriage of convenience is never very – palatable.'

Scott's knuckles gleamed white on the steering wheel. 'Need it be only that? We're always at each other's throats, but even you must admit there is a certain physical attraction apparent. We could be quite – compatible – if you weren't always so uppish, on the defensive. A good, full-blooded love affair might well clear the system of past illusions. Marriage makes it legal.'

Her voice came whisperingly tight. 'Get married in order to obtain a housekeeper or nursemaid sounds quite logical, compared to the monstrous suggestion you've just made. Are you so desperate for – for sex – that you would

153

forgo your freedom for such—'

'I was thinking of you, nymph. Could you ever feel the way I – can't you see I – I—'

Theresa interrupted with a fury that deepened her eyes to sparkling violet. 'I could not and would not dream of satisfying your desires, however much you insist they're mine. How very thoughtful and conscientious of you to think only of my wellbeing, Scott Milward, even to the extent of making it legal! Look for your full-blooded affair elsewhere. I'm resigning my position and will leave as soon as we get back. I don't even need to go back, there's a hospital right here where I can offer my services.' She stopped for breath.

The car came to a stop and Scott turned to her, a whimsical twist to his mouth. 'I did put that rather badly. What an obstructionist you are, honey! Fury becomes you as much as blushes, and if you don't calm down quickly my wish to start a love-affair may well begin right now. Shall we make a bet that, given a moment's persuasion, you will be as passionately eager as I?'

The shock of his arrogant complacency held her witlessly silent while she fought against the magnetism of smoky eyes drawing hers, so compellingly. . . .

A muscle, or nerve, was visibly throbbing in a brown cheek when Scott turned away at last and dipped his hand in his pocket for his lighter. The keyed-up feeling became a sudden void under her ribs.

He said, 'You're halfway to being in love already, Theresa Stanton. What I feel is not the most important thing at present, but we're still going to be married tomorrow afternoon, for the original protection of Melinda. Forget the love-affair suggestion. It can wait. I'll not provoke you again, and if you ever feel you – need me – well, it will be your move. No more nonsense about resignations. Our being engaged puts you under my care and marriage will ensure a comfortable future for you.'

'You're determined on your course, to hold me to my silly statement to Elaine? Why?'

The muscle jerked again. 'Need I explain – don't be so obtuse. Sorry, Theresa. Let's settle it as an eminently suitable arrangement. You may not think so now, but later, you will accept it.'

Theresa knew that it would be easy to refute his words. He had no hold on her, she was a free agent, the engagement was phony and she could walk out when and where she pleased. For some obscure reason he wanted this marriage to take place and was banking on her natural integrity, to keep her word once it was given.

Melinda's plea echoed back. 'Please, Tresa, don't ever go away!' Love for this lean, hardboned man at her side had caused her passionate outburst, because he treated, thought of marriage as a convenience and his suggestion of an affair was proposed so lightly, so casually, as if it were a mere infection that needed a certain treatment, to clear the system. And yet her inner being yearned to accept because, even if he never touched her, she would be near to him. In little ways, he would rely on her and their relationship would be cemented by mutual love for his daughter.

Theresa realized she had thought this way once before. So far it hadn't helped, but with the added spur of matrimony, Elaine obviously out of his life, finer and deeper feelings could emerge from a closer, happier relationship. He had stated that what he felt was not important, but her physical attraction for him could be the start of a deeper, spiritual love. She would try very hard to make it so. . . .

'Are these second thoughts – don't deny that you *are* thinking mighty hard – more agreeable?' His voice quickened the slow excitement that had stirred her, as if he could almost read those thoughts.

'I believe they are. As you pointed out, romance is not so important, I'm very fond of Melinda and she of me, and if we keep out of each other's hair, I guess everything should work out and my future comfort be assured. That last item is a great worry to any single girl—'

'Mercenary hussy! Did that decide you?' He was coolly amused.

' – so I will accept your offer before you change that volatile mind again.'

'Thanks. My state of wealth did the trick. I forgot that a woman can be more easily swayed by monetary gains than by passionate declarations.' Scott started the car and took the highway.

Theresa said with sweet candour, 'Your own words, sir,

were that love is illusory, an explosion that fizzles out. I'm being as realistic as you.'

He answered gruffly, 'I'm pleased that we're agreeing at last. 'Church or register office?' His eyes flicked her startled face. 'Church it will be ... our denominations, fortunately, are the same.' Stopping in the driveway, he leaned over to open the door and handed her an envelope. 'This is all yours, to buy your wedding fripperies. I'll have to move, lots of things to see to, before I go back to the sales. Enjoy yourself, little bride-to-be!' The wheels sang as he pulled away.

Val came down the steps and draped an arm across Theresa's shoulders. 'What's that dazed look for? What are you holding as if it's red-hot, and have you been kissed lately?'

'How – how is Melinda?' Bewildered blue eyes looked through her. 'I'm going to be married – tomorrow – and I think this contains the – er – wedding outfit.'

'You think? Married tomorrow? Hark at the girl! Come in. I personally think you have a touch of the sun.'

In the cool of her room Theresa gathered her wits, and told Val of Scott's decision to marry while they were here now, as he could not consider another long trip for quite some time. (Surreptitiously crossed fingers at one more untruth!)

Val laughed delightedly. 'When Scott Milward makes up his mind about a thing, it's as good as done! No wonder you look dazed. Did you know about this last night?'

'No, he – we spoke about it on the way to Miss Matilda's.'

'Ah, the spark of romance is still there, under that austere manner. . . . You haven't very much time, we'll have a hasty snack and then hare down to the salon. Are you going to wear a veil?'

'No!' The negative shot out, uncontrolled. Theresa lowered to her normal tone. 'No, Val. I would prefer a simple dress and hat.'

'How prosaic! Oh well, it's your show,' Val mourned.

A willing babysitter was once more called for, Theresa having the fear of encountering Elaine in the town and feeling it wiser to leave the child safely at home.

They eventually settled on a slim, ivory sheath dress with

a confection of a hat and shoes that were the exact colour of hyacinth eyes. Scott's cheque was blank and Val persuaded Theresa to buy sheerest hose and underwear. 'What about a going-away outfit? You never even told me where you're going to honeymoon.'

'Back to Windimount, most probably, so I won't need a costume. Slacks are comfortable for the trip and I have those in my bags. Nothing more, thank you,' Theresa said firmly to the hovering saleslady.

By mutual consent the two girls made for a nearby restaurant, where they sank down gratefully in the cool dimness, to quench their thirst. After that Val insisted that Theresa remain right there, while she popped over to the jewellers to collect her watch, her real object being a wedding gift for Scott and Theresa.

Theresa was deep in thought, having a quiet cigarette, when Derek asked politely, 'May I join you, Terry?'

She assented stiffly, for this man's hasty judgment of her still rankled.

'Unexpectedly nice to see you again, Terry. You were looking rather pensive just now. May I ask, as a friend, what are you doing here in Rhodesia, are you on holiday or following your nursing career?'

'I told you in my letter I was staying with Mary and Dan.'

'Was? Are you not with them any more?'

Theresa bit her lip and answered carefully, 'I'm getting married tomorrow, so will return with Scott to his home—'

'Tomorrow? You didn't tell me last night.' Derek looked put out at her omission.

'I didn't know—' she hastily repeated, 'I didn't think it would interest you, Derek.'

He looked at her intently. 'Are you very sure this is the real thing, girl? Don't blunder into anything without deep thought, deep sureness that it is what you want, really want.'

'Thank you for your concern. I *am* quite sure.' Her answer came steadily.

Derek covered her hand with slim, surgeon's fingers. 'My blunder made me lose you, and regret will always be there.

It has taught me one thing every doctor knows but seldom practises, in his private life ... not to jump to hasty conclusions.'

'Diagnosis is cold and clinical while emotions are not so easily charted, Derek. I'm fair-minded and can see the unequivocal position you were in. The fact is quite clear and simple: you were not really in love with me.'

'And now you've also found true love. It cuts both ways, my dear. You didn't love me enough to wait and forgive. Let's call it hurt pride, both ways.'

'And they do say that pride comes before a fall, doctor?' the cold voice of Scott Milward inquired.

Theresa drew her hand guiltily from Derek's clasp and he stood up to meet the cold grey eyes.

'So I found, to my cost and your good fortune, Milward. Terry tells me you're to be married tomorrow. Every happiness you wish for yourself, Terry dear, and to you, sir, treat her gently.' And Derek walked, erect and proper, out of her life.

'How touching!' Scott drawled.

'I didn't even offer him refreshment—'

'Again, how touching. Too busy letting him down gently, or are there further meetings on the horizon?' he inquired caustically.

'Jealousy gets you nowhere, sir,' Theresa retorted spiritedly, then lowered her voice timidly. 'I didn't expect you to finish so early, nor did I expect to see you here ...'

'Hence the cosy tête-à-tête!'

'Forgive me Scott, it was irresistible.' Lowered lashes fanned darkly on her cheeks and a dimple became alluringly elusive.

Scott watched her with hooded eyes. 'I can't fathom you, Theresa Stanton. You're a sly witch and I don't believe you—'

A breathless Val Martin plumped into the seat next to him. 'Hello, Scott. Did I keep you waiting long, Theresa, so sorry. What are you doing here, groom-to-be?'

'Keeping tabs on my future.'

'You're a secretive devil to spring surprises on us like this. One thing is puzzling me. Theresa informed me that you're going straight back to Windimount after the wedding ...

won't that be rather late? Fancy driving through the night with a new bride at your side and a child and elderly lady on the back seat! You simply can't—'

'Pipe down, nag-bag, all has been arranged. We're certainly not spending the night at your house. I've noticed the sad lack of door-keys! With your dear husband's help, we tracked down a cosy little place in the hills, just right for – newlyweds. They even have trout-fishing. I regret, though, that time is short and duty calls. We'll have to leave there very early in order to pick up our entourage and so on to home.' Scott sat back languidly.

'Trout? You think of trout, while – oh!' Words were beyond Mrs. Martin.

Theresa sat up, she had not given a thought to that problem. So this was his discreet way of solving it, for if they stayed at David's house it would look distinctly odd not sharing a room on their wedding night. She returned his glance, an odd smile curving the corners of her lips. Trust this lean, arrogant man to think of everything!

No answer being forthcoming, Val put up her hands in mock despair. 'Theresa, are you coming back with me, or this great fisherman?'

'With you, of course.' Theresa hurriedly grabbed her purse.

'Methinks the lady hath great fear of being—' Scott paused, and she interjected quickly, 'Not ravished, but of being led along more devilish and devious paths.' She smiled sweetly at him in passing, a slightly dazed Val in her wake.

Scott Milward sat, deep in thought, until David appeared. 'You car is ready, Scott, serviced and cleaned, ready for the great event. I'll drop you at the garage.'

'Thanks. Theresa and Val have just left.'

'Didn't they offer you a lift home?'

'They never even guessed that I was stranded.' Scott grinned boyishly at his friend.

That evening Val ordered her husband to take Scott out. 'Have dinner or a splurge at the club, or any other place. Have you all forgotten tradition, that it's bad luck for the groom to see his future bride on the night before the wedding?' Theresa started to protest, but was hushed determinedly. 'None of you are worrying about anything, I've never seen such a dull lot! Why, Scott, I had to force that young woman to use your lovely blank cheque. Firstly, she reckoned she didn't need a wedding dress, one of her old frocks would do. Secondly, she had money of her own, to pay her way. My goodness, if I had free access to a blank cheque! But then my good spouse knows me, I'll never have that privilege. . . . Well, anyway, this tradition jazz, I may be a square and superstitious, but that's how it's going to be.'

Theresa was angry with her for bringing up the subject of Scott's cheque so blithely. As she saw anger in his face too, her chin came up a trifle and she stared back at him defiantly. He confounded her by suddenly dropping an eyelid in an unmistakable wink.

David reluctantly left his comfortable armchair. 'We'd better obey my charming wife, Scott. Let's gather the boys anl have a real tonk, mourning your loss of freedom, in our cups.'

'I'm with you, Dave. By jove, I didn't realize there was so much entailed. Chasing after the minister fagged me at the start.'

'It was your idea, all this haste, darling.' Theresa emphasized the endearment with tender venom and was instantly alarmed when Scott stepped nearer with a mocking smile.

'Shall I give you a taste now of the reason for my haste, sweetheart?' Mimicking her, he also put emphasis on the last word.

She hurriedly left the room, speaking over her shoulder, 'I'm sure I heard Melinda call—'

Later, while she was preparing for bed, Val gave a light tap on the door and entered, carrying a beribboned blue garter and dainty handkerchief. 'Something borrowed, something blue, Theresa, you're all set now.'

Theresa felt a lump in her throat and sudden moisture clouded her eyes. 'Thank you, Val, you're very sweet – I only wish I could—' she reached for a tissue and buried her face in it.

'Mop up, honey. We can't have you getting all red-eyed at this stage.' Val's own eyes burned in sympathy and she also grabbed a tissue. 'Bother it, my hay-fever is coming on again! Now, into bed with you, have a good sleep and there's no need to get up too early. I'm going to have the pleasure of bringing your breakfast to you and you're not to put your nose out of this door before that time.' A strangely tender kiss was planted on Theresa's cheek and Val walked quickly out of the bedroom.

Midnight chimed as David's car returned and a wakeful girl listened to the hushed voices of the two men. Then the house settled into the silence of the night.

CHAPTER NINE

THE wedding of Theresa Stanton and Scott Milward was suitably solemn, without noticeable incident, except for the bride's paleness when the ring was slipped on to her finger and when her husband kissed her tenderly while the Reverend Mr. Baker chaffed her on the forcefulness of her groom's behaviour in practically shanghaiing him into marrying them, at such short notice. David and Val were best man and matron of honour respectively.

Miss Matilda Todmore had charge of Melinda, who sat big-eyed with suppressed excitement throughout the ceremony. A few selected friends of the Martins and Scott attended. Elaine, obviously cognisant of the facts through mutual acquaintances, showed good taste by her absence, for which both Scott and Theresa were extremely thankful, Melinda being present.

The guests were invited to the house for a champagne toast and David Martin gravely did the honours. Scott stood, tall and proud, at his wife's side and took the ribbing of his friends with superb good humour.

It was over at last and Theresa, sitting next to her new husband, watched the passing scenery as the car purred over parallel strips of concrete. Finally, slowing down at a signboard, they turned off the highway on to a lesser, gravelled road. The shadows were lengthening and the pink glow of a setting sun veiled deep, mountainous valleys through which they now travelled.

Scott sat relaxed behind the wheel and, apart from inquiries concerning her comfort, remained quietly preoccupied. Theresa was content to study the wonderful flora and terrain, almost afraid to shatter the peace by some remark that might start a sardonic comeback. Inevitably, her eyes turned to rest on the lean contours of his face. He had removed his jacket but not his tie and he looked incredibly handsome, distant, in sharp contrast to the man of Windimount, to the Scott who wore open-necked shirts and tight-hipped khaki trousers, with a hat that usually balanced pre-

cariously on the back of his head. Now the dark, unruly fall
of hair was neatly brushed back and his long-sleeved shirt
gleamed immaculately white against tanned neck and hands.
. . . The girl at his side sighed involuntarily and he turned
immediately.

'Surely not bored, Mrs. Milward, on the most exciting
day of any girl's life?'

'Not bored at all, Scott. The scenery is beautiful – I guess
I'm a wee bit tired.' An infinitesimal thrill shot through her
at his use of her married title.

'Another five miles approximately you can relax to a
quiet dinner. After that—' he hesitated and she waited for
the familiar mockery, ' – a nice hot bath will set you right
for a sound sleep and our early start back in the morning.
What you need most of all is a few calories tucked under
your belt, right now.' His talk was light, with no evidence of
mockery.

'Yes, I am starving. It's been quite a day.' Relief made the
words rush out.

Scott's eyes flicked her profile briefly as he answered
gravely, 'That's no lie. The gnawing against my backbone
can only be hunger . . . look at that stream on your side,
believe it or not, that shallow water is teeming with trout.
We'll most likely have it on the menu tonight.'

'Mmm, delicious . . . are you fond of fishing, Scott?'

'Fairly, but opportunities are few and far between. I've
done some camping at Kariba, did a trip on the Zambezi
and sea fishing along the north coast of Natal. Once, a
couple of my cronies and I flew over to Bazaruta.'

'That must have been fabulous . . . I've heard of Paradise
Island. Mary and Dan went there for their honeymoon.'

Scott's lips quirked. 'Sorry I couldn't lay it on for you.
Maybe one day, when the chores are not so overwhelming,
we can do a trip to see if it's all it's cracked up to be.'

'Oh, I'm not that interested. Any place would be heavenly
if you – when you're in—'

'In love? he caught her up swiftly. 'But you're not, hence
the disinterest? There's the chalet, ahead of us.'

The hotel did indeed resemble a Swiss chalet, clinging to
the side of the hill up which they were now curving. Pink-
washed walls with facings of dark timber, a light already

twinkling from an attic window that nestled under tilted eaves and a tiled roof. Scott stopped the car in the narrow driveway which sloped down again on the far side to a swimming pool and tennis courts. Incredibly green lawns, dotted with indigenous shrubs and trees, clung to gentle slopes.

Flashingly white teeth were very evident as the dark-skinned waiter ushered them into the foyer which served, jointly, as cocktail bar and lounge. The walls were lined with treated splitpoles, the rough bark showing and heavy, dark beams criss-crossed overhead. Native craft was displayed to advantage, light came from bulbs ingeniously attached to a huge wagon-wheel suspended on brass chains and hanging from the central beam, the effect of Swiss architecture and African decoration being most intriguing and well balanced.

Scott and Theresa followed the waiter up the beamed stair case to a door on the split-level upper floor. They entered, and she felt flags of scarlet flushing in her cheeks as she met Scott's whimsical gaze. He tipped the waiter and laconically surveyed the room.

'Ah, that's what I was looking for.' Striding forward, he opened an interleading door. 'Come and see my monk's hole, it has only one bed. Very unfair! You can always move from one to the other, if they're lumpy, while I'll have to suffer in silence.' He did not move and she had to duck under his outstretched arm resting across the open doorway. The colour had cooled in her cheeks at his words.

Theresa studied the smaller room and walked to the curved window. 'You have a gorgeous view from this angle.'

Scott muttered an inaudible profanity. She raised an inquiring eyebrow and he spoke louder. 'A lovely view is all I need to make everything "luverly" in my private garden. Oh yes indeed!'

Ignoring his sarcasm, Theresa walked back into the other room. 'I'm going in search of a bathroom.'

He watched from the door, as she gathered soap and towels. 'No need to change your frock, precious. Mustn't look too newly-wed or someone will wonder why the two rooms . . . rather awkward explaining that my bride is awfully shy . . . much better to let 'em think my old spouse can't abide my snoring!'

'Much better, and you do snore, old man,' she retorted. Her ears felt hot as she walked down the passage to the bathroom.

Individual table candles lighted the dining-room, giving it a softly intimate atmosphere. The tiny flame on their table reflected gold in blue pools as Theresa's eyes wandered from her table companion to the delicious food, her surroundings and then back to the lean, dark man. Sure enough, trout was served and as delicious as they had anticipated. Muted radio music provided a soothing background.

The Swiss proprietor joined Scott and Theresa in the lounge for after-dinner liqueurs. Any friend of David Martin (who had not told him that the couple were newly married) was welcome and did not need recommendation, so he did not question the unusual arrangement of bedrooms. He kept them entertained with tales of South-west Africa, from whence he had come, to settle and start his little hotel, Cloud's End, in the hills of Rhodesia.

Theresa was startled out of a relaxed interlude when Scott glanced at his watch and commented on the late hour. 'We have to make an early start, so let's catch some shut-eye. You go up, honey, while I settle with Mr. Jergens.'

Clad in shortie pyjamas and blue gown, Theresa brushed her hair until it sparked with static. She decided on the bed nearest the window – farthest from that interleading door. As she heard sounds on the other side, her gown was hastily discarded and she slipped between the pink sheets. Her heart started an irregular beat as a light tap came on the door and Scott said softly, 'Theresa? I'm coming in.' He waited a moment before suiting action to words. Two large, apprehensive blue eyes met his above the tightly held sheet.

Scott grinned as he approached. 'Your eyes should be pink, you resemble a very scared rabbit.' He sat down on the foot-end of her bed, took a pack of cigarettes from the pocket of his dark blue dressing-gown and offered them. She shook her head and he lit one for himself. The smoke curled lazily upwards as grey eyes surveyed her dispassionately.

Tongue-tied, Theresa could only gaze back at him, hoping the pink covering did not reveal a betraying thud in her breast. Silence lengthened while Scott remained in the same position and finished his smoke at leisure. At last he stood up to press the stub into the ashtray on her side-table. Leaning over suddenly, he touched the soft curve of her lips with his own.

'Sleep without fear, little Rabbit Milward, the fox will not hunt tonight.' At the door he turned. 'Even though he has a licence!'

Theresa battled with conflicting, chaotic emotions, afraid of any advances, yet betraying heart and body yearned for the embraces that were never offered. Shame at her longing buried burning eyes deep in her pillow, severe chastisement of self made not an iota of difference in stemming the flames coursing through her body. To think that she would welcome an embrace that had no spiritual loving, only physical attraction. . . . Where were her ideals, her self-control, that this man could turn them to nothing just by his very presence? What of his indifference to test the strength of her capitulation against his advances (what would have happened yesterday, if he had carried out his threats to start a love-affair, and how much persuasion would she have needed?) This love was bitter-sweet anguish. Just kiss your brand-new wife goodnight, Mr. Impartial Milward, and let her sleep the sleep of the innocent. Damn the innocent, damn you, Scott Milward! Long lashes were damp fans on her cheeks when at last white knuckles relaxed and Theresa slept.

Scarce had her eyes closed, or so it seemed, when a tap at her door awakened her and she lifted heavy eyelids. The waiter murmured a polite good morning and deposited the tea-tray on a low table under the window. Scott, fully dressed, followed on his heels.

'Leave it there, Manuel, madam will pour, thank you.' He waited for the door to close, then handed her dressing-gown to the sleepy girl who had struggled to a sitting position.

'Morning, wife, it's a crying shame to wake you so early, but duty calls.' He took the gown out of her hands and held it up, perforce she had to slip out of bed to put her arms into the garment. Scott fumbled with the buttons and she pushed his hands away as awareness cleared her tired brain.

'I'll manage, thanks,' she said in irritation.

'Hmm, not even a "good morning" for me? I'm learning fast! You're not a cheerful waker-upper, evidently.'

' 'Morning, Scott, I'm still drugged with sleep.' Theresa excused her behaviour. Fastening the last button, she pushed tumbled hair off her face and walked barefooted to the tea-tray.

Scott waited in patient amusement as she battled with cups and tea-pot while unruly hair obscured her vision. Aware of his tantalizing gaze, she straightened up. 'My first chore, when we get back, will be to chop off this mop.'

'Oh no, you don't! It's lovely, and I like my women with long tresses. Nothing doing!'

'Stop ordering and bossing so early, Scott Milward, I can't take it. Drink your tea.' Theresa sank into a chair and sipped her tea. 'I'm not one of your women,' she added belatedly.

'I query that statement . . . as of yesterday you belong to me, lock, stock and barrel, hair and all. My chattel, in fact.' Scott posed loftily.

'Movable property?' she defined, and yawned daintily. 'If you don't vamoose very quickly, I shall dive back into that bed, and nothing on earth will move me then!'

Scott took indolent steps to the door. 'As you're my property, I'm at liberty to move wheresoever it moves, so take care, girl. Twenty minutes to pack!'

The Martin household were up and waiting when Scott stopped in their driveway. Miss Matilda had slept in Theresa's room. She sat primly on the verandah with all the luggage stacked in readiness. Scott's daughter ran down the steps to greet them. 'Where have you and Tresa been, Daddy? Have you been away all night?'

'Yes, Poppet.'

'Did you take Theresa 'cos you got married?'

'Er – yes, Poppet.' Tanned cheeks became slightly red.

Melinda stamped her foot and declared, 'I'll marry Tresa too and then you must take me with you next time, Dad.'

'What about me, Melinda?' Miss Matilda inquired mischievously.

'You can marry Daddy as well.' Pleased at this solution, Melinda smiled importantly.

'One lovely marry-go-round!' Scott mispronounced.

'Lock, stock and chattels.' Theresa's gibe reached only his ears.

He sent her a dark look – 'Women!' and walked round the car to open the boot.

A quick breakfast, interposed with wicked innuendoes from David and Val's shining eyes on the flushed cheeks of the new Mrs. Milward, and then Scott and his entourage were on their way home. Midday brought them to Umtali where they stopped for lunch. Miss Matilda and Melinda dozed on the back seat as they continued their journey. Soon, with Scott's deft handling of the car, they left the highroad to traverse a lesser road under the shadowed Mtanda ranges. Again Scott kept her enthralled, this time on the great project, Kariba, one of the world's largest artificial lakes, and its power station also one of man's greatest achievements.

He spoke of the fantastic fighting tiger-fish, a fisherman's ultimate, objective dream. Kariba could be reached by land, air and water, and his promise to take her there one day was stored in Theresa's memory, for did not all these promises mean that he was content to have her at Windimount indefinitely?

Theresa hugged the thought tenderly and vowed that she would make them come true, somehow. . . . Her heart leapt with a true homecoming feeling as she glimpsed the house through the avenue of trees. Everybody seemed to share that feeling. The elderly Matilda's eyes glistened with unshed tears, Melinda shouted to a beaming Cleo and Scott stretched his arms contentedly before taking a firm hold of the old lady's arm, to help her up the steps.

The servants' joy when they heard of their boss's marriage was high, somewhat mitigated by Cleo's disapproval, when she was told quite firmly by her new madam that she would not vacate her own bedroom to share the master's bedroom. Clucking in disgust at 'white ways and habits', she took Melinda for her bath.

At dinner, Theresa suddenly suspended her fork halfway to her mouth and looked so dumbstruck that Scott lowered his own and leaned forward anxiously.

'Mary and Dan!' she gasped.

'Mary and Dan?' Scott repeated, looking around in a puzzled way.

'What are they going to say, about us – ? Oh, heavens, what am I going to do – to say? Mary is my best friend,' Theresa stammered while her eyes, if possible, grew larger.

Scott relaxed, whistled through his teeth. 'I thought, for a moment, you were on the verge of having a fit – don't *do* that – look how pale our Matilda is. Mary and Dan – I presume you are aghast at their reactions when you disclose our hasty marriage?

'Oh, Scott!' she wailed. 'You're going to tell them, not me. Mary will flay me alive for not even sending a telegram, or letting her be the first to know – but I didn't even know myself. We didn't even let on about our temporary – I mean—' flushing, she glanced at Miss Matilda, 'our engagement. What am I going to do? Mary is almost family to me—'

'Hush up, girl, pull yourself together. We can't hide behind a phone call, so a nice little ride is indicated, to face the lion in his den.'

'Right now? No, Scott, I couldn't—'

'You can. We'll finish our dinner first. Matilda won't mind, I'm sure . . . eat up now. You can stand behind my broad, manly back while I drop the bombshell.'

Blue eyes looked at him, mutely appealing. Grey ones crinkled back in smiling assurance.

'You two run along, Melinda is perfectly safe with me. After all, Scott will grab every chance of being alone with his new bride and I will efface myself as much as possible, so as not to spoil the new bliss. Just pretend I'm not here.' Miss Matilda's appeal was uttered earnestly, but the twinkle of curiosity in her eyes belied the docile manner.

It was a very reluctant girl who preceded Scott into the Rourkes' sitting-room. Mary jumped up, a smile of delighted welcome on her lips. Dan looked equally pleased.

Hugging Theresa, she excaimed, 'How very nice of you both to come over, I didn't expect to see you so soon. Did you enjoy the trip, honey?' Mary held the girl at arm's length, studying her. 'You look a wee bit fagged. It looks as if you need to recuperate – you must have had a high time, mmm, Scott?'

'Well, I thought it best to – er—' Scott dithering!

Dan looked astonished at this phenomenon. 'Well, you're here, and we're pleased indeed to see you. Sit you down, Terry. Would you like a sherry?'

Scott tried again. 'We had a very good trip, thanks, so good, in fact, that we – er – we – that is, Theresa and I are—' He stopped.

Astonishment turned to disbelief at the sight of cool, assured Scott Milward actually stammering!

Into the thick silence Theresa cut, clearly and calmly, 'We're married, Scott and I.' Instinctively she moved nearer to her husband and his arm came up in a protective gesture round her shoulders.

The Rourkes' gaze swivelled from one to the other, as one would look at normally sane friends who had suddenly gone crazily mad right under their noses. Hysteria was apparent as Mary turned to her Dan. 'Not sherry, dear, I think there's a bottle of champagne in the back of the lower shelf.' She trailed off in a whisper. 'Joke is over?'

Scott regained control. 'No joke, Mary. Look pleased and congratulate us, even if it is only out of politeness. Theresa was terrified of your reaction, and yet when it came to facing you, she was braver than I.'

'They're not mad, Mary, they really mean it. For a moment my mind ran on "mad dogs and Englishmen" – the sun is very hot, but both of them at once? No. Their embarrassment points to the truth.' Dan took a lean brown hand in his and kissed Theresa. 'May you both be very happy,' he added, with a grave simplicity.

The dazed look cleared as Mary followed suit. 'Forgive me, it was sprung so suddenly. I never dreamt – I couldn't have wished for anything better to happen to you both. Give me time to assimilate. . . . Ah, Terry, don't worry about Dan and me being hurt, I'll bet it was as sudden for you as well. Scott Milward can be a swift, menacing juggernaut, believe me!'

Scott dropped her at the front steps and drove off to garage the car. When he walked into the house, Theresa had already closed her bedroom door. He hesitated a moment, walked to his own room and stood at the open window for a long time smoking one cigarette after another.

The days fell into routine and Theresa found plenty to occupy herself with in the house and gardens. She unpacked shelves, took inventories, tidied and mended, so that when day was done she was exhausted and retired as early as possible. She dreaded the nights, for then, inevitably, her mind and heart dwelt on her love. Suffering longing and yearning took possession, for the man who was so near and yet so far.

She took great care to avoid direct physical contact with him during the day, although certain inadvertent brushes were unavoidable, and then her senses would feel with the same sharp impact as before. Scott had a manner of appearing suddenly and flicking loose tendrils of her hair across her face with casual fingers. She hated it, for the simple reason that the gesture exploded the cocoon of withdrawal she was constantly weaving around her emotions.

Three weeks after their marriage Scott announced, after dinner, that he would be going to Fort Victoria on the following day, and would the women want anything from the shops? They considered and declared 'No, thanks, not a thing!' Later, however, when Miss Matilda had gone to bed Theresa took courage and joined him in the sitting-room where he was reading a journal and smoking his pipe. He looked up as she stood hesitantly before him.

'Scott, will it be possible for you to buy new curtains for this room? These are impossibly heavy and suffocating.'

Scott glanced from her to the offending drapes, drew deeply on his pipe.

Theresa rushed on before he could speak, 'I know it's presumptuous of me, as it's your home. If you're satisfied with all this heavy stuff please don't think you have to—' The spate of words came to a stop as he unwound from his chair and came closer.

'My dear girl, my house is your home, remember? If it looks lousy in your eyes by all means change it. Tell me roughly what you need and I'll supply, if possible.'

'It's not lousy, only I think a hot climate calls for lighter, cooler furnishings.'

'You may be right at that. I'll see what can be done. Don't be nervous about asking for anything, Theresa ... as my wife you have every right, remember.'

'I'm apt to forget, quite often. I feel more like an unpaid nurse and housekeeper,' she rejoined lightly, but unconscious bitterness coloured her tone.

Scott towered over her. 'Are you in need? I never gave a thought to any requirements, of your wardrobe or other things a woman may need.' He took her arm in a rough grip. 'Tell me, girl, are you unhappy with our present arrangements?'

'Are you, Scott?' Theresa countered quietly, forcing down an irregularity in her breast.

'Don't prevaricate, answer me,' he ordered, and as she stood, dumbly still, he took her in his arms and pressed her head against his shoulder. 'What must I do to make you happy, make you feel like a wife? Buy new curtains or – perhaps this—' A hand lifted her chin. Scott's eyes lit with flame as he pressed his mouth on hers with deep urgency.

The kiss had a fierce, sweet quality. Through drowning senses Theresa forced her mind to remember that this man did not love her, that this was his generous way of trying to make her happy. . . . Curtains or kisses?

Passion flowed from his mouth, his seeking hands, and the girl's head swam as she moaned an insistent 'No, Scott, no!' against his lips.

'Yes, yes, darling, don't be so adorably obstinate. . . . You want me as much as I've wanted you . . . you're my wife and I need you.' He kissed the quickening pulse in the hollow of her throat.

Through a mist of leaping responses, one sane thought hammered. No word of love from his questing lips, only want and need – just say it once, 'Nymph darling, I love you' just once and nothing in this wide world will matter. Her heart pleaded while lips remained silent.

Scott did not say it. . . .

Coldness settled around her heart and chilled her spine. Her body lost its ardour, she stood limp, and numbed and despairing. Scott became aware of the change in her and let her go, stepping back a pace. 'Not satisfactory?'

'Not without love, Scott,' Theresa whispered, and waited, giving him another chance to say what she most wanted to hear.

'That's rather unfortunate, isn't it?' Sarcasm was in the husky tones. 'Maybe I could have that answer now. What do you want, need, to make you happy?'

'Curtains,' Theresa voiced woodenly.

'One commodity being unobtainable, curtains it shall be. Write down the measurements, etc.' With that rather cryptic statement he turned away, dismissal in the uncompromising back.

'Goodnight, Scott.' Small and slim, she walked out.

Theresa threw herself into furious activity the next morning, after Scott had left, the cause being mainly the shock of his parting words – 'I'll be at my solicitors, to finalize monetary affairs concerning Elaine. She'll most likely be there as well. Might take a day or two, so expect me back when you see me. Sam's got everything under control here, refer to him if any difficulties arise.'

An urgent desire to get away, be on her own, motivated her actions, and in the late afternoon she left Miss Matilda to watch Melinda and set off in the utility jeep. A few miles of abstracted driving brought her to a huddle of blue-gum trees where she stopped the jeep and sat for a long while, smoking cigarette after cigarette. Impulsively she decided to carry on and visit Mary. Thoughts of Scott and his ex-wife were resolutely pushed aside.

Mary was tidying her bedroom cupboards. Theresa entreated her not to stop, Rina could serve the tea right there. The girls chattered for a while and Mary surveyed the pile of discarded clothing on the carpet. 'One never knows what to do, discard or keep for another wear or two.' Innocently she queried, 'What are you doing about your clothes? Have you kept your room on as a dressing-room – I happen to know that Scott's bedroom is large, but his wardrobes are not big enough to hold—Terry love!'

For a welled-up heart had at last burst its banks and Theresa put her head into Mary's pillow and sobbed heartbreakingly, unable to control herself or to hide her misery any longer from her friend. Mary sat beside her, stroked the fair head in silent compassion, until the racking shoulders gradually subsided.

Theresa could not, was not going to deceive any longer.

In words that choked her at times, she told the whole story of her love for Scott, the phoney engagement and subsequent events leading up to their marriage. '—and I love him so desperately – it hurts to be near him. I want to touch him, run my fingers through dusty hair when he comes in, trace the line of his mouth, help him to unlace riding boots. ... Dear heaven, Mary, will it be better or worse if I leave him, never to see the sun crinkles at the corners of proud grey eyes, not have the indescribable joy of mixing a drink for him and feel the warm touch of his hand when I hand it to him. . . . And that tender look he has for Melinda – turn to indifference when it settles on me?' Her shoulders shook again in an agony of remembering.

'Heavens, honey, you've fallen desperately hard. It's real, this time.' A tender arm circled the girl's shoulders. 'Have you considered why he's gone to the lengths of marrying you? Could it be that he loves you too? The question of protection or scandal wouldn't swerve Scott Milward to that extent . . . he's a law unto himself and would treat all that with the contempt it deserves. Maybe he does love you, Terry, but can't show it through that hard crust of control he's built around himself, ever since Elaine disillusioned him so badly. If you could crash that obstacle, you would no doubt find a warm, generous, loving man – for he can be that, I know—'

'He's a hateful, arrogantly conceited man who thinks a girl has only to be kissed by him for her to melt and succumb—'

'Is he, Terry?' Mary interposed quietly.

'No – yes. He's all that, a wonderful devil, and I love him to distraction – and he doesn't love me. Now he's with Elaine—' words failed her, misery darkened eyes to a tear-drenched violet.

'I honestly believe *that* shouldn't worry you at all. Even if he did have some feelings for her, they were surely and certainly blotted out after Elaine's mucky dig about Melinda. You must do something drastic, to make Scott reveal himself, to show his true feelings soon, otherwise you'll be climbing the wall – with all this love and misery bottled up inside you!'

'I'll do no such thing, for if I do anything drastic and find he doesn't love me, what then? My own love isn't going to lessen.'

'And if you find that he does love you?'

The stars that shone from glistening eyes almost blinded Mary – and then were gone again. 'That would be the most lovely moment of my life. I shan't do anything drastic, though, I'm tired of deception. Thank you, Mary, for seeing me through all this. I – I feel much better now, partly relief and mostly because I hated deceiving you. So now you know. I'd better fly back before Miss Matilda starts panicking.'

At home again, Theresa flew to answer the shrilling code ring of the telephone. Georgia's voice came. 'Terry, we're engaged!'

'Engaged?'

'Yes, engaged, e.n.g.a.g.e.d.'

'Oh, engaged. To whom are we engaged?'

'Not you, nitwit. Me, to Hugh. Hugh to me.'

Theresa came alive. 'How perfectly wonderful! I just knew a bit of manipulation—'

'Just you wait, Mrs. Milward, just you wait! . . . That will be tomorrow. Hugh is bringing me out, in the afternoon.'

'Lovely, Georgia dear!'

'And you're going to spill everything about your whirlwind romance as well. The whole town's agog. I suppose you've had visitors by the gallon?'

'A few, yes. Mostly calls from Scott's friends, with good wishes.' Theresa spoke with sudden effort.

Georgia's tone was mysterious before she rang off. 'See that you have on your prettiest dress. I have my reasons. 'Bye now!'

CHAPTER TEN

BREAKFAST over, Theresa had the heavy curtains taken down in the sitting-room, thus exposing the white terylene drop which she left hanging. The difference in light and air was amazing. She fitted the two cretonne slip-covers, that she had cut and stitched herself, over two armchairs and stepped back to survey her handiwork. Miss Matilda and Melinda gave their full approval; already the room appeared gayer and a low vase of yellow chrysanthemums on a corner table effected a bright finishing touch.

In the afternoon Theresa showered and chose a cool blue linen dress. She combed her hair to a shining topknot and slipped her feet into low-heeled sandals which matched her dress. While dressing, she wondered about Georgia's request that she wear her prettiest dress (a certain other call had been waited for, in vain).

Her wondering ceased when she went out to watch as Mary, Lily and Georgia piled out of Hugh Lessing's car and she saw the dust of other cars arriving. The ladies of the community had come to call on her!

Hugh waved self-consciously and disappeared in the direction of the paddocks, followed by other men drivers. The ladies, arms laden with goodies, bottles and parcels, crowded Theresa back into the room, delighted at the surprise on her face.

Mary looked anxiously at her friend and managed a quiet aside, 'I didn't know a thing about this until they stopped by, Terry. Georgia pointedly omitted to tell me, fearing I would give you the tip ... it's a belated linen tea, for you. You're doing nicely, keep that chin up my brave one....'

The traditional fun and jokes, at her expense, began then, and Theresa met new faces and acquaintances with superb aplomb, taking their ribbing in the spirit it was given. Cleo received a couple of mystery baskets, with orders to unpack them into the refrigerator.

Theresa was made to open the other parcels, some with notes which made for more hilarity, and the pile of linen disclosed grew at her feet. Tears almost overcame her at one stage, but Lily de Wet declared wickedly, 'Too late for tears, woman, you've been an' gorn an' done it. Right under our noses too! Did you marry him after all to fix this sitting-room – I notice those dark drapes have vanished?'

Theresa agreed solemnly, 'Just for that did I snag the man.'

'Ha! We'll wait a wee while, then make you eat those wild words, at your next party. Stork business thrives!'

The stricken girl blushed furiously and was saved further taunting by the entrance of Cleo and Daniel, laden with trays of tea and home-made cakes. Theresa made her little speech, thanking them all in a rather husky, small voice.

A setting sun was the cue for the men to make their appearance. They had been prepared to spend the earlier part of the day with Scott, unaware of his absence, so Sam had entertained them instead, in the barn. Besides Sam and Hugh were four others whom Theresa vaguely remembered seeing at the barbecue. They all paid respects, bemoaning the fact that Scott was away.

Hugh and Georgia now came in for their share of good wishes. Theresa suddenly found a brimming glass of champagne thrust into her hand and everybody drank to the couple's health. The glasses were refilled and they toasted the absent one and his wife, who had to drain her glass to shouts of 'Down, down, down!'

Feeling slightly light-headed, Theresa started down the passage towards the kitchen, but was headed back by Lily and Sam, both carrying trays loaded with savouries and jugs of iced lemon drinks, quite evidently the contents of the mystery baskets. She managed to snatch a minute square of cheese and two olives.

The company were discussing the new craze for folk dancing and Sam boldly declared that he was an authority on same. At Theresa's nod of consent, the pile of linen was removed, the carpet rolled up and a blushing Sam was ordered to demonstrate. Someone had brought the appropriate records and the ensuing hour was earnestly passed with everyone following Sam's calls. Hugh changed the music to a deep, sensuous rumba, and Theresa found herself in his arms and they started to dance while the others watched.

Scott Milward stopped his car and gazed in alarm at the vehicles in the driveway. He shot out of the seat and took the steps on the double, came to a halt at the doorway and watched his wife and the doctor doing an exhibition dance. A cold rage filled him as he walked in, calmly manoeuvred Hugh aside and took over. 'Let me show you how it's done, old chap. Hello, darling.'

Joy coursed through the girl's body, making her more lightheaded than ever. Surely she had drunk too much – this was a lovely hallucination? Scott was home again, she was dancing in his arms and he had called her 'darling' – what more could a girl want! She smiled dreamily up at him, 'Hello, my love.'

Oblivious of onlookers, he held her closer as he saw joyous welcome in blue eyes. The champagne and his closeness gave her a heady moment and she missed a step. Righting her in an instant, Scott looked closer and discovered that his wife was slightly tipsy.

'Well, I'll be damned!' he exclaimed under his breath. The joy in her eyes was induced from a glass, not because of his unexpected presence. . . . As the music came to a stop he deliberately claimed her mouth.

Theresa closed her eyes, blissfully unaware of anyone but the man holding her. Dawning realization came, of mockery, when he let her go and bowed solemnly to the clapping of hands.

A glass was thrust into Scott's hand, another toast given and accepted. The object of the party was explained and he drew his wife to his side with an arm around her waist, while he smilingly thanked them all.

Only the girl at his side detected the grim line of mouth and the faint pulse in his cheek as he spoke and smiled. He was not pleased with her, that was for sure, she could feel it. Well, they were his friends too. Why did he call her 'darling' as if he meant it, and almost immediately become displeased with her? Still somewhat lightheaded, Theresa murmured inaudibly, 'Damn your vacillating moods, rajah, see if I care!'

'I beg your pardon, Theresa?' Scott bent courteously.

She smiled sweetly. 'How was your – business trip? Did things go satisfactorily?'

178

Scott stiffened, answered curtly, 'Fair, thanks.'

'Did you see the – fair lady?'

'I did. She sends venomous regards and tells me she has a doll which resembles you. She's got it stuck full of pins. Pardon me, please, I want to pass on some information to Sam, before it slips my mind.'

His terse reply startled Theresa and her bemused mind speculated bitterly. There were several ways to accept this man's inconsistent behaviour; consolation with Elaine had made it harder to tolerate his new wife; he might have had a difficult time with his solicitor and ex-wife and consequent bad temper covered her, Theresa, as well. . . .

Obligingly, their friends left early, under the impression that Scott was tired and wanted time to spend with his pretty wife after being away two whole days.

Miss Matilda and Scott sat down for a nightcap while Theresa busied herself empting ashtrays and tidying the room. Laughter and chatter came from the kitchen where Cleo and Daniel were washing glasses and dishes.

'Do sit down and drink yours too.' The old lady sighed. 'That was a lovely surprise, Scott, you should see the lovely things they brought for Theresa and you.'

'Linen stuff, I believe. Theresa can show it tomorrow.'

Theresa stacked the records, switched off the radio, turned and tripped slightly on the edge of the carpet that had been rolled back. Scott eyed her warily.

'I wouldn't take another drink if I were you. Champagne and gin and tonic don't mix well.'

'Well, you're not me, and I'm not under the influence,' she retorted spiritedly. Sudden revolt at his manner, her own uncertainty of the outcome of his trip made her feel reckless, at the end of her tether. 'A simple gin and tonic will not affect me any further, and being in my own home I'll drink gallons if I want to and still stagger on my own two feet to my bed. Don't be afraid your strength will be called upon to carry me. Save it for other trips – other things!'

'Theresa!' Miss Matilda looked shocked.

'Theresa!' Scott mimicked, amusement lurking in his eyes.

'Theresa, Theresa – I'm sick of that name. "Theresa, I

wouldn't do this, Theresa, don't do that, follow my orders, Theresa"!'

Scott watched in surprise as she actually stamped her foot. He said mildly, 'Temper, love? I guess this isn't an appropriate moment to show you the new curtains.'

Theresa stared at him in angry frustration and brought a clenched fist to her mouth. 'You can keep them, Scott Milward!' she enunciated clearly, and walked out of the room.

Dead silence reigned. Miss Matilda clucked reprovingly and whispered a goodnight to the silent man. He did not answer, and she stopped at the doorway. 'You've finally met your match, boy, so put that in your pipe and draw deeply.'

'Traitor!' His husky whisper followed her down the passage.

A sleepless night had shown Theresa clearly what course she must take. She must leave Windimount.

She must give Scott an opportunity to assess facts, without her worrying presence to distract him. Being a full-blooded, virile male, he would naturally want and seek female contact sooner or later. She was not prepared to be that woman, not without his full love. If he wanted Elaine, or someone else for that matter, she would leave him free to choose. His quixotic gesture in marrying her need not make him feel bound to her. She would try hard to get over the loss of Melinda – and him.

Theresa did not dare allow herself to even dream that Scott might seek her out, might discover that it was she he loved, fully and eternally. She would ride to her private dream-place and consider ways, means by which this heart-break course she had decided on could be carried out. . . . Deliberately, she stayed in her room until she heard Scott leave in the utility jeep.

He must think she was suffering from a hangover, but she found it impossible to face him, after last night's inelegant outburst, of which she was mightily ashamed. Her invidious position was already showing a change in temperament, nature. Any more of this and Theresa Milward would become a sharp-tongued, sour old nag-bag!

Melinda came looking for her and she reluctantly left the safety of her room to see and help open the box of curtains. The firm had made them up, ready to hang. Soft autumn colours matched the green in the cretonne chair-covers and blended satisfyingly with the tan of the other chairs. Theresa forced down her enthusiasm. After all, soon she would not be here to enjoy relaxing with the family of an evening. Someone else, perhaps, would enjoy or change it again. What did it matter to her?

Miss Matilda was guiding Melinda's hands on her tiny sewing-machine, Cleo and Daniel were cleaning the store-pantry, no one was about when Theresa saddled up and cantered off. Neither Sam or any stockboys were in evidence, for which she was thankful, not wanting anyone tagging for her. The particular place she had in mind was much farther from Scott's homestead than Mary's. No matter, she didn't care if she stayed away all day. Melinda had Matilda, Scott was self-sufficient, in fact, she was beginning to feel miserably redundant. . . .

Theresa checked this dangerous self-pity and headed for the distant blue mountains. Noon found her in the foothills. She studied the sun-limned outlines while drinking from her water-bag. A bank of clouds was rising swiftly in the east. This seemed to be a roundabout way. She glimpsed a line of green – that would be the river – and the outcrops looked familiar. It was not too late to make for them; she could have a peaceful afternoon and be back by sunset. She came out on the ridge where she had seen Scott on that far-off day of their memorable ride, and there was her 'treasure house'.

The horse lapped thirstily at the river bank where the water ran cool and clear. Theresa walked him back, tethered the reins firmly under a shady mimosa, then started her walk up to the outcrop where she settled down, to think . . . to grieve awhile. Her lilies had died down, only the leaves and fern were still green. Her heart would lie buried here too, in the land she had come to love. But the flowers would bloom again next season while that heart would remain arid, un-loved, with no spring rains to revive it, no all-powerful love to burst the chrysalis and let it take wing.

The girl closed her eyes and blank numbness enveloped

her. Ways and means were forgotten while her tired brain succumbed to misery and heartbreak. A pregnant stillness in the air opened her eyes at last. The sun had disappeared behind a dark, heavy blanket of clouds. Theresa sat up slowly, so much for planning – the simplest course would be to pack her bags and tell Scott she yearned for her home town. That she, like Elaine, did not care for this sort of life, or rather the lack of life and bright lights. Scott's arrogant nature would spurn any idea of holding her against her will, his contempt for a weak nature would show and hurt, but she could think of no other way.

She scrambled up the clefted rock to the top and stood straight while a wayward wind caressed her loosened hair. A measure of peace came then, she would always have this to remember. ... Thunder clapped sharp and sudden and forked lightning split the skies.

Theresa climbed down carefully under a hang of rock, back on to the clefted boulder. Her riding-boot slipped on the smooth surface and she came down with a sharp bump, one foot imprisoned in the narrow cleft. In trying to free her foot she only forced it farther down to below her knee. A fierce struggle followed while she endeavoured to get her hand in, to unlace the boot. If that could be done, her foot could be slipped out of the confining space. She was in a sitting position under the overhang of rock. One leg remained free while the other, fortunately unhurt, was wedged firmly in the narrow cleft and there was not room enough to admit her hand, to manipulate the bootlaces. If only she possessed a knife she could cut them loose; her boot had prevented scratches and possible damage to her leg; it was also a hindrance.

Theresa tried again, her panic rising as the thunder rolled and zig-zag lightning seemed to strike the very rocks of her prison. And then the rain came, hard and fast. It came from the rear and the rock at her back partly shielded her from the terrific onslaught. She cowered back as far as possible, but within seconds her clothing had become soaking wet.

Not a soul knew where she had gone, the horse was securely fastened, and unless he reared hard enough to break the reins she could not even hope that his riderless appearance would set a search party out for her.

Another brilliant shaft of lightning split the heavens and mounting panic threatened menacingly.

In desperation she closed her eyes, willing her thoughts away from the frightening elements, to conjure up comforting pictures of Melinda in the safely warm homestead; Mary Rourke and little Theresa happily playing on the rug in the nursery. She had some super denim remnants and simply must get down making those cute little play-suits for her namesake ... that is, when she was settled again, in Pretoria ... or anywhere. ...

Maybe, right now, Melinda would be lounging in her favourite stance, against the bathroom door, watching her precious daddy while he washed his hands ... that was her favourite pastime too, watching her daddy. Theresa saw it quite clearly ... 'Tresa gone 'way, Daddy.' 'Did she go for a walk, Poppet?' 'I not know.' Scott would be troubled enough to question the piccanin, who would volunteer, 'Missy don take the horse.'

Her husband (what sweet heartbreak in one word) would look across the paddock, down the avenue, up at the darkening skies; most surely he would have some pretty grim thoughts on the uncaring, silly behaviour of a certain female!

Brave resolutions dissolved as Theresa pictured the angular brown face, the sun wrinkles deepening at the corners of smoky grey eyes. Her head drooped wearily and prickles started needling up her leg. She massaged it halfheartedly and wiggled her toes in an effort to keep up the circulation.

Scott would come to the conclusion that she would be taking shelter at Mary's and Miss Matilda would grumble that 'the naughty lass' had been gone for ages, committing the unpardonable crime of not telling anyone where she was going.

Quite likely – please make it very likely – he would phone through to the Rourke household and Mary might remember that she, Theresa, was fond of going to the river.

Scott might not even be home yet ... just when would someone finally become concerned?

She never knew if it was tears or rain on her face when the

muffled whinny and drumming sound of a fast-moving horse reached her thunder-deafened ears. Seconds later Scott materialized and, to her blurred gaze, looked infinitely large, very dear and welcome in his streaming black slicker.

And very angry?

Theresa lifted rainwashed lashes and spoke through blue lips. 'I'm glad you've come, Scott. I knew you would, sooner or later. I was beginning to feel awfully cold, wet, and lonely. P-please don't be angry!'

Relief roughened his voice. 'Why didn't you come home? Or go to Mary, instead of sitting it out here, like a foolish child—'

Theresa interrupted in a tone pitched higher than normal, 'I do regret I was unable, Mr. Milward, to quote Miss Otis—'

He caught sight of her imprisoned leg and came down instantly on to his knees beside her, asked quietly, 'Does it hurt, Theresa?'

'No-o, not at a-all,' she stuttered, near to tears again, now that help had arrived. The storm had seeped her will-power, she had cowered in absolute terror as shafts of lightning had danced around her semi-shelter to the accompaniment of clapping thunder.

Scott explored the crevice. His warm fingers touched her knee and she shivered as the pins-and-needles started again in her cramped foot. The man took another look at her bed-raggled hair, blue lips and wet clothes. He vanished below the rock, appearing moments later with flask, sweater and first-aid kit. The box was opened and he took out a small flask of brandy, tilted a stiff tot into the cup and filled it with hot black tea. He put an arm around her shoulders.

'Drink this.'

Theresa spluttered at the strength of the mixture. He waited until she had drained the contents, then proceeded to unbutton her shirt. Peeling it off, Scott hesitated, raised an inquiring eyebrow as he surveyed wet, flimsy underthings. The water splattered from her hair as she shook her head, so he shrugged his shoulders and a whimsical smile turned his lips as he slipped the thick sweater over her head.

The rain stopped suddenly. Scott handed the girl a large handkerchief. 'Rub your hair while I see what's to be done about this foot. Are you quite sure it's not hurting?'

'Quite sure. I'm sorry to cause you all this t-trouble.'

He did not answer, but looked up for a moment. The flare in his grey eyes, inexplicable yet gentle, warmed her far more than the laced tea. He turned to the bag and extracted a long pointed pair of scissors, slipped it down until the points contacted her bootlaces. Grasping firmly, he managed to cut them almost to her instep. 'Try now, nymph.'

Theresa tugged, to no avail. 'It's no use, my toes seemed to have become wedged in a small crevice at the bottom.'

Scott studied the cleft intently. 'Hold it, I have an idea,' he smiled encouragingly. 'Don't go away,' planted a swift kiss on her warming lips and disappeared again.

Theresa's lips curved upwards at this order and she brought cold fingers to touch her mouth, to feel the comforting warmth.

He was back. 'Thanks be for a rancher's saddlebags. You'd be surprised what's in 'em, at all times. This hammer and chisel ... it's only a wood chisel but will last out. I'm going to hammer bits of rock away until we can get that silly foot out.' Suiting action to words, he continued casually, 'Of course you must let me know if I happen to chisel through your leg, my darling, and – there, that's a small piece off. I mustn't let it fall in, otherwise ... don't ever let me go mad with worry again. This could only happen to you – good, another sliver off. Whoops! sorry, lass, that was very close, I'd not be much good as a sculptor. I've been such a blind fool, Theresa, fighting against my feelings. I was, quite possibly, sunk that very first time I saw you, a golden nymph on a wayside station. I am ashamed to admit that I sneered at that feeling; it was only attraction, a trap. But the compulsion came later, to keep you, to bind you closer to me.'

Theresa sat absolutely still and watched the strong brown hand falter for a moment. Scott carefully retrieved the sliver of stone that had slipped past his questing fingers.

'I can't begin to convey how uneasy I felt when Melinda told me that her Tresa had gone away ... more so when I observed the darkening sky and the stablehand said you'd taken a horse. I tried to get through to Mary, but the blasted line was down. That was when I got the wind up and sent the men in all directions while I grabbed the jeep to Dan's house . . . and you were not there.'

Theresa sat, fascinated and bemused. Just so had she visualized his actions.

'I collected horse, sweater, tea and first-aid stuff. Mary told me about this, your favourite hideout – I should have known, I found you here once before, remember? My one desperate hope was that you wouldn't take shelter under trees . . . they attract lightning like a magnet . . . that's a nice chunk out, hmmm? Do you also realize that I've lived in a private hell of my own, knowing that you didn't return the love I have for you?'

Theresa's lower lip trembled alarmingly. 'Scott, I was going to . . . I mean, I'd—'

'Save your breath, honey, scold me later. I've got it coming and will try not to chicken out. Right now I want to get things off my chest. I guess my conceited arrogance was a cover-up, to hide former disillusionments or to blind myself to what was happening to me . . . I didn't want it to happen . . . So, while I was searching for you, I thought of what Mary had told me. Oh yes, she told me, very succinctly, the truth about your heartbreak over Derek. And another interesting disclosure, which I'm struggling hard to believe—' Scott stopped and looked up for the first time.

Theresa's eyes had widened considerably and now her cheeks raised banners of delicious colour. 'She told you . . . Mary Rourke went and told you—' She was unable to continue and Scott gave a small smile as he dropped his eyes to the work in hand.

'Now I realize only too well what compelled me to force our engagement – and marriage. It was my heart, urging me, to hold on to something very precious. I was madly jealous of Derek Mann, that he could have the power to hurt you. Even jealous of Hugh when I watched you dancing so happily. Forgive me, I have to tell you all this, although it doesn't excuse my behaviour. So, when Mary told me that you loved me, I could scarcely believe her. I love you, Theresa. If Mary is mistaken, and you don't love me, well then, my very dearest, I won't hold you, add to the burdens you already have by forcing my will on you. You're free to choose your way, darling.' Scott added, almost as an afterthought, 'Melinda loves you too.'

'Scott!' Theresa sat up and firmly straightened a back that had suddenly lost its ache.

'Yes, Theresa?'

She looked at the top of a dark head, bent as if in humility, almost as if he was afraid to look up, afraid to read the wrong answer in hyacinth eyes. Theresa put out her hand and clutched a fistful of hair, gently forced his head back.

What he read in her face and eyes, so close to his own, was greatly enlightening. Tools were downed as Scott Milward took his wife in his arms, holding her head close to his fast beating heart while one unbelieving hand stroked damp, honeyed hair.

'Mary was right, bless her. Say it, darling, let me hear it from your lips and heart.' He spoke deeply, urgently.

'I love you, my rajah.' Theresa was breathlessly recovering from his casual chattering. Chatter that had made her whole world come singingly, vibrantly alive. Now she could keep her promise to Melinda. How close she had come to nearly losing everything!

'How and when did this wonderful phenomenon happen? I thought you hated my touch – you said so once, without love, remember?'

'I did love you then – I meant without your love I couldn't – if only you'd said it, the way you wanted me to say it now.'

'Darling, you mean we've wasted all this time because I was too dumb to utter a few vital words . . . darling nymph, come closer.'

Their embrace was a miracle of awakening, seeking love between two people who had held emotions in check, long and unneedfully.

Theresa drew back breathlessly. 'My foot, Scott!'

Scott rubbed his chin along the soft skin under her ear and murmured thickly, 'Yes, my love. It's a very pretty foot, I love it too.'

'It's still stuck, you know,' Theresa whispered conversationally.

Her husband reached reluctantly for hammer and chisel. He sighed, but remarked with the wisdom of a sage, 'Quite the cunningest, wisest little ole foot I've ever come across in all my born days!'

FREE! Harlequin Romance Catalogue

Here is a wonderful opportunity to read many of the Harlequin Romances you may have missed.

The HARLEQUIN ROMANCE CATALOGUE lists hundreds of titles which possibly are no longer available at your local bookseller. To receive your copy, just fill out the coupon below, mail it to us, and we'll rush your catalogue to you!

Following this page you'll find a sampling of a few of the Harlequin Romances listed in the catalogue. Should you wish to order any of these immediately, kindly check the titles desired and mail with coupon.

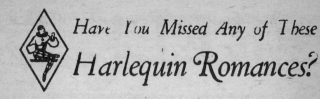

Have You Missed Any of These Harlequin Romances?

All books are 60c Please use the handy order coupon

GG

Have You Missed Any of These
Harlequin Romances?

All books are 60c. Please use the handy order coupon.

Have You Missed Any of These
Harlequin Romances?

All books are 60c. Please use the handy order coupon.

HH